SPINE-
TALES

A Ghostly Combination of

A FIT OF SHIVERS
Joan Aiken

and

IN BLACK AND WHITE
Jan Mark

Illustrated by Neil Reed

PUFFIN BOOKS

Published by the Penguin Group
Penguin Books Ltd, 27 Wrights Lane, London W8 5TZ, England
Penguin Books USA Inc., 375 Hudson Street, New York, New York 10014, USA
Penguin Books Australia Ltd, Ringwood, Victoria, Australia
Penguin Books Canada Ltd, 10 Alcorn Avenue, Toronto, Ontario, Canada M4V 3B2
Penguin Books (NZ) Ltd, 182–190 Wairau Road, Auckland 10, New Zealand

Penguin Books Ltd, Registered Offices: Harmondsworth, Middlesex, England

A Fit of Shivers first published by Victor Gollancz Ltd 1990
Published in Penguin Books 1992
In Black and White and Other Stories first published by Viking 1991
Published in Puffin Books 1992
A Puffin Book exclusively for School Book Fairs 1995
1 3 5 7 9 10 8 6 4 2

A Fit of Shivers copyright © Joan Aiken Enterprises Ltd, 1990
In Black and White and Other Stories text copyright © Jan Mark,
1980, 1981 1983, 1986, 1991
Illustrations copyright © Neil Reed, 1991

The following stories in *In Black and White and Other Stories*
have been previously published:
'Nule' first published in *Nothing To Be Afraid Of* (Viking Kestrel) 1980;
'They Wait' first published in *They Wait* (Pepper Press) 1983;
'Who's a Pretty Boy, Then?' first published in *Black Eyes* (Pepper Press) 1981;
'Welcome, Yule' first published in *An Oxford Book of Christmas Stories* (Hamish Hamilton) 1986;
'Efflorescence' first published in *Beware, Beware* (Oxford University Press) 1986.
All rights reserved

A FIT OF SHIVERS
Joan Aiken

Contents

Number Four, Bowstring Lane

In Crowbridge, a small town not far from the English
Channel, the boards of estate agents blossom like hollyhocks
among the pointed red roofs, the Tudor chimney-pots, the
pantiles, wrought-ironwork, and cobbled walks. Crowbridge, so cute, so gracious, so full of raftered pubs and
gate-legged tables, boasts more retired gentry per square
foot of ground than any other borough in south-east England;
it also possesses more ghosts. Nearly every diamond-paned
cottage claims to have been occupied, at one time or another,
by some historical character of note or notoriety; and, dying,
whether respectably or amid scenes of drama and scandal
(for Crowbridge, full of urban virtue and sobriety now, has
known its fair share of skulduggery and crime)—dying, the
former residents conferred a legacy of perturbed spirits who
moan, squeak, gibber, jabber, rap, rattle, clank, wail, keen,
and scrabble every night and all night, beginning promptly
at midnight and keeping up their cacophonous chorus until
the formal signal of cock-crow calls a sudden halt to the racket.
(Fortunately Crowbridge is a very compact little conurbation
with green marshes encircling its ancient walls; farms,
equipped with veritable roosters lie within earshot of the
townspeople in their neat houses.)

The death-rate among the inhabitants of Crowbridge is
unusually high; not from disturbed nights or lack of sleep
(they all wear ear-plugs), nor due to any insalubrity of the
locality or climate (indeed Crowbridge is billed as one of
the healthiest burghs in south-east England), but simply
because most of the householders are senior citizens of ample

means who retire to pass their declining days in this peaceful and picturesque spot; the actual number of declining days not infrequently proves to be a great deal less than the quality, and often some elderly nabob has done little more than decorate his dwelling to his own taste and plant a few bulbs in the garden before natural mortality carries him off and his demesne is once again on the market, of course at an increased price; house agents turn over a rapid business here, and seven of them have large handsomely-furnished offices in the High Street, while another nine occupy ex-market stalls and smaller inferior premises in Station Approach.

It was to one of these lesser offices that Marcus Fantail repaired on a Saturday morning, having reached Crowbridge for the first time by train. Travel by public transport was a complete novelty to Marcus, and so was the prospect of early retirement from his well-established position in television. An unsuspected affliction of the heart, making its unwelcome presence known by severe and sudden chest pains, had brought his professional life to an abrupt close. For twelve years he had been one of the best-known names in the business, controlling a wide spectrum of popular and successful drama programmes. He was a big jolly man, his face well known both on screen and in the press. The best-known of his programmes, *A Phantom at the Fireside*, a series of half-hour humorous ghost plays, had been running, to wide acclaim and impressive ratings, for the last eight years.

It was a natural progression, therefore, that Marcus, having gone through the regular list of amenities, up-to-date fitted kitchen with tiles and dresser, central heat, paved garden, two bath, four b., garage, dining area and recep., should inquire, concerning the cottage he was proposing to purchase:

"And of course it has a ghost?"

Young Mr Teazel, of Teazel and Gritchby, appeared a little embarrassed.

"Well, sir, I'm afraid, at this present moment in time that, no, just now it does not have one. But that might possibly be a matter of arrangement."

(It was taken as a matter of course that intending purchasers of house property in Crowbridge would prefer and expect the property to be haunted; that the premises should be shared with some ghostly resident was a desideratum; in fact properties lacking this amenity were rated lower, priced lower, and their owners shared a similarly humble place in the social rating of the town.)

"That," explained young Mr Teazel, allowing a slightly condescending note to enter his voice, "is why the little property is available on such favourable terms. You would not find another in Crowbridge, I assure you, Mr Fantail, at anything like this price. It is—" he lowered his voice still further, "a snip. But why not stroll round and have a look at it, sir? It is a most attractive little place, I assure you."

Selecting a bunch of keys from a large board, Mr Teazel led his client out, along the wide station approach, pleasantly bordered with pollarded limes, along Wharf Way, up Dolphin Passage, with its cobbles and bow-windows, through a narrow alley known as The Spindles, which smelt of coffee from all the little tea-places that graced its length, and so into Bowstring Lane, where four brick-and-tile cottages with neat front gardens faced out across a short, broad footway and a low stone parapet on to a wide vista of green marshland terminating in a silvery line of distant sea.

"Delightful prospect southwards as you see, Mr Fantail," said Mr Teazel, throwing open one of the neat front gates and fitting a fine new Chubb key into a shining new lock in the ancient oaken door. "The garden requires only minimal

upkeep, an advantage for a gentleman in your—er—state
of health, sir, and the rest of the premises are in first-rate
condition having been recently redecorated."

Marcus could see that this was so. The little house was
pristine: windows fitted, plumbing worked, paint gleamed,
glass shone, and all the electrical equipment appeared to
have been newly installed.

"The last owner had not—been here very long?" he
suggested.

"Lord Woolsack, sir, a most distinguished old gentleman,
we are handling the property on behalf of his grandchildren," divulged Mr Teazel, shaking his head. "Aged
ninety-two when he retired from the bench, hardly had time
to do more than plant a few pansies in the window-boxes
when *Anno Domini* caught up with him. Sad, very sad. He
really loved the little house. But he had left it so late. Now,
you, sir . . ."

Tact brought him to a halt for a moment, then he recom-
menced. "You, sir, still in your fifties, will surely have plenty
of time to enjoy living in Crowbridge," he said kindly.

"Lord Woolsack then did not object to the lack of a
ghost?" inquired Marcus, casting his eye up a definitively
Tudor, but well-swept chimney.

"Why, no, sir. He said that he had enough memories of
shady deeds and wicked goings-on from his years in court;
he made no complaint. And, of course, a gentleman of his
standing would be certain to find a sufficiently eminent
place in the society of the town—if he wished it—without
the need for, as it were, supernatural assistance."

Mr Teazel here paused again delicately. Both he and his
client were quite aware that television, though undeniably
well paid and ranking foremost among callings conspicuous
in the public eye, did not by any means command such a
high place on the scale of social values then obtaining in

Crowbridge; in fact it cut very little ice, ranking as grocery might have done a hundred years earlier. To be a TV controller in Crowbridge was to be graded little better than a plumber; unless you possessed some other asset.

"You said something before," recalled Marcus, withdrawing his head from the chimney. "About a ghost. Not at present, you said, but it might be subject to arrangement. What did you mean by that?"

"Why, sir, there is a lady, a Mrs Spearpoint, a long-standing resident in the town, who is, who finds herself able to supply such deficiencies. More or less to the customer's requirements."

"Indeed? She is a medium?"

"Something of the kind, sir."

"You see—I do *like* the house. It is charming. And the price suits my pocket." Mr Teazel nodded sympathetically. Marcus did not mention his circumstances, but they had found their way sufficiently often into the popular press. Alimony payments constituted a colossal drain on his resources. His ex-wife, an ex-actress twenty years younger than himself, showed no signs of ever intending to remarry or re-enter her former profession.

Marcus went on: "I like the house. The price is right. But —in view of my best-known programmes—a ghost would certainly be expected. It would be humiliating to occupy the only unhaunted cottage in a town otherwise infested by spooks. It would not do."

"Then," said Mr Teazel, "I have no hesitation in recommending the services of Mrs Spearpoint. If that is the only problem, consider the deal clinched, Mr Fantail!"

Mrs Spearpoint occupied picturesque premises just beyond the venerable grey stone towers and arch of the Land Gate. Her shop was bow-windowed, bristling with coloured raffia mats, gleaming with lustreware jugs, Indian silks, rustling with everlasting flowers; a large green-and-red parrot occupied a perch over a sign that said NOT FOR SALE. Mrs Spearpoint, in contrast to her wares, was a pale, attenuated, soft, silvery muted lady, in the borderland between middle-aged and elderly. But the beam of attention that she trained on Marcus Fantail was like a lighthouse ray; her awareness of him appeared to be total. And in her silences could be heard echoes of sounds otherwise impossibly faint and far-away, like the pulsing of distant deeply-buried underground waters.

"So you are in need of an entity, Mr Fantail?" was what she said. "Can you tell me why?"

Very slightly embarrassed, he explained the social and professional nature of his need. It was soon evident to him that Mrs Spearpoint never watched television, did not understand the ABC of his references, had never even heard of *A Phantom at the Fireside*; however, her lightning-swift, razor-sharp intelligence obviated the need for any complicated explanations. Marcus did, though, to his own surprise, find that he was giving her an account of why a man in his otherwise favourable financial position could not at this time afford one of the more expensive, ready-haunted mansions that stood so much higher in the town's hierarchy.

"Your wife Gloria. I perfectly understand—and have you been parted for long?"

"For the last ten years. Ever—ever since my son, our son —ever since our son died."

He did not expand on that, and she did not inquire.

With a somewhat startling switch to rapid, businesslike efficiency, she began to lay before him the various choices with which he was presented, going into poltergeist, banshee, footsteps, psychic cold, elementals, howls, tele-

kinesis, appearances, disappearances, supernatural flames
—a whole catalogue of paranormal phenomena.

"These can all be introduced at will?"

"Oh, my dear sir—" Mrs Spearpoint kindly overlooked
the note of scepticism in his tone. "You must understand
that—to persons of perception—this whole planet is
packed, is lined, is layered with such emanations. Imagine
a suitcase completely filled with spiders' webs, crammed
so that the lid will hardly shut. Remember the countless
millennia that have passed—the infinity of spirits that have
been liberated from their earthly envelopes. Where are they?
All around us. And all that you request is for just *one* to be
transferred—decanted, as it were, from one location to
another."

In spite of himself, Marcus began to find her convincing.

"Put like that it does sound simple," he admitted. "So
when—when can you do it? Ideally, I should like to move
in next month."

"No problem, my dear Mr Fantail. No problem at all."

By what means Mrs Spearpoint went about her business,
Marcus was not informed, nor did he inquire. He preferred,
in fact, not to know. The process of his departure from
Hyperion TV, the business of closing his Marylebone flat,
disposing of his assets, transporting his furniture, occupied
all his energies, nowadays also much depleted by the disease
of the aorta which had necessitated his early retirement.

He settled Mrs Spearpoint's four-figure account without
a murmur, being of the type that is impressed and convinced
by any price if only it is high enough. And after all, he
thought comfortably, I can always sue the old girl if nothing
turns up.

Before leaving Marylebone he had an acrimonious conversation with Gloria, who had of course read about his
early retirement in the daily press, and telephoned him to

make sure that her allowance would not lapse from its present level.

"How come you can afford to move to a fancy little dump like Crowbridge?" she inquired disagreeably. "I know about that place. Glenda Pilbeam lived there with her second husband."

"Don't worry, don't worry—" he suppressed the words "you bloodsucking bitch", his doctor had warned that any strong emotion such as anger would be very deleterious in his condition. He told her mildly that he expected the town's ambience would produce many ideas for future free-lance television work.

"Oh, I see," she said, sounding relieved, but then added spitefully, "How you can go on doing that kind of thing— how you can bear to make a living from all that revolting melodrama—when your own son—" her voice ran up to a high pitch.

"That's enough, Gloria! That's quite enough! We won't go into that again. You had your hand in it too. If you had been—a different kind of mother—"

She began screaming. "You drove that boy to do what he did. If you had ever talked to Mark—"

"I can't stand this," he said, and put down the receiver.

Their rare conversations always ended in the same way.

Marcus unplugged the television, locked the door of the Marylebone flat for the last time, and made his way down to the hired limousine which, since he could no longer drive, awaited him in the street.

The trip to Crowbridge took two-and-a-half hours, through pleasant hazy autumn weather, past gold and tawny oakwoods and grey dismantled hopfields. Riding thus in unwonted freedom and relaxation, Marcus began, after all, to look forward to his retirement with its idle pleasures. I shall potter, he thought peacefully, I shall play records

and tapes and talk to the neighbours. "If you had ever
talked to Mark——" Gloria's furious words came back to
him. How hideously unfair she was, he thought. In the old
days, before Mark had become an alien, he and the boy had
talked and talked for hours together, ranging over every
possible topic. He remembered at random one of their
discussions, on holiday, it must have been, when the boy
still went on holidays with them, one rainy day on Skye.
It had been about body-language: the differing codes of
manners to be found in different civilisations. Body-
language, he had said, was extremely important in TV
programmes, you could not hope to sell anything world-wide
if it violated some powerful unspoken rule of conduct—"like
showing the soles of your feet to somebody," he remembered
Mark suggesting, that would be a shocking insult in some
oriental countries, and the conversation had ended in
laughter as they envisaged other such gestures and the
situations in which they might, inadvertently, occur. Do
ghosts have body-language? Are there codes of conduct for
dwellers in the supernatural world?

Number Four, Bowstring Lane looked peaceful and inviting when Marcus reached it: late roses still bloomed in the
tiny front garden, a light shone in the window. Mrs Frint,
the new daily woman, would have turned on the heat and
left a meal ready for him.

Unlocking the ancient oak door with his bright key,
Marcus speculated rather cheerfully on what form Mrs
Spearpoint's psychic phenomenon might take. In the end
he had left the choice to her. "Only I would rather it were
not *noisy*," he stipulated. "That is unfair to the neighbours,
and I personally don't care for loud bangs, or howls, or
rappings."

And she had set down a note on her businesslike memo
pad.

The cottage was warm, tranquil, friendly. Bypassing the lounge, doubtless, he thought, the site of any manifestation, Marcus went carefully up the short stair to the master bedroom, pushed open the door, and switched on the light.

And saw before him on Lord Woolsack's green carpet, which he had purchased, the soles of two dirty bare feet, the toes turning outwards into a terrible caricature of peace and relaxation . . .

Gasping, with his hand to his heart, Marcus turned and fell headlong down the stair.

"Poor gentleman, them steps must have been just too much for him, after his journey," said Mrs Frint who found him next morning, after she had dutifully summoned the police and local doctor. "Such a shame when he hadn't even moved in yet; and the house all so neat and tidy a-waiting for him—not a speck out of place!"

Number Four, Bowstring Lane is again on the market.

Earrings

When Aunt Dimsie got married to Mr Goss, I heard Ma
say to Father that it was really a mercy, in some ways, that
little Marjorie wasn't still alive, as, between them, Marjorie
and Mr Goss would have torn Aunt Dimsie in half.

"Marjorie wouldn't have been prepared to share her
mother with a strange man," Ma said. "She was always
such a demanding child, from the day she was born. Poor
Dimsie—I don't know—perhaps it's better this way."

Pondering over the interesting picture of Marjorie and
Mr Goss each with an arm and a leg, I found myself in
disagreement with Mother. I thought: if Marjorie were still
alive, Aunt Dimsie wouldn't have married Mr Goss. No
way. Marjorie would have prevented it.

Marjorie *loathed* Mr Goss.

And, although I'd never been too wild about my cousin
Marjorie, who kept pet doves in a dovecot, totally preferred
birds to humans, and called me a stupid sop because I wasn't
keen to go on ten-mile-hikes through rain and brambles to
look for a marsh warbler's nest, when it came to the question
of Mr Goss I was heart and soul on Marjorie's side. Herbert
Goss was big and massive and red-faced, baldish, with
a ginger moustache, and had made his money, a whole
lot of it, from inventing some nasty weapon, a kind
of pocket machine-gun, that he sold to foreigners and
terrorists so that they could kill each other with greater ease
and speed.

Mr Goss had retired from active business now (though
he still derived a big income from his gun) so he'd have all

the time in the world to shout at Aunt Dimsie and bully her.

"I do pity her, poor woman, I must say," said Father. "She'd certainly have had an easier life being trampled underfoot by Marjorie."

Aunt Dimsie's first husband, Father's brother Christy, had been killed five years ago in an air crash. When Marjorie was nine. She'd have been fourteen, the week of the wedding.

There was a tentative suggestion that I should be bridesmaid in Marjorie's place. I think it was Mr Goss's idea. Ma thought it in shockingly poor taste.

"So soon after the tragedy—disgraceful! What about poor Dimsie's feelings?"

"Well, he still wants the big slap-up wedding with all the trimmings," said Father.

"I expect it's because they had the bridesmaid's dress all ready," I said. "Those blue and white stripes. Marjorie said she wouldn't be seen dead in them. Anyway I shan't accept. I don't want to walk along the aisle behind Mr Goss. He's just like a big shark—teeth and all."

So, in the end, they managed without a bridesmaid.

We went to the wedding, of course.

It was a *terrible* day. Rain from day-break on, not just ordinary rain but real hard torrents of it, bucketing down. All through the wedding service you could hear it drumming and thundering on the church roof (and finding its way through, here and there—Tench Underhill church was built in 1100 and is in urgent need of repair; you could hear squeaks and moans from the congregation every once in a while, as a big drop hit somebody's bald pate or feather hat). The inside of the church was as dim and misty as a bathroom full of steam; you could hardly see up the aisle. After the signing ceremony in the vestry there was no question of photographs at the church door—everybody simply made a bolt for their waiting cars.

"I really think I must need a holiday," muttered Ma, when we were in our Renault driving glumly through the downpour. "It was so dark in the church—and stuffy— that several times I felt as if I might pass out. Once or twice —believe it or not—I could have sworn that I saw Marjorie standing behind Dimsie. In that blue and white dress."

"She'd never have worn it," I said. "She said it looked like a cleaning rag."

I didn't add that I thought I had seen Marjorie too. Holding a bouquet of gentians and freesias, scowling horribly at Mr Goss.

The reception was held, not at Aunt Dimsie's little house, which was to be sold, but at Pine Hill, Mr Goss's great place. It was large enough to house a trade union conference, all polished, yellow wood floors and square banister rails and massive newel posts and suits of false-looking armour, and stained-glass windows in every room, including loos. The wedding breakfast was served in a barnlike room with a minstrel's gallery and two grand pianos, one at each end.

There was a great deal of jollity and a great many of Mr Goss's friends, who were either built on his pattern, with big square business faces and thinning streaks of hair draped carefully over the tops of their heads—or they were small and dark and ugly with unpronounceable names. I began to feel desperately sorry for Aunt Dimsie; and all the champagne in the world couldn't stop Ma from looking more and more depressed.

She and I went to help Aunt Dimsie change into her powder-blue going-away suit, in a bedroom the size of an airport runway with massive stone balconies outside the windows and a view of rain-drenched lawns and rhododendrons beyond, stretching away into the misty distance.

"It seems so cold in this house," said Aunt Dimsie shivering.

"Well, of course you are bound to catch the wind here, in winter, up on this hilltop," agreed Ma. "But I'm sure Mr Goss can afford the very best kind of central heating. Here, just turn round while I button you at the back."

"Oh Edna—did I do right? Tell me I did! I d-do so miss d-darling Christy—and poor little M-Marjorie—and Linnet Cottage—"

"Of course you did right," said Ma in the sort of scolding voice she puts on when she really isn't so certain about something. "Herbert can give you a wonderful time. Now you need a bit of make-up—you're far too pale—"

"I keep thinking about Marjorie. Do you know—Herbert did such a kind thing—he moved all Marjorie's nesting boxes from Linnet into the shrubbery here. Wasn't that sweet of him?"

"It was indeed," Ma said rather drily.

"He knew how much I'd be missing Marjorie. I think, n-now she's gone," said Aunt Dimsie in a faltering voice, "Herbert appreciates her qualities more."

"I'm sure he does, my dear." Mother did not allude to the terrible things Marjorie used to say about Mr Goss, or his retaliations. "There—now you look very nice. Which earrings are you going to wear?"

"Oh—that reminds me." Aunt Dimsie turned and rummaged in her little going-away case. "Here, Lucy darling—these are for you. Marjorie was—she was to have worn them as bridesmaid—her godmother, my friend Geraldine left them to her. Now I want you to have them."

"Oh, Aunt Dimsie—thank you!" I stammered. "They—they are beautiful."

"Geraldine brought them back from one of her field

trips," said Aunt Dimsie. "They were made by the Skahoe
Indians."

They were long, dangling complicated spirals—two
spirals, one inside the other—made of delicate silver with
tiny green stones.

Geraldine Stannery had been Aunt Dimsie's greatest
friend. They had met at college and kept up ever since,
seeing each other every couple of weeks, corresponding
when apart. Geraldine was an anthropologist and spent
years of her life studying the habits of primitive tribes.
In the end she just didn't return from one of her long
field trips. (Just as well, maybe, for she and Mr Goss
didn't get on at all.) It was odd that she and Dimsie should
have been so devoted, when you think how different they
were.

"There was another thing that went with the earrings,"
said Dimsie. "Here it is."

She handed me a circlet about five inches in circumfer-
ence, made of thin, stiff bark. Across it, criss-cross, was
woven a network of fine grasses.

"It's a Dream Catcher," said Dimsie. "You put it by
your bed, Geraldine told me, and it is supposed to drive
away bad dreams. And bring pleasant ones."

She smiled at me wanly. I wondered if she had been using
it herself. If so, she wasn't a particularly good advertisement
for its magic power.

"DIM—SIE!" yelled Herbert Goss. "Aren't you ready
yet? Get a move on! We're going to miss that plane!"

We heard him come thumping up the wide pine stairs
and Aunt Dimsie quivered a little, then gulped and hugged
Ma.

"Goodbye, darling Edna—thanks for everything—Goodbye, Lucy dear—keep an eye on Marjorie's doves in their
nesting boxes, will you, if you have time—?"

She pulled herself away from us and made for the door, just as Herbert came bursting in.

"Ready at last? So I should hope! Come on, then!"

He whisked her round and almost shoved her down the stairs.

Mother and I followed more slowly, Ma turning first to give a slow, puzzled stare round the big shiny room with its four-poster bed, glass-topped furnishings, velvet curtains and furry white carpet.

There was a white quilted stool in front of the dressing-table with its huge triple mirror. I wondered if Ma had thought she saw what *I* thought I had seen: the reflection, in the glass, of my cousin Marjorie, squatting on the padded stool, her arms round her knees, directing a silent, malignant glare towards Herbert Goss.

But I said nothing to my mother, nor she to me.

By the time we loitered downstairs the goodbyes had already been said, and the married pair, in their Rolls, were being driven away through the deluge.

We didn't linger on with the rest of the invitees, drinking more champagne, but made for our own small messy car.

"Thank the lord that's over," said my father. "Now I can put my best suit back into moth-balls for another nine years."

"I do hope to goodness Dimsie doesn't regret it," Ma was muttering as the windscreen wipers scraped and squeaked.

"Well at least she's not our worry any more," said Father rather heartlessly.

When we got back to the house, Mother made me hand over Aunt Dimsie's earrings in their little silk-lined box. "Far too good for you just yet. Perhaps when you are a year or two older . . ."

In a way, I wasn't sorry. Although they were very beautiful, there was something snaky and hypnotic about th concentric spirals; they almost seemed to move and squirm by themselves as they lay in their silk nest. And they were so long that I thought they might be a nuisance, even dangerous; they would dangle and swing and catch in my hair or collar.

"Besides, you haven't had your ears pierced yet," Ma went on.

I resolved to have this remedied without delay—most of my friends already had—and also to switch to a shorter hair-style; both of which programmes I carried out. Yet I never got round to reminding Mother about the earrings; although it wasn't that I didn't think of them, from time to time, lying there quietly in her top left-hand drawer.

Once in a while I'd go and look at them, when Ma and Father were out and I was alone in the house.

There they lay.

In the course of time Aunt Dimsie and (as we were now instructed to call him) Uncle Herbert came home to Pine Hill. His wedding gift to her had been a trip round the world, so by the time they got back they were tanned and weathered, and full of stories about disastrous flights and magnificent beaches. Herbert was several inches fatter, whereas Dimsie seemed to have shrunk—she looked as thin, brown, and gnarled as one of those dwarf Japanese trees people plant in rock gardens. Ma had to suppress a yelp of horror at the sight of her.

Herbert, however, was thoroughly pleased with himself.

"Just the right time of year to come home." (It was April.) "Had a first-class garden firm come last autumn and put in thousands of bulbs at Pine Hill. Really paid off. It's a grand sight now—good as a bulb catalogue."

I knew that, because I'd walked across the valley now and then to check on Marjorie's nesting boxes. Acres of huge double daffodils the colour of mustard sauce, masses of hyacinths, bigger than chimney pots, in violent pinks, blues, and mauves; hideous little miniature double pink cherry trees like marshmallow explosions.

"Pine Hill really is a sight," Herbert said again complacently. "You must all come over to lunch on Saturday and enjoy it."

Father said, terribly sorry, he had a complicated case on at the assize court, needed a lot of reading, couldn't make it. Which left Ma and me to go dismally on our own. Dimsie, at parting, had given us such fervent beseeching hugs that we couldn't deny her.

"Please come! It's so wonderful to see you again," she said, looking at us piteously out of eyes that seemed disproportionately large, sunk in their shadowy netted pits in her drawn face. "Do you wear Marjorie's earrings sometimes?" she asked me.

"Er—well—I keep them for special occasions," I mumbled.

"Do wear them on Saturday, dearie—I'd love to see them being used. They'll remind me of Marjorie and my darling Geraldine."

"Darling Geraldine!" scoffed Herbert, overhearing. There was a disagreeable sneer on his face. "Now *there* was an old witch if ever there was one. I don't suppose anybody cried buckets at her end, when she was eaten by the Yamahazbecs (or whoever finished her off)—except poor old Dimsie here who, let's face it, hasn't much judgment when it comes to picking friends. Geraldine! She's no loss to the world." And he went on in this vein for several minutes more

Poor old Dimsie cringed, gave us a hunted, harassed look and allowed herself to be shovelled into the car.

That was enough to make Ma get out the earrings, later

and say to me, "You'd better wear these on Saturday, Lucy. But mind you take good care of them . . ."

"Of course I'll wear them," I said. "I'd planned to."

"What's this?" Ma fished out a flat tissue-paper package from under the earring box and eyed it in bafflement. "Oh, I know, it's that other thing Dimsie gave you. I forget now what she said."

"A Dream Catcher. Drives away bad dreams and brings good ones. I wonder how you are supposed to use it?"

Mother, abandoning interest, went away to telephone her sister Sylvia and tell her about the hideous effect that marriage to Herbert had had on poor Aunt Dimsie; I took the earrings and the Dream Catcher off to my bedroom. I studied the earrings in their box—touched them a little to see them shimmer—but decided not to put them on at present. Not just yet. The Dream Catcher I hung on a thread over the head of my bed. No reason why that shouldn't be put to use. Not that, in the general way, I do have bad dreams; on the whole I greatly enjoy my dreams, which are full of unexpected events and interesting people. In the old days I used to relate them to Marjorie who, poor thing, could never come up with anything half as entertaining. Hers were mostly about birds. And she found mine terribly tedious.

But that night I had a real monster of a dream.

I was falling down a dark, soft precipice. There was nothing to grab on to, except friable, black crumbly stuff that came away in my fingers as I touched it. And there was nothing to breathe, except the same black horrible stuff, which poured into eyes, mouth, nose and lungs, blinding, choking and suffocating. I was falling, sliding, choking, *done for*. I was going to die. And I *did* die. The dream did not end in a scream, hurling myself out of bed and into wakefulness, as my infrequent nightmares tend to, but just moved on into sleep, so that next morning I had it clear, whole, and dreadful in my mind the very instant I woke.

Now, *now* I knew just how Marjorie had felt as she died.

We had known the bare facts of the story before, of course. She had taken refuge from a thunderstorm (it was assumed) in a farmer's haybarn about five miles from home when she was off on one of her bird-watching hikes. Climbed on top of the hay, which was last year's, old and mouldy, accidentally slipped down in the deep crevice between hay and barn wall, and somehow asphyxiated from the fumes of the decomposing stuff. Not found until several days later. A dreadful, dreadful tragedy, as everyone agreed, but at least the poor girl can't have suffered much; her lungs were full of hay, she was almost certainly unconscious and never realised what was happening to her. That was what people said.

But now, I knew better.

The morning was grey, overcast and sultry, not like a spring day, more like one in August when a storm's due. I felt, not unwell, but just wretched, the way one does after getting a horrible piece of bad news, the knowledge of which will always be there from now on, inescapable, colouring everything else.

When Mother said, "What are you going to wear?" I almost growled at her, "Oh, what does it matter what we wear?"

In the end I chose a green pleated silky dress Aunt Dimsie had given me last year, one of a pair she brought back from a Venetian holiday with Geraldine Stannery. She had given Marjorie the other dress. Green suited Marjorie's dark colouring. I don't care for the colour, and hardly ever wore the dress.

"A very tactful thought," said Ma approvingly. "And it will go with the earrings."

I left putting them on till the last minute before we started. They were surprisingly heavy. I could feel them swing and dangle and twirl as I walked to the car; I had the rather crazy impression that two tiny people were hanging from my ear lobes.

There was another very odd thing which I soon noticed about them, and so did Ma.

"What's that whistling noise?" she said, getting out her car keys.

"It's these earrings. They seem to catch the wind. Like Chinese windbells."

"But there isn't any wind, to speak of."

It was a still, heavy, hushed day, more like midsummer than April.

"Why should *you* have the earrings?" whispered Marjorie's voice in my ear, as we drove along. "They weren't bought for you. You've no right to them. And I never liked you, anyway."

The leaves on the trees were still tiny, pale-green and glistening—until we drove up the approach to Pine Hill, where huge rhododendrons with dark foliage and flowers the colour of blood rose up like ramparts on either side of the drive. Then, beyond them, we saw the massed mustard-yellow and washing-powder-white of the daffs and narcissi, stretching away in lavish carpets.

And all along the drive Marjorie's earrings were whispering and nagging in my ears.

"He did it, he did it, Herbert did it! He gave me a packet of drugged nuts, he knew I couldn't resist macadamia nuts. And when I got drowsy he took me to that place and pushed me down. He did it. Herbert killed me."

"Do stop whistling under your breath, Lucy," Ma said. "I can't stand it as I drive."

"I'm not whistling . . ."

Herbert was there to meet us at the portico, all jollity and hostliness.

"Before you come indoors, walk round the side and see the daffs on the south lawn," he boomed. "If you think these are spectacular, just you wait!"

After one rather startled glance at me, he kept his eyes firmly on Ma, but Aunt Dimsie, behind him, said, "Oh, how nice you look, Lucy dear, in that dress. And I am so pleased to see you wearing the earrings."

I wondered if Dimsie could hear them as well as see them. Their whisper was now a hiss, loud as the sound of wind through dry rushes: "Herbert, Herbert, Herbert, Herbert, killed me, killed me, killed me, killed me."

"I think I'm going to have to take them off," I mumbled unhappily. "I'm not used to wearing such heavy ones."

"Just wait, dear, till we are in the house. Then you can come to my room."

The room, I remembered, where I had seen Marjorie reflected in the triple mirror. And yet she had never set foot inside Pine Hill.

As I thought that, I saw Marjorie, herself, wearing a green dress the twin of mine, move out of a door in a wall enclosing a vegetable garden, and walk along, just behind Uncle Herbert.

We were following a neatly-tended gravel path between the great yellow plastic plains of daffodils. It led towards a shrubbery. More rhododendrons grew there, scarlet, flame-coloured, and salmon-pink.

I saw Ma give Marjorie a quick, puzzled glance, and then look hastily back at me. Aunt Dimsie, apparently unaware of anything unusual, was talking in a breathless, feverish twitter, about the flowers they had seen on their travels.

"Put a sock in it, can't you, woman?" Herbert called back impatiently. "Let the guests get a word in edgeways."

His mood seemed suddenly to have shot downhill.

At the entrance to the shrubbery he turned and said, "I'm bringing you this way because Dimsie is always going on about how I didn't love her precious little Marjie. I'm taking you to show you what I did in memory of her precious little Marjie. And then you can decide for yourselves if I am such a mean old stick as Dimsie is always making out."

"I never, never said, Herbert—" Dimsie began timidly, but he had turned and was striding on. He appeared not to see Marjorie, in her green dress, silently keeping pace just behind him. Nor, it appeared, did Aunt Dimsie see her daughter, though once she did put out her hand in a puzzled, beseeching gesture.

We came to a clearing in the shrubbery. It was like a little courtyard, paved with cobbles, walled with yew hedges. All around it had been set up Marjorie's nesting boxes for the doves. I had been here once or twice in the course of the spring, and knew that the doves were nesting well, seemingly not bothered by their change of habitat. Flocks of the white creatures, more, I thought, than ever before, were fluttering about, bustling back and forth, taking off on excursions over the rhododendrons, returning again to their nests.

But there was something new since I had been here before: in the centre, a grey marble statue of Marjorie, standing, hands on hips in a characteristic posture, looking up at her bird-boxes.

"There! Had that done as a surprise for Dimsie, while we were away! That chap Fenimoore who does them from photos. Remarkable likeness—ain't it?" demanded Herbert, recovering his joviality.

It *was* a good likeness. It cruelly rendered all Marjorie's plainness—her glasses, big nose, bad skin, hair scraped ungracefully back, thickset body, shapeless legs. She was wearing a school tunic, most hideous and unbecoming of garments, wrinkled socks, and sneakers with the laces coming undone.

"*Marvellous* likeness—ain't it?" repeated Herbert fondly.

By now the earrings in my ears were fairly yelling: "He killed me, he killed me, *Herbert killed me!*" I saw Ma turn and throw me a startled look. Beyond her I saw Marjorie, in the green dress, walk between the doves' boxes into the middle of the circle and give the statue an angry push. It fell over, as if it were made of *papier-mâché*, with a loud crash and a cloud of dust.

Herbert spun round, his mouth wide open.

Marjorie now stood where the statue had been, in precisely the same attitude, hands on hips. Then she clapped her hands together sharply, once.

All the doves rose up together in a mob—a white, flapping, whirling, raucous mob—they sounded more like a swarm of rowdy rooks than a decorous flock of demure white doves. Next, with one accord, they swooped down upon Herbert.

In a moment he was covered all over with the white things—face, head, eyes, arms, hands. He looked like a big macaroon that has been rolled on coconut flakes.

He began to scream. "Get them off! Get them bloody off! Help me! Help me get rid of the buggers!" His words were muffled by feathers, by birds. Then he rushed away, beating with his arms, down one of the paths that led away from the clearing. The doves went along too, perching, swooping, and pecking. In a moment they were out of sight. We heard him screaming in the distance.

Dimsie fainted, dead away, on the cobbles.

"Help me get her back to the house," said Ma, white-lipped. Her teeth were chattering, and so were mine.

I carried Dimsie's feet, Ma her shoulders. A gardener met us half-way and offered to take Dimsie, but Ma told him he'd better go and help Mr Goss, who was having trouble with the birds. Off he went and we, once indoors, assisted by Mrs Wade the housekeeper, gave Dimsie brandy, and held ammonia under her nose.

After a while she came to, looked at us in a puzzled way, and said, "I saw Marjorie. In the shrubbery. I saw my daughter Marjorie."

"Just take it easy now, dear," said Mrs Wade, slipping in another spoonful of brandy.

By and by the gardener came in, white as paint. "What is it, Wilkins?" snapped the housekeeper. "You shouldn't be in here."

"I can't find Mr Goss," said the man hoarsely. "All I could find—well, mum, I think you'd best come and see."

Mother and I went with him, both of us walking slowly on legs that trembled a good deal. And he showed us, at the far end of the shrubbery, a patch of blood on the path. The blood had soaked into the gravel, and the patch was the size and shape of a man. That was all there was to see —blood, and a few shreds of leather and tweed. And a belt buckle.

No further trace of Herbert ever came to light.

Later on, I gave the earrings back to Aunt Dimsie.

They were beautiful, but too heavy for me, I said.

An L-shaped Grave

The artist's name was Luna Knox, and the show of sculptures was billed simply as 'self-portraits'. And it was being held in a most inaccessible part of town, thought Maurice Hart, the art critic, staring irritably out of the dirty train window at monotonous rows of suburban roofs slipping past with their dank December gardens and grey leafless trees. One of the houses, to Hart's mild wonder, had a moosehead attached to its wall, the kind of trophy usually to be found indoors, in hunting lodges and baronial halls; how very singular to set it up out of doors, he mused; but then it occurred to him that a moose is, after all, an outdoor animal, accustomed to life in the wild; the oddity, really, is in fetching the beast inside four walls. Another house, a short distance further on, had a sign: "Mathematics Lessons: call 03339-9966." How many rail passengers would be in need of maths lessons and would trouble to call that number, activated by a sign seen so briefly through grimed, rain-streaked glass? But many people, he supposed, travelled to and from their work along this piece of track ten times every week; to them the moose, the maths lessons, must be an accustomed part of their daily ritual.

Gresham Common, Lordsfield, Crittleworth . . . and now the track, taking a wide curve on its raised embankment, circled back towards the river, into a region that must once have been tidal marshes, but now, long reclaimed, held docks and warehouses. Ancient rusty derricks loomed among grass-grown, littered trackways and half-derelict buildings. The district was, in fact, being transformed yet again, as waterborne trade took to the air and shipping sadly declined; now the spacious, lofty warehouses were being converted into art galleries and artists' studios, rents were soaring, and ships' chandler's stores were experiencing a new lease of life as expensive boutiques offering frivolous unpractical luxuries and exotic trifles, in place of their former sternly utilitarian wares; the principal virtue of the new goods offered for sale was that they could be billed as 'ethnic'; the actual source of origin was of little importance so long as it was somewhere overseas.

Hopford Dock: Maurice Hart stood up, buttoned his raincoat and, with considerable reluctance, left the warmth of the stuffy carriage. Hopford Dock station was no more than a halt, a one-walled shelter with steps leading down to the unexplored wilderness below.

Dusk had already begun to fall, though it was hardly past three on a disagreeable afternoon. Hart wished that he could have come by car, but an unfortunate drunk-driving episode had rendered him subject to a three-month ban; hoisting his shoulders, turning up his collar, he strode out along a roadway bordered on both sides by the bulky rectangular shapes of storehouses or factories—how to find street names in this derelict area? Impatiently he hurried on, occasionally consulting the small conventional map printed on his card of invitation, realising with added annoyance that he might as well have quitted the train at the previous stop and saved himself a walk: there was the house with the moose, getting sleeker with wet all the time. At last he came to a street sign, *Rope Walk*, and was able to orient himself. He took a left turn, then a right, and suddenly found himself among people and lights; brilliant shop windows were filled with glistening swathes of fabric, dazzling pyramids of crystal, colours that appeared to seethe and bubble as elixirs might in the alchemist's crucible. The people in this thoroughfare, which had apparently been closed to wheeled traffic, were all young, their clothes ran to the wildest extreme of contemporary taste: they wore huge hats, high-heeled boots, shawls, turbans, dhotis, breeches, cloaks, serapes, bustles, pelisses whose gaudy hues throbbed like the music of tom-toms in the dusk and drizzle.

"Is this Watergate Lane?" Hart asked. "I'm looking for the Crane Galleries."

"Right there, man! Right ahead of you!"—and in the same moment he saw it, a wrought-iron strip-sign which, in eccentric lettering, spelt out the word CRANE up the side of a narrow, lofty building.

Hart showed his card, after passing through a massive glass door that opened to him automatically, then signed his name in a book that lay on a large metal barrel. Behind the barrel was what appeared to be an organ constructed out of monumental steam-pipes and valves left over from some discarded piece of machinery. He noted this with slight disapproval, and proceeded through an inner door into the gallery itself, where he was immediately handed a large glass of red wine.

So far, so good, he thought drily, sipping the beverage (which, he must admit, was not bad at all, powerful and with an excellent bouquet).

The building was full of people, yet so very capacious that the crowd was of little more importance than acorns on the floor of a forest. Once the place had been a warehouse, the ceiling, almost out of sight, supported by mighty cast-iron pillars with filigree ornamentation and Corinthian capitals. These, and the walls and ceiling, had been painted stark, arctic white; and the floor, composed of some hard, resonant wood, was polished to an arctic glitter. Yet the enormous bare room was not cold. Nor was it noisy; the voices of the guests became muted, soft, and awestruck as they strolled and wandered with glasses in their hands. Tiny sparks of red light, reflected from the wine in the glasses, moved and flickered on the white walls. The light came from lustres which were hung, rather frivolously and eccentrically, on twenty to thirty pairs of deer's antlers, which had been suspended on white ropes, high above the guests and the exhibits.

These were what Hart had come to see, and what he noticed last. Yet, once he had taken them in, he ceased to observe anything else at all: the white walls, the large mirrors on the walls, the monumental white pillars, the black lumpy shapes of the crowding people, the red-flashing reflections, all sank through his mind like salt dissolving in water.

The pieces, of which there might have been twenty or so, were from six to seven feet high, and they had been constructed, Hart read, consulting his card, from epoxy, cloth, and bronze or aluminium powder. The cloth had been somehow impregnated with the glue and powdered metal, then coaxed into folds and drapings, then left to harden. The material, thus stiffened, suggested the outline of a figure inside; but the figure was lacking. Here was a cloaked, hooded massive woman: but the space below the browband of the hood was vacant, merely a dark hole; no eyes looked out. Folds of grey cloth conveyed the shape of a breast, a nipple; but a slit down the side of the robe, from armpit to ankle, showed dark emptiness inside. Draperies blown back on a ship's figure-head outlined a graceful torso, but stepping behind this figure, Hart found it to be concave at the rear, no more than a hollow shell.

"Hey, Hart, me old son!" said a voice in his ear. "What do you think of them?" and, turning, he saw the face of a fellow critic, a man called McDougal who wrote a weekly column for the *Sunday Landmark*. "What d'you think?"

McDougal repeated. "Not bad? You gave the girl a real pasting last time, didn't you? Heroic groups, wasn't it then, all made out of hemp?"

"These are better. Clever," admitted Hart, a shade reluctantly. "Frozen motion. Not a new idea, but she's done it capably, I must admit—"

"But—?"

"But—don't you feel there is an element missing?—And I *don't* mean just the bodies inside," he added defensively.

"What, then?"

"What's between dark and light, between moonbeams and sunshine?"

"Much too philosophical for me, old boy," said McDougal, clapping him on the shoulder. "And you better not speak too loud, the lady herself is somewhere about, I saw her just now."

"Oh? I've never met her. What sort of age?"

"Hard to say. She might reasonably feel she has a grudge against you—after what you wrote last time. I've heard she can be quite tough with fellows who get into her bad books. You better give her a nice boost this time."

"Can't promise," snapped Hart. "I can only say what I think, can't I? I came to her flaming show, didn't I? And a nice trip I had of it, all the way out to this god-forsaken spot. Anyway, I don't wholly dislike them—they're better than the last lot at least—there is something a bit mysterious about them—"

Then he realised that McDougal had stepped away, and that he was addressing instead the back of some female in a black dress who stood with her head turned away from him. Her hair was black too, and there must have been yards of it, enough to reach to her ankles if it had been let down, but it was coiled and plaited into an intricate structure, a kind of coronet on the back of her head, and two long twisted locks fell on either side of her face. The face, he now discovered, was dimly discernible to him in the mirror on the wall beyond her; he could see sparks of light reflected in her eyes and some kind of a sparkling crescent pinned on the crown of hair. She began to speak without turning round and, from her tone of mockery, he supposed that her words were intended for him.

"So you actually came all the way out to this god-forsaken spot, Mr Hart, did you? And you like these better than the last lot? I wonder by which god do you suppose this spot *was* forsaken, Mr Hart? By Apollo, perhaps? Or by Wotan? Or Allah? Or Jehovah?"

"Oh, just a manner of speech, you know," he said uncomfortably. "Are you—am I right in guessing that you are Luna Knox? The pieces are quite original—you heard me say there was something mysterious about them—"

"Yes, and something missing as well; I wonder what that something can be, Mr Hart?"

Still she went on admonishing him in the glass, with her back turned, and he exclaimed angrily, "I wish you would turn round and talk to me properly! This is an idiotic way to hold a conversation."

"You wish that I would speak to you directly? Oh, but that wouldn't do, Mr Hart, that wouldn't do at all. No, I fear you must look for me in the mirror—I very much fear that if you looked at me directly, something unfortunate might happen. People have been blinded who stared into the naked light of the sun, Mr Hart. Perhaps that is why I leave something out of my works. No, I am afraid you might find the sight of my face much too disturbing—"

With a furious exclamation he laid his hand on her shoulder and pulled her round to face him.

Heads turned in the crowd at the clatter of broken glass and a series of cataclysmic screams. Startled guests jumped aside as Hart, flailing with his fists, staggering, lurching, made his way to the lobby and out through the automatic doors, which mockingly parted to permit his exit.

All the way along the street his shrieks continued: "My head, my head, oh god, my head!"

When he was picked up, at the end of Watergate Lane, he was clasping his temples with both hands, as if to contain intolerable agony. And he had grown a full-size pair of elk's antlers; it was thought his death must have been caused by a brain haemorrhage.

The antlers were so large, indeed, that it was necessary to dig an L-shaped grave in order to accommodate both him and them.

Something

When the thing happened for the first time I was digging up wild lilies to plant in my own little garden. Digging up wild lilies. A happy task. They are dark orange and grow down by the narrow shallow brook that freezes solid in winter. On that day it was babbling and murmuring placidly and I sang a song, which I made up as I went along, to keep company with its murmur. "Wild lilies I find, wild lilies I bring, wild lilies, wild lilies, to flower in the spring." Overhead the alder trees arched, and water-birds, becoming used to my harmless presence, called their short gargling answers. Once or twice a kingfisher flashed. There were trout in the water, but only tiny ones; I could feel them brush against my bare legs every now and then as I waded knee-deep along the course of the brook, which made an easier route than the tangled banks.

At the end of a whole afternoon spent in this manner my mind felt bare, washed clean, like the stones in the brook.

And then—suddenly: fear. Where did it come from? I had no means of knowing. *Menace*. Cold fear was all around me—in the dark arch of the trees, the tunnel they made (into which the stream vanished), the sharp croak of birds, the icy grip of the water on my calves, the gritty scour of the mud on my grimed and scraped hands. But, most of all, in my own mind, as if, down at the back of it, stood something hidden, watchful, *waiting*. In another minute I would see it and know what it was. In another minute I would go mad from terror.

Frenzied with haste to be away from there I scrambled

up the bank, snatching my trowel and the wooden bucket in which I had been putting my lily roots—dropping half of them; panic-stricken, never looking back, I thrust and battered a track through alders and brambles, tearing my shirt, scratching my arms and face. Mother would be furious, but I never gave that a thought. All my need was to get home—home—home to Grandfather's comforting presence.

Barefoot I ran over the ploughed field, stubbing my toes on flints, reckless of sharp stubble-ends and dry thistles with their lancing spines. Tonight I would need to spend hours squeezing them out, painfully one by one. Tonight was not now. Now if I did not find Grandfather I would die of fear.

Luckily he was always to be found in the same place: placid on a backless chair with his dog Flag beside him, outside the smithy where my uncles Josef and Willi clanked on the anvil and roared on the bellows. A great grey cart-horse waited patiently, one hoof tipped forward. A cone of fire burned bright in the dim forge, and there was Uncle Josef in his black leather apron, holding the gold and blazing shoe in his long tongs. For once I didn't wait and watch. I ran and clung tight to Grandfather. He felt frail and bony, and smelt, as always, of straw and old-man's-odour, and sweet tobacco.

"Grandfather—Grandfather—" I gulped.

Holding me in thin strong old hands he looked at me long and shrewdly with his faded shrunken eyes.

"So it's happened, has it?"

"Yes. Yes. It has. But what *is* it, Grandfather? *What* has happened?"

"Easy. Easy!" He soothed me with his voice as if I had been a panicky foal. "It was bound to come. It always does. Your father—your brothers—now you. All our family. It always happens, sooner or later."

"But what? But what?"

A terrific fusillade of clangs came from the forge. Uncle Josef had the shoe back on the anvil and was reshaping it with powerful blows of his hammer. A fan of sparks rained out, making the cart-horse stamp and whinny.

"Come along," said my grandfather. "We'll walk to the church." He put his hand on my shoulder to hoist himself into a walking position, then kept it there, for balance. He was very stooped, and walked with a limp; still, for his years, he was as strong as an old root.

We went slowly along the village street. Marigolds blazed, nasturtiums climbed up the sides of the ancient timbered houses. Apples on the trees were almost ripe. The sky, though cloudless and blue as a gentian, was covered with a light haze; in the mornings and evenings now, mist lay thick in the valley. It was September.

"Winter is coming," said my grandfather.

"Yes, Grandfather."

"Winter is a kind of night," he said. "For months we are prisoners here in the village. As, at night, we are shut in our homes. The next village is a world's end away."

It was true. Our village lies in a deep valley. Often in winter the roads are blocked with snow for weeks, sometimes for months. Up to now I had never minded this. It was good fun, being closed away from the world. We had huge stacks of firewood—cellars full of wine and flour. The cows and sheep were stabled safely. We had dried fruits, stored apples, fiddles, music, jokes, and a few books. We had each other. What more did we need? Up to now I had loved the winter. But at this moment I shivered, as I pictured miles of gale-scoured hills, the snow sent by wind into long curving drifts, with never a human footprint. Darkness over the mountains for thirteen hours, from sunset to sunrise.

"Night is a kind of death," said my grandfather. And then: "You know that I have bad dreams."

Indeed I *did*. His yells when he woke from one of those legendary dreams were terrible to hear; they almost made the blood run backwards in your veins. Yet he would never tell us what the dream had been about; he would sit (once he was awake) white, panting, shaking, gasping, by his bed; sometimes he might have hurled himself right out of his cot, an arm's length away from it, and, next day, would be covered in black bruises, and his eyes sunken in deep grey hollows.

But what the dream was about, he would never reveal. Except perhaps to his old dog Flag, who had trotted behind us, never more than a yard away, along the village street. During the hours of daylight, Flag never left my grandfather; and at night, when all the dogs were left downstairs to guard the house and the livestock in the back stable, Flag invariably seemed to know beforehand, if my grandfather was going to have one of his bad dreams; in his own sleep he would whine and snuffle; or, often, he would be awake and trembling at the stairfoot all night long. And, next day, Grandfather, bruised, breathless, staring and shaky as he was, would be especially kind to Flag and feed him crusts of brown bread dipped in schnapps and honey.

"You know that I have bad dreams," repeated my grandfather.

"Yes, Opar; I know that. We all know it. And we are very sorry for you."

It seemed unfair that such a good, kind man should have such dreadful dreams. All his harmless life had been lived in the village. All his deeds were known. Never had he raised his hand unjustly or spoken in malice against another man. Why should *he* have to suffer such an affliction?

We came to the small graveyard where, under wooden

crosses and between browsing goats lay his father, my great-grandfather, and *his* father, and all my great-uncles and great-great-uncles and so on, back into the past for hundreds of years.

My grandfather looked gravely and gently at the crosses, as if they were old companions from a whole series of hard-fought battles.

"What do we know about being dead?" he said. "Nothing, really."

Old Flag lay down, panting, and Grandfather sat on the low wall. Then he gave me a severe look.

"You don't have any friends," he said.

"Well—how can I, Grandfather? There just isn't anybody of my age. Everybody else in the village is either too old for me, or too young."

He sighed. "Yes; that's true enough. But tell me now—and tell the truth—when you are by yourself, as you were this afternoon, do you have a made-up friend in your own mind, a dream friend, a wish friend, who comes and talks to you?"

I blushed.

"Yes—well—just sometimes—not very often—"

"One friend—or several?"

"One."

My imaginary friend, Milo, who kept me company sometimes, and laughed at my jokes, and praised me if I had done well in my lessons with Father Tomas.

"Send that being away!" said my grandfather strongly. "Send him away and never never let him come again. Such friends are—can be—very, very dangerous!"

"But, Grandfather, why?"

"Have you ever thought about your brothers?" he said. "Have you ever wondered why Anatol went to be a monk, why Peter joined the army?"

My brothers were many years older than myself. To be honest, I had never wondered about them at all.

"To be like my father—like Uncle Christian?" I suggested.

Grandfather carefully filled his pipe with strong, sweet-smelling tobacco.

"To be like them—yes," he said between puffs as he lit it. "But also for the same reason. No doubt your brother Peter will be killed, as your father was. No doubt Anatol will be lost to us, as your uncle Christian was. But *this* is the reason why they went: a soldier is never alone, for he is always surrounded by other soldiers. Likewise, a monk is never alone, for he is with other monks."

"And in the company of God, too?" I suggested.

"Humph! That depends on the man, I'd say." Grandfather stared, frowning, at the small ancient church, as if he did not quite know where to fit it into the picture that was forming in his mind. Then he went on, "The men of our family do not dare to be alone."

"I don't understand—"

"Something happened, once, to our ancestor—"

"Which ancestor?"

"Nobody knows. It was many generations ago. He was a clever man, whoever he was, much more book-learned than the people of his time. He found out something he should not have."

"What sort of thing? What did he find out?"

"We don't know. But it made him, the first in the family, terrified to be alone."

Impulsively, I started to speak, then closed my mouth. I myself had just encountered that fear, for the first time; I did not wish even to think of it.

"Has it ever occurred to you to wonder," said my grandfather, "what it would be like if you were alone in the world in an empty room, in an empty house, in a deserted town; if you had reason to be certain that nowhere, not anywhere in the whole world, was there another living being?"

I had never thought of such a possibility. I did now, and shivered at the chill of it.

"There you are," said my grandfather, "waiting in the empty house, in the empty street, in the empty world. And yet, now, *something* comes and taps on the door."

I clutched his hand.

"How *can* it? What *is* that Something?"

"That Something," said my grandfather, "is what stands waiting, now, down in the deepest cellar of your mind."

I let out a sharp cry.

"No! It has no right! I won't have it! I can't bear it!"

"You have to bear it," said Grandfather. "There is no reason to suppose that you, out of the whole family, will be spared."

"Then I'll—I'll—I'll join the army. Like Father, like Peter."

But I knew I would not.

"No," he said. "You have to stay and work the smithy. With your mother's brothers."

"But what *is* the Something? Why is it so dreadful? Is it," I said hopefully, "is it just because we don't know what it is, that it seems dreadful?"

"No," said Grandfather, quenching that hope. "It *is* dreadful. My dreams tell me that. It is dreadful, and it waits for all of us."

It has waited a long time for you, Grandfather, I thought. Ninety years.

And he spoke, echoing my thought.

"It has waited ninety years for me."

"But perhaps it won't ever get you, after all, Grandfather."

Flag whimpered dolefully at our feet, and Grandfather looked down and rubbed his ears.

"We must go home," he said. "It will be supper-time, and your mother will be wondering where you have got to."

"But what can I do about the—the thing, Grandfather? What can I do?"

"You can be brave," he said.

We walked back between the old houses with their gay flowers. Twilight was thickening in the air. My uncles had long done shoeing the cart-horse and the forge fire had been banked for the night; the tools were put away. I picked up my basket of dried, shrivelled lily roots and trudged beside my grandfather in silence.

"Grandfather?" I said after a while.

"Well?"

"Why no imaginary friends?"

"Because," he said, "because—knowing your deep need —they could gain great power over you. And might in the end become the Terror themselves. You must learn to stand quite alone."

"I can't bear it," I said again, and he said again, "You have to bear it."

My grandfather died that night, quickly and quietly, in his sleep. Uncle Josef discovered him in the morning, cold and stiff already; lying straight in his bed for once, with his hands composedly crossed on his breast.

For three days I felt unbelievably wretched, as if my own two hands had been cut off at the wrist. Grandfather had told me so many things, had looked after me so long, had treated me more like a son than a grandson; how could I ever get along in life without him?

And then, too, there was the aching sense of guilt and worry; had I, with my questions and confessions, with my clamour and my need, somehow laid too heavy a load on him and so hastened his end?

But Father Tomas the priest told me that Grandfather was a man of sterling qualities, a brave, thoughtful, honest, generous man who died in the fullness of years; we should not grieve too much for him, but should be proud of his life and happy that he had gone to a better place.

This comforted me, for a while.

We have this custom when somebody dies, that for three days they lie in the church, on a stone bier, with the empty coffin waiting below. Then the priest blesses the coffin, and the burial takes place.

So it was with Grandfather. For three days he lay in the church. Every morning the people who had loved him came to cover his body with new flowers, asters and late roses and marigolds and trails of scarlet briony berries and bunches of golden cherry leaves. He looked like a warrior garlanded with wreaths of victory.

And during that time I thought, all is well with Grandfather.

But on the third night old Flag, who had lain for days like a stone dog, with his head on his paws, who would not eat nor drink nor let out any sound—on the third evening Flag began to howl. At the stairfoot he howled and howled, dementedly, until Uncle Josef said at last, "For God's sake, put the beast outside, this is not to be borne!"

So he was turned loose in the street, and ran back and forth along the village all night, howling as if a pack of fiends were at his heels.

In the morning I found him crouched against the church door, shivering and whining. I tied him to a tree and raced to fetch Father Tomas, who unlocked the church door and went inside.

Waiting on the step, I heard him let out a great cry, and

so I followed him into the church, my heart thudding.

There lay Grandfather on the stone floor, a whole man's length away from the bier. The dead flowers were scattered about him, some crushed beneath him.

He must have hurled himself off the stone table, and clean over his coffin, which lay on the floor below.

He must have had another dream.

"But he was dead. He was *dead*. I should know, I have seen so many dead people. He has been dead for three days," Father Tomas kept repeating, and he crossed himself, over and over.

He sprinkled Grandfather's body with holy water, and the uncles came and helped him put it into the coffin. And nail down the lid.

The funeral was a hasty, furtive affair. Nobody looked at anybody else. Nobody spoke, apart from the usual prayers and psalms. And when it was over the people dispersed to their own homes without the usual feast, without even loitering for conversation.

Back at home, I huddled in a corner, with my arms round old Flag, and fed him bread dipped in honey and schnapps.

"What did he dream, old Flag? Do you know? Did he dream about Something?"

But old Flag only whined in reply.

I have a puppy now, one of his children's children, and he follows me wherever I go. And I am glad of his company against the day, not too far now, I think, when it will be my turn to dream about Something.

Birthday Gifts

The two sisters, Imelda and Catherine Dounraigh, had been, all their lives, in continual, if unavowed, competition. Ever since the early days when their father, Professor Dounraigh, had addressed them impartially as Boots and Snooks, and took no notice of either. The youngest son, Conor, was the only child in whom he showed the slightest interest; but unfortunately Conor, a brilliant boy, died untimely of Asian flu while in the sixth form at Bramchester; his elder sisters, by now at Leeds and Durham universities respectively, were from then on completely ignored by their father, who withdrew, after that day, into a cloud of angry grief. Their mother's timid sympathy and partisanship had never been of the least importance to either of them; Mrs Dounraigh, a gentle unassuming person, had always been morally trampled underfoot by her husband who, until the boy's death, had been a formidably successful mathematician; as a result of the tragedy, for which, in some obscure way he blamed her, she developed premature senility and had to be packed off into a Home.

Imelda was of the opinion that her mother had done it on purpose.

"Mother was never anything but totally ineffectual," she used to say, in her clipped impatient way. "This is just her means of opting out."

From age five (when her brother was born) Imelda had regarded life as a kind of obstacle course in which it was incumbent on the entrants to vault higher, run faster, leap farther, than anybody else; if you did not do that, what was the point of it at all? She had taken an excellent degree in physics, switched over to biology, discovered an unknown genetic factor in weasels, and was now the acknowledged authority on a new and obscure form of computer virus.

She had always treated her sister Catherine with the same tolerant scorn accorded to her female parent. Father and Conor were the only ones who counted in the family. So it was a cause of genuine (if undisclosed) satisfaction that for some years Catherine's career seemed at a standstill; she appeared to be destined for the same kind of tame, domestic, undistinguished obscurity that had enmeshed their mother. After taking a moderate arts degree at Durham, she went on to a worthy but unremarkable art school, did nothing very notable there, and then retired to a cottage in East Anglia which had been bequeathed her by a sister of their mother's, and settled down to a life of what Imelda described as "the worst kind of boring, amateur rusticity. She makes *pots*, believe it or not, and *weaves*, and embroiders. It really is quite a waste. After all, when she was at school and university, she did have some kind of a *mind*."

Catherine's failure to marry had increased the gulf between the two sisters; Imelda, while still at university, had contracted an alliance with a brilliant chemist (who then went into politics by way of television) and proceeded to give birth to three highly-intelligent children, who soon distinguished themselves at school and later in every possible way. The boys had medical careers, the girl took up dress design after gaining a first-class history degree.

When they were small, it had been convenient for their mother, in school holidays, to despatch the children to their Aunt Cathy, in her rural retreat, where they could enjoy the advantages of riding and sea-bathing, but after they were in their teens such contacts became a thing of the past; as ponies and windswept Suffolk beaches lost their appeal, visits to Aunt Cathy became condemned by Imelda's brood as boring. "Just an old cottage. Nothing to do in it." "What *does* she do with herself all day long?" her sister once asked, with fascinated distaste. "*I* dunno. Reads, or embroiders in that studio of hers. We hardly see her."

It had never been inquired whether Catherine enjoyed the incursions of her niece and nephews; Imelda naturally assumed that the young people's visits would furnish an interesting and lively distraction to their aunt's quiet existence.

At last intercourse between the sisters had been reduced to six-monthly telephone conversations during which Imelda, ringing up, would recount her family's latest triumphs in case Catherine had missed reading them in *The Times*: Graham's new job as Adviser to the Cabinet on the Distribution of Science Funds; her own honorary degrees from Adelaide, Tokyo, and Lausanne; Susannah's gold medal and commission to design clothes for small Royals; the boys' academic and professional successes.

Then, most unexpectedly, the balance tipped in the other direction: Catherine Dounraigh had spent, it seemed, the last ten years in researching, assembling, and processing the material for a monumental study of Lethargy, which was published by Cambridge University Press, and which received respectfully awestruck notices in the press; not only was it acclaimed by scholars, but the actual text was so witty, stylishly-written and absorbing that the book became, incredibly, a national bestseller, topped publishers' lists for weeks and months, was translated into Spanish, German, and Chinese, and made for its writer a substantial fortune, besides catapulting her into the public eye as an English picturesque country eccentric in the finest tradition. Catherine Dounraigh's Victorian cotton country dresses, rescued from East Anglian attics, her herb garden, her vegetarian

cookery, the fact that her aunt, previous owner of the
cottage, was reputed to have been a witch, her expertise on
that obscure instrument, the baryton, her intelligent views
on autism, hyperactivity, and other related topics, but,
above all, her truly remarkable tapestries, a combination of
paint, collage, and embroidery, were endlessly described,
discussed, and portrayed in colour supplements, TV programmes, and journals of every calibre from *Private Eye* to
Goody Gumboots' Gossip Weekly.

The tapestries were to be seen on view at Versailles,
where they attracted so much acclaim that the Prado, the
Cloisters, the Cluny, and several other museums were soon
hotly engaged in outbidding one another (the Prado finally
acquired them in the teeth of an anonymous Japanese
bidder).

Imelda was at first, not unnaturally, somewhat stunned
by all this celebrity and limelight focused so unexpectedly on
her humdrum sister; but she appeared to take it graciously
enough: "In our family we are all achievers, of course;
except for poor mother; so it isn't at all surprising, really,
that Catherine should produce something at last . . ." she
explained to various of her acquaintances who had expressed
some surprise, remembering her frequent previous strictures
and slighting references to "poor Cathy, Father used to say
she was practically retarded, IQ barely normal." Whereas
nowadays, recalling her father, Imelda tended to say, "He
talked a great deal to me, latterly; I was the only one he
could talk to, he used to say. Conor was bright, of course,
but shallow; probably had one of those flash-in-the-pan
brains that often fizzle out later. It may have been a mercy
that he died when he did. Father would have been so
disappointed if he hadn't fulfilled his early promise. Father
always thought that Catherine might be a late starter . . ."

Professor Dounraigh had died at the time of Imelda's

marriage, so there was nobody to contradict these reminiscences.

Fortunately for Imelda, the balance was to some extent righted at this juncture by the publication of a book on Freud's obsession with maps, by Jonas, the elder of her two sons, both of whom had gone into popular psychiatry; while the daughter Susannah announced her engagement to the youngest son of a duke; so honours might have been considered even, except that the book on Freud was somewhat dismissively reviewed by several experts. 'Shallow' 'frothy' 'lacking in depth' were comments calculated to give the mother of the writer no particular pleasure.

The sisters' birthdays, both in June, were only a week apart, and, when they were small these anniversaries had, much to their annoyance, been, as a matter of convenience, celebrated together on a day midway between the two dates—as if they were not of sufficient importance to be considered worth taking separately. While Conor, whose birthday fell in October, had a festival all of his own.

It had been the sisters' habit, since they were grown, and possibly even before that, to give each other birthday presents that were ingeniously calculated to annoy. Clothes that were expensive, fitted well, but were unbecoming, records of composers known to be disliked, *objets d'art* so inappropriate as obviously to have been chosen out of malice or bought at charity sales, hideous foreign peasant artefacts, unreadable books. Once, three years in succession, Imelda had given her sister sets of lace-edged table doilies. "I don't use doilies, you know," Catherine had been driven to say on the third occasion. "Oh—don't you?" Imelda had answered vaguely. "I thought, somehow, that you did . . ."

It was felt, tacitly, that she had scored a point on that anniversary in the unacknowledged duel that was forever being waged between them.

This summer Imelda's husband Graham Klopstock (now Sir Graham) had suffered a mild lung-infection and was ordered rest in bracing sea air. His wife therefore proposed that the couple should come down to Suffolk for a week and the two sisters celebrate their birthdays together, a thing they had not done since their teens.

The plan may have had a certain basis in Imelda's wish to demonstrate to her acquaintance that she and her sister were on the most cordial of terms after the latter's unexpected fame, that envy or jealousy played no part in their relationship.

"Do you mean actually *stay* with your sister?" Sir Graham had demanded, in alarm. "No, no, *no*, we'll stay at the Walberswick Arms, of course, I don't know if Catherine even has a spare room any more, the whole cottage is probably elbow-deep in art supplies and embroidery things. Characteristic of Catherine that if she had to take to an art form it should be such a typically feminine one," remarked Imelda who like her father before her had a somewhat pejorative and puritanical attitude towards the arts.

So long as he was assured of residence at a comfortable hotel, Graham did not make any objections; his apprehensions had been raised by memories of his children's reports on Aunt Cathy's cottage "full of tables covered with typed pages and unfolded ironing-boards with bits of material trailing everywhere." He had never been invited to the place himself; had, indeed, met his sister-in-law on only two other occasions, at his own wedding and his father-in-law's funeral. (His mother-in-law, in her Home, was still alive, but people tended to forget her existence for years together. A Trust took care of her expenses.)

Surprised at the suggestion, but graciously assenting, Catherine booked a suite for the Klopstocks at the hotel and made arrangements to take them out to dinner on Imelda's birthday (which came first) at a local vegetarian restaurant of good repute. Neither of the visitors was a vegetarian. "But," as Catherine observed, "since I will have to come off my Vegan diet for the meal, we are all making some concessions." "Of course," kindly assented Imelda, while Graham, looking depressed, said nothing.

"It really is a very lucky thing," added Catherine, "that you came down here for your birthday, since the present I found for you is so valuable that I should have hesitated to entrust it to the post."

This gift turned out to be, when duly presented on the day, a Victorian night-dress of such amplitude, so tucked, rucked, frilled, ruched, adorned with broderie anglaise and insertions of narrow ribbon, so flounced, pounced, fringed, and trimmed, that it seemed made rather for some gigantic creation of antiquity, such as the Sphinx, than for human form.

"Thank you, my dear," faintly declared Imelda, whose taste for stark simplicity, based on the elegant fashions of her daughter, were, she fancied, well understood in the family.

"Knowing your fondness for lace-edged doilies I knew it couldn't fail to please," Catherine blandly told her. "Besides, it has a most unusual and distinctive history; it belonged, believe it or not, to Florence Nightingale. The pedigree is absolutely authenticated. Nightingale gave it to an old and much-loved nurse, who retired here to Suffolk and never wore it but kept it as a family treasure. I thought, since you are such an advocate of women's advancement, that you would be specially interested in wearing a garment that had belonged to so notable a pioneer."

"I appreciate the thought very much."

"Mind you do wear it, now! You'll see that she does, won't you, Graham? This very night!"

"Certainly I will. Though," Imelda's husband added, bursting into laughter, "she will look just like a pregnant bracket fungus in it, won't you, darling?"

Imelda, tending to bony gauntness when young, had become, in middle age, almost square in shape; "having," as she impatiently said, "no time to indulge in all those self-preservative exercises with which some women seem to take up all their days."

She now studied the Victorian night-dress with silent dislike, wondering how soon it would be safe to give it, either to her daughter Susannah (though Susannah did not share the current trendy passion for such articles) or, preferably, to some folk museum. But would Catherine be likely to inquire after it? No use saying it had worn out. Its construction seemed guaranteed to defy time; it looked built to last for ever.

Graham was vaguely wondering what kind of a garment his sister-in-law wore in bed. She was a strange-looking, eldritch little creature, with pointed features, wispy grey hair, and burning grey eyes; her clothes were amazingly nondescript but contrived to hang round her in picturesque folds, a feature which had been turned to full advantage by the Sunday colour supplements. They looked as if they had been bought at jumble sales and doubtless had been; Graham decided that Catherine probably retired to bed in a man's flannel night-shirt.

Arrangements for her birthday were now under discussion. "The boys are bringing down your present," said Imelda. "It is to be a surprise. Con and Jonas have arranged it between them."

The boys, now two handsome successful young doctors in their early thirties, duly arrived on Catherine's birthday. (Susannah was unable to appear, being about to give birth to a ducal grandchild.) The whole party dined at the Walberswick Arms, Catherine eating nothing but grapefruit, undressed salad, and some of her own goats' cheese which she had brought with her. She did, however, drink a little champagne.

Imelda was in a rather strange state; had been, indeed, for the last three days.

"For Christ's sake, Ma, what *is* it?" demanded Jonas as soon as he first laid eyes on her. "You look as if you've had a breakdown."

"I'm glad *someone* takes it seriously. Your father just thought it a load of nonsense. All *he* said was for heaven's sake don't talk about it to the PM."

The PM was a great friend of Sir Graham and Lady Klopstock.

"He would," said Con. "But what *happened* to you?"

"It was that night-dress your aunt Cathy gave me for my birthday. I wore it that night. One night! If I'd slept in it again I think I'd have died."

"For crying out loud! What did it do, give you dreams?"

"No, not dreams. Just moods, impressions. Utter, *utter* despair. Giving up. I could perfectly understand why Florence Nightingale retired to her bed and never got out of it again."

"She did quite a lot while she was *in* bed, mind," pointed out Jonas. "But still, I suppose in a way she did give up. Who else had the night-dress, after her?"

"I don't know. But I'm sure whoever did just pined away and died of hopelessness."

"*Accidie*," said Con cheerfully. "One of the Seven Deadly Sins. What Aunt Cathy's an expert on. I must say, it was rather naughty of her to give it to you."

"Oh," said Imelda vaguely—she felt better now she had been able to talk about her experience, and have it discussed, instead of laughed at—"very likely Cathy didn't know about its effect. How should she? I don't suppose she wore it."

"I wonder," said Jonas, inspecting the garment. "Well: maybe we can try it on some of our patients. Be an interesting experiment."

He and his brother were now jointly running a clinic near Bury St Edmunds for artistically creative psychotics—a picturesque venture that attracted a lot of publicity and funding.

"In the meantime, you go and pick up Aunt Cathy for dinner, and Con and I will drop the present round at her cottage after you've gone, so as to give her a surprise when she gets home. Then we'll follow you to the Arms for dinner."

This programme was duly carried out. The dinner was adequately festive, thanks to the high spirits of Jonas and Con, who teased their aunt in a fairly friendly way about her recent intellectual success.

"Number One on the bestseller list four months running! Put Ma's nose right out of joint. Hasn't it, Ma?"

Since Imelda's only published works were learned monographs on weasel genetics and computer viruses, this was regarded as a pleasantry and received with gracious humour.

After dinner they all adjourned to Catherine's cottage for coffee and liqueurs.

A wet June evening had succeeded a cold June day, and uneven shapes of misty rain wavered uneasily among the lilac, syringa bushes, and apple trees which screened Catherine's unassuming, grassy garden plot from the flat East Anglian landscape that lay beyond. It could not, as Jonas assured his brother in an undertone and with a nudge, have been better conditions for their surprise. Dark had not yet fallen—would not for another hour—but nobody could have said that the visibility was one hundred per cent.

"Is that somebody upstairs?" said Imelda.

"Probably one of my cats," said Catherine.

"Here you are, Aunt Catherine," said Jonas, "a drop of Benedictine, just right for your Vegan diet. Remember how you used to take us out gathering mussels when we were young and un-diet-conscious?—My goodness me, Auntie, you certainly have some hardy and weather-proof friends! Who's *that*, out there in your garden?"

Catherine looked where he pointed, and dropped her glass, which smashed on the stone flags.

The illusion was complete. It was only a dummy figure, cast in concrete, disposed on a metal office-chair; but, at a distance, through the wavering skeins of moist drizzle, against the mass of lilac bushes, it had exactly the appearance of a dead person. Or some aged, incapacitated figure, unable to get up and move . . .

"It looks like *Conor*!" said Catherine, white to the lips. "How did—"

"No, it ain't, Aunt Cath! It's a model of Jonas there. Isn't it lifelike, though? Won't it make a conversation piece in your boring little garden? Just you wait, Auntie, till the colour supplements see *him*!"

Young Con had fetched a dustpan and swept up the shards of glass. Catherine, with her colour slowly coming back, was able to sip another drink and congratulate her relatives on a most original present.

"He weighs about a ton," said Con. "Don't try shifting him yourself, Aunt Cath, or you'll slip a disc for sure. He'll be company for you, out there! Just as good as a husband."

They all laughed.

"Even better," said Catherine, whose lips were still pale. "For I can always draw the curtains."

"He was made by one of our patients—a dear, sweet, creative fellow—only he *can* be rather naughty when the mood is on him. But he has a real gift for sculpture at other times. It's a grand likeness of Jonas, isn't it?"

"I never noticed before," said Catherine, giving her nephew a slow scan, "how like your uncle Conor you were."

"Catherine must have detested her brother," said Sir Graham, later, at the Walberswick Arms.

"Oh no—I don't think so," answered his wife vaguely, taking off her glasses. "It's just that he was the only one to whom Father ever spoke."

After the Klopstock family had returned to town, Catherine Dounraigh made a strong and determined effort, which was on the whole successful, to ignore the piece of sculpture that occupied her garden.

The task was not easy. For the piece was quite large— slightly above life-size—and was so uncomfortably realistic. Rain or fine, there it sat, grey and patient in its metal chair, waiting. But for what? She might draw the curtains, but then it was still there, outside, waiting, whatever the weather. Lying in bed she thought of it every night, sitting out there in the wet. She could have called in a neighbouring farmer to remove it, with tractor and winch, drop it into one of the deep ponds for which Suffolk is well known—but that would be an admission of defeat.

Imelda had won another point, Catherine was obliged to acknowledge.

Moreover, as the months passed, Catherine observed something else, for which she could hardly give Imelda the credit.

Slowly, month by month, the concrete image was drawing closer to the house. For several weeks it would remain in the same spot—becalmed—and then, one day, she would discover that it had shifted, was a foot farther from the lilacs, a foot closer to the lily bed.

Autumn drew in, the dark fell earlier.

Catherine, who fortunately had learned method during her researches into the history of lassitude, now observed that the statue always seemed to make its move on the same night—a Sunday night before the first Monday in the month.

Armed with this useful and reassuring piece of solid fact, she kept impassive watch, concealed in a thick and screening clump of Dutch firs. And presently she was rewarded by the sight of her two nephews, parking their estate car in the adjoining stubble-field, and coming through the hedge with a jack and a trolley, evidently to move the statue, with a great many smothered chuckles.

One must pay this tribute to the Dounraigh family, thought Catherine: even their practical jokes are carried out with fanatical efficiency. If on a somewhat juvenile level.

But when they approached more closely to the figure on the chair, she heard one of them let out a smothered shriek; and then they were both running for dear life to the boundary hedge, whimpering and moaning with fright.

Catherine stepped out from cover and impaled them on the brilliant beam of her police torch, ordering them to stop.

"Or I'll shoot!" she called.

Shamefaced, the brothers slowed to a standstill. A strong whiff of alcohol floated from them.

"Oh—it's you, Aunt Cath," Con gulped, mortally embarrassed.

"Whom did you think it was?"

"I—we—*that*—"

"A fine pair you are. Two doctors!" She looked at them scornfully. "You look like two twelve-year-olds. How long do you think it took me to work out that you visit the clinic at Saxingby on the first Monday of every month? You ought to be ashamed of yourselves. How would you like this to get into the papers?"

"Aunt Cath—" Jonas glanced behind him. "Who the *hell* have you got sitting on that chair?"

Catherine glanced towards the chair. The figure on it—now voluminously robed in some kind of white enveloping garment—had risen cumbrously to its feet and taken one or two slow paces towards them. Jonas let out another little whine of terror—he was plainly the more inebriated of the two—bolted through the scanty hedge and disappeared from view. A moment later they heard the sound of the motor starting.

"He's got no guts at all, has he?" said Catherine acidly. "At least you didn't run, Con. Don't you want to come and meet your grandmother?"

With his legs barely supporting him, Con lurched forward until he could get a focused view of the massive figure, wrapped in pale fur, with its blurred features and melancholy puzzled eyes.

"I've had her living with me for the past year-and-a-half," said Catherine. "Take her arm, will you, Con; that's right. And she's a lot better, now—aren't you, Mother?—than she was at the start. Shall we go back to the house, now, Mother?"

"Yes, dear; if you say so . . ."

The body of Jonas, still in his car, was found at the bottom of one of the deep Suffolk ponds next day. Catherine felt badly about that. She had not anticipated such a drastic outcome. But, as he had been the one to plan the practical joke with the statue, she felt that the blame for his death must be at least partly his own.

The two sisters never communicated again. But Mrs

Dounraigh made a modest recovery under her daughter's patient care; and is now able to read large type, embroider, and knit.

The Rose-garden Dream

My brother Skid can do this queer thing.

Could do.

He only did it twice, that I know of; but twice is twice more than probably any other person in the whole world.

And I've dreamed of him doing it, other times. And I think sometimes my dreams of him are true. Can't say for sure, as I haven't seen him since he left home. He don't write to me, and I don't write him, for I've no address to send to.

Skid can just *go* . . .

Of course there has to be a looking-glass in the room, or a bowl of water. Something that reflects.

The first time he done it, was when we were in Primary. We're twins, see, that's why we dream the same dreams. "What happened after we walked in the door?" Skid'd say, putting on his socks in the morning, and I'd say, "Don't you remember? We looked about and saw the wallpaper was all blue and white flowers," and he'd say, "Oh yes, now I got it."

Of course our best dream, the one we had regular, it might be as often as twice a month, was the Garden of Roses dream. We never tired of that one. And Skid didn't need reminding about it; I reckon we both of us just about know it by heart.

It never changed, see.

Anyway, back to Primary School. Herdman Road Infants, it was. I started there six weeks before Skid, cos he got asthma very bad and had to stay home. He was always getting asthma, and it used to rile Dad, he said Skid could easily snap out of it if he — — chose. Our elder brothers didn't get asthma, why should he? Dad used to get very mad and slap him about. Nothing to what he done later, though.

So, anyway, I'd got used to the school six weeks before Skid turned up, and that wasn't a bad thing; I knew, and I could tell him, which doors to go through, things like that, which of the big ones was horrible, which weren't so bad as they looked, and which teachers to keep clear of.

Bad luck for Skid, he got there three days before our birthday.

Girls didn't have it as bad on their birthdays. But with the boys, for some reason, Mr Goadby (he was one to keep clear of), he used to make the birthday kid come out in front of his class and then, don't ask me why, he'd pull the kid's hair and ears, and thump him on the head with a bible. Thumped really hard, too. All meant in fun, he *said*, but lots of the boys hated it, some of them yelled.

And, when I told Skid what he had to expect, I could see he was dreading it. Really dreading it. He was little and skinny, covered in bruises anyway because of our Dad having it in for him at home, and he was timid. Things like that upset him more than they done other boys.

So, on our birthday, going to school, he was white as Mother's Pride already and I could see the beads of sweat all over his spotty, scurfy little forehead.

"Does it happen right away?" he asked, licking his lips as if they were flaky-dry.

"Can't tell," I says. "Sometimes first thing. Sometimes old Goader takes a fancy to do it at the end of the period. But don't you be scared, boy. Just stand there, don't show him you're bothered. Cos then he only goes on more. Remember, now!"

"Come out there, now, the birthday lad!" roars out Goadby, half-way through, and I was glad for Skid so he'd get it over with.

A couple of others pushed him out from the boys' side of the room and he stood in front, flinching, sort of, and squinting sideways up at Goadby, who's tall and bony and red-headed.

"Ah, yes. Our dear little Skidmore Weatherby. A most distinguished patro-nymic," says Goadby, kind of smacking his lips and glowering at the same time. "Pity you don't *look* the part more, eh? Eh? *Stand up straight, boy!*" he suddenly barked, and made Skid start so much he nearly fell over, and the current of air, when he jumped, must have affected a small round shaving mirror what was dangling on a string from the ceiling (for some project the bigger ones had been doing) and it turned slowly round, flashing as it caught a ray of the sun, then tipping lop-sided so it happened to catch Skid's terrified eye as he gazed upwards, waiting for the punishment to begin.

And—suddenly—he wasn't there.

Goadby had looked away for a second, when the flash from the mirror caught *his* eye. And when he looked back, Skid was gone.

"Hey, *you*! Come back!" bawls Goadby. "I hadn't finished with you yet. Devil take it, where *is* the brat? Where's he hiding? Who's sheltering him? Come out from under that desk, I can see you!"

He prowled all over the classroom (it wasn't very big) while we all sat paralysed. *Nobody* was going to say "Skid took and vanished" because, for a start, we didn't believe it ourselves. Things like that just don't happen. And, secondly, if anyone was such a clunch as to say it, he'd have had Goadby down on him like the Last Trump.

So we sat mum and mute, and squinted at each other out

of the corners of our eyes. And presently, looking out of the window, Goadby says, "Why, there *is* the little caffler, out there in the playground. That boy will grow into a cat-burglar. How did he get out there? I never saw a get-away to beat it. Go out there and fetch him back, Blaydon."

But luckily at that moment the bell rang for end of period, and we all scarpered off, and even Goadby didn't try to take it any further.

I said to Skid in the playground, "What *happened*?"

He was looking dazed. He said, "I dunno. I was lookin' in the glass—we was both lookin' in the glass, him an' me —an' I could see the playground in the glass as well, over his shoulder, like—an' then I was *there*. Out there. In the playground."

"You didn't go through the door?"

"Don't remember," he said, looking doubtful.

I could tell he didn't like being asked about it. We didn't say anything about it to Mam, and we *certainly* didn't tell our Dad. And, as no one at school believed what they'd seen, no one talked about it after that.

Skid never done well at school, and his asthma got worse. And he used to get terrible pains in the belly and couldn't eat. That made Dad really wild. "If you don't eat your dinner today," he used to tell Skid, "then you'll get it tomorrow. And so on till you do finish it." Breathing heavily down on the kid, smelling of beer. Sometimes the same plate of stew would come out, day after day, till it got to look really nasty, kind of wrinkled and buckled and grainy, as if at any moment the whole plateful might begin to heave about. It made you gulp just to see it. Mam wasn't much of a cook at best. And nobody's stew is up to much after our days.

So one afternoon Skid was stuck in the back kitchen with plate of stuff like that. Mam couldn't stand it—our Dad

was just as hard on her as on the rest of us—and she'd gone
down the yard with a basket of wash to hang up.

"Now: I'm going upstairs to get my Sunday belt," says
Dad—his Sunday belt was the one he used to tan us with,
cos it was thicker—"I'm going to get my Sunday belt and
if that stew's not et up by the time I'm back, my boy, you're
going to be sorry. Very sorry."

He walked up the stairs, slow and heavy. Skid gave a
kind of panic-stricken stare round our back kitchen. Brick
floor, table, chairs, sink. Our row of boots by the back door.
Quick as a flash, Skid poured the plate of stew (it was quite
runny) into his boots. He done it very neat, considering.
There was just enough to fill both boots. They weren't very
big. Then he's at the table again, sitting in front of the
empty plate, when Dad comes back.

I was rinsing socks under the tap, sick with fright.

Dad looks at the plate and does a double take.

"You never et that in the time, boy, don't try to fool me,"
he says, and his eye roams slowly round the room, kettle on
the hob, old Jip in his dog-basket, clock on the mantel,
calendar on the wall. Then it comes to the boots.

"Aha!" says Dad as if satisfied. "Thought you'd be one
too many for me, did you, young man? Well—I'm about to
show you that you are WRONG!"

He starts off slow and quiet, but ends on a shout, with
his face dark red, and beery breath coming quick.

Skid sits at the table, petrified.

"Get out o' the way, you," Dad says, elbowing me away
from the sink, and he fills the washing-up pan with water
and sets it on the table. Then he picks up one of the boots
full of cold stew.

"Now, my boy," he says, walking slow towards Skid,
"you are going to swallow down this stew, if I have to tip
it all down your skinny throat. Then you are going to

swallow what's in the other boot. And then you are going to wash those boots—your good boots, what cost money—in that pan of water. And *then* you are going to get such a tanning—"

As he moved towards Skid, I saw my brother's eyes shoot wildly about the kitchen, and come to rest on the pan of water. It reflected the sky, and the branches of the big old cherry tree in the yard.

Next moment, Skid's gone. Like a pricked bubble.

There's Dad, standing by the table, with the boot full of stew in his hand, looking dumbstruck.

Next minute we hears a shriek and something big and dark falls past the window. I hear Mam's voice outside in the yard calling, "Bert! Bert! Sal! Come quick! Skid's fallen! He's hurted himself! *Quick!*"

"What the — — —!" says Dad; and, after a moment or two, staring about him as if he's just come out from under gas, he stumbles out the back door.

I take the chance, while there's no one about, to tip the stew from both boots into Jip's tin dinner-pan. Jip gives me a grateful look and starts in eating it in big gulps. (Jip's always raving hungry and not particular.) I rinse Skid's boots in the pan of water and run out after Dad.

He and Mam are having a big stand-up argument.

"I saw him fall, I tell you!" she yells at him. "Out of the cherry tree! Go and fetch the doctor. Hurry! He may have busted something. I'm not shifting him till the doctor's seen him. Very like he's got concussion. Look at the way he lies!"

Then I saw Skid, flat out in the grubby flower-bed full of snail shells outside the kitchen window where Mam tries to grow mint and parsley. Skid didn't move at all. And one of his arms was doubled back in a queer way.

"What *I* want to know is," said Dad, "how the — blazes did he get there when he was indoors just now?"

"How should *I* know?" says Mam, short and wild. "Maybe you throwed him there." And, under her breath, I hear her mutter, "One o' these days you'll go too far—"

Dad, looking angry and mazed, goes for the doc. Who says that Skid's got concussion and a busted arm. So he's in bed for a bit; and the boots and the stew's not spoken of, though we all know Dad'll have it in for Skid even worse when he does get up.

"What happened *that* time?" I ask Skid a couple of days later, one evening when we're alone in the bedroom, Mam and Dad down the pub.

"I saw the tree's branches . . . in the water . . . and next minute I was *in* them. That's all. I don't want to talk about it," says Skid. "Let's talk about our garden."

So we talked about that instead.

It's always the same, our dream. First, walking up the path to this mountain. Steep path, rocky, spiky mountain. Blue and bony against the pale sky. Then we get to the gates. There's four of 'em, all gold, solid gold. Big and splendid, flashing. Like the gates to a palace. Higher than your head. Funny thing, there's no fence. Just a silk thread running from one pair of gates to the next. You'd think anybody could get in. But they can't, only us. There's something queer about that thread. Maybe it's electrified. No one can get past it. You touch it, your hand comes off. Or whatever you touched it with. "I wish Dad would touch it," Skid said once, kind of dreamy.

But, mostly, when we are there, we don't think about anything at home.

We go through one of the gates, it don't matter which, they open for us as we come to them, like the doors of the Welcome Supermarket. And then we're inside. First thing you notice is the scent of the roses. They're everywhere.

huge tall rose trees, higher than houses, all covered with big open roses, wide open and sweet-smelling. Not the kind you see at Green Alley Florist's, tight and narrow and wrapped up with no scent to 'em; these ones have a big open patch of gold in the middle, round as an eye, and the scent's enough to turn you giddy.

There's narrow paths winding everywhere, among the big old rose trees, and birds singing. Not birds we know, foreign ones, and you can't see 'em, but their voices are loud and sweet, they're all singing their hearts out.

Skid and I wander about in there—sometimes it seems like hours, sometimes only five or ten minutes; then, slowly, a cold mist comes along the paths, and the bushes begin to dim away into it, and the birds' voices aren't so loud, and then—all of a sudden—it's gone, and we're outside in the cold. And I can't find words to tell *how* cold and sad that is. For each time we're there, we believe that *this* time we'll be able to stay, and not ever, ever go back.

But, of course, we never can.

"Some day I will, though," says Skid. "Some day I'm going to pick one of the roses. If we could only do that, I reckon we could get to stay."

"Roses are hard to pick. You need scissors or clippers. Or a knife."

"Well, I'll take one." And, for a while, Skid took to hiding a little penknife under his pillow, one our brother Bob gave him for Christmas. But it never works. When we have our rose-garden dream the knife stays behind, at home, under the pillow.

And maybe, I think, that's just as well. For if Skid managed to pick one of the roses, it might work the other way. It might break the spell. He might never get back to the garden again.

*

Our garden never changed. But we changed. We got bigger,
and Dad got angrier. Time we got to fifteen, Dad was laying
into Skid just about every time they was together. Hurt him
real bad, sometimes.

So in the end, Skid run off.

What else could he do?

There's no jobs round where we live, so he couldn't have
got one anyway. It's a case of signing on and lining up.
That's all they ever do. Skid couldn't stand for that, not
and then come home to be knocked about by our Dad. So
he run off, up to the big city.

I reckon so, at least. That's what he said he'd do. And I
often dream about him. I can see him trudging about the
streets; he looks thin and pale, with his fair hair getting
longer and greasier. Mostly he's hungry, got nothing to eat.
Skid wouldn't mind that part of it too much, for he never
did eat a lot. But I worry, cos he's getting *ever* so thin.

And, at night, I see him and all the other kids—sometimes
there's scores of 'em—lying under these arches, if it's wet
weather, or along by the river, under a bridge. Some of 'em
has newspapers wrapped round, some has sleeping-bags;
more has nothing at all.

Night after night I get this dream of Skid and all the
others, most of them as young as him, lying there side by
side, like sardines, under the greeny, greasy light of the
streetlamp.

Sometimes Skid is dreaming our dream. And sometimes
I dream it too; but not so often, now. More often, now, I'm
dreaming about *him*.

So, one night, along the street comes this old cove. He's
blind, you can tell, for he has a white stick, ivory, with a
silver handle, and he goes tap, tap. But he's well-dressed
quite grand, in a coat with a fur collar, and a hat, and has
another big feller with him, who seems like a servant. Yo

can tell. They go along, slow, looking down at all the sleepers lined up along the pavement.

Every now and then, the one with the stick stops, and gives a poke to one o' the sleepers, and says to him, "Quick: tell us what you are dreaming about!"

And, mostly, the sleeping guy will wriggle and curse and mumble some rubbish, or just growl "Go to hell! Leave me be!" and then the two wakeful ones will go on their way.

But, every now and then, one of the sleepers will say something that makes the big feller snap on a tape recorder he carries on a strap round his neck. And then they listen real careful.

And so they come along, and they get to Skid.

Skid is sleeping very peaceful and, right away, I know he's dreaming the rose-garden dream. I can tell it by the happy look on his face and the way he lies, his hands relaxed, breathing so quietly. And when the guy touches him with his stick and says, "Quick! Tell me what you are dreaming!" Skid rolls on to his back and begins to talk, in a clear voice and very fast, on and on, as if he's one of those radio announcers giving the forecast. But what he says is just double-dutch, not even English, but a kind of nonsense language; abana teapotty throumi tirpan weeho—or something just as crazy as that. Whatever it is, the big guy snaps on his tape recorder and catches it all. And the blind cove seems to get very excited, and by and by wakes Skid by giving him a sharp poke with the ivory cane.

"Hey! Don't *do* that!" yells Skid, looking up, confused and blinking, at the two above him. "Why the plague did you have to wake me? Who are you? I wasn't doing anything wrong."

"No, no, of course not," says the blind guy. He speaks very posh and calm, like a TV news reader. "And we don't mean you any harm."

"Well, then, leave me alone!"

Skid is sore, because of being woke from his dream. I can see that.

"I'd like you to come to my studio," says the blind guy. "It's just along here. We'll give you a bit of supper. And there's money in it for you. Come along with us, now."

They've got a car, a big old Rolls, and somehow they manage to coax Skid into it. Next thing I see them bring him into this big room, with a huge high ceiling, and window looking out over the river. "This used to be what's-his-name's studio," says the blind guy. Some name like Rosy. Didn't mean nothing to me, nor to Skid, who was looking sort of scared and panicky.

"What d'you *want* with me?" he keeps saying. "Leave me alone!"

"No harm, I promise. I'm doing research," says the blind guy, soothing as the doctor when he's going to stick a dirty great needle in your backside. And, in fact, when they give Skid a sandwich and a glass of Coke, I see the big bloke slip a shot of something into the Coke, out of a little bottle. And, very soon, Skid starts to fall asleep, lying back on a kind of sofa they call a shay zlong. Up on the wall at the end of the room is a huge old silvery mirror that shows the river outside, and tugboats and police launches going past.

You can feel it's very late, after midnight.

"Just lie back now, comfortable," says the blind guy, and, for the third time, he says "We don't mean you any harm."

"What *do* you want, then?" mumbles Skid, and the guy says, "I collect dreams, that's all."

"*Well, you're not going to collect mine!*" shrieks Skid, suddenly wide awake and panicking. "My dream's all I ever had, and *you're not getting it off me!*"—and suddenly he's gone, clean out of the room, and the two guys looking at each other, utterly scared and shook and puzzled, like Dad or Mr

Goadby back in Herdman Road Infants. There's nothing between them but the empty leather sofa.

So what I see next is people on the river bank, pulling something ashore. There's cops, and torches, and the splash of water and thump of oars against concrete piling.

And there's Skid, laid out on the bank, white and wet and silent in the blue light of the police lamp. Dead as a mackerel on a fishmonger's slab.

And in his clenched fingers is a big pink open rose.

All this is only my dream! All this is only my dream!

Watkyn, Comma

When Miss Harriet Sibley, not in her first youth, received an unexpected legacy from a great-uncle she had never met, there was not a single moment's hesitation in her mind. I shall give up my job in the bank, she thought, and live by making cakes.

Miss Sibley had never baked a cake in her life, nor was she even a great cake-eater; once in a way, perhaps, she might nibble a thin slice of Madeira, or a plain rice bun; but rice buns were becoming exceedingly hard to find.

All the more reason why I should start up a little baking business, thought Miss Sibley triumphantly. I need not have a shop. I can do it from home. Word about good cakes very soon gets passed around.

And she began hunting for suitable premises.

Due to soaring house prices she encountered considerable difficulty in finding anything that lay within her means. For months every Saturday and Sunday was passed in the search. From cottages she turned to warehouses, from warehouses to barns. Even a ruined barn, these days, fetched hundreds of thousands.

But at last she came across exactly what she wanted, and the price, amazingly, was not unreasonable. Miss Sibley did not waste any time investigating possible disagreeable reasons for this; if there are drawbacks, I will deal with them as they come up, she decided, in her usual swift and forthright way, and she made an offer for the ruins of Hasworth Mill. Her offer was instantly accepted, and she engaged a firm of local builders to render the ruins habitable.

The building stood on a small island, with the River Neap on one side, describing a semicircle, and the mill-race on the other, spanned by a three-arched bridge.

What better place to bake cakes than a mill? thought Miss Sibley.

When she inquired why the place had remained uninhabited for so long, she received a variety of answers. The mill itself had ceased to grind corn after the closure of Hasworth Station and its branch railway line, which had made the transport of corn and flour so much more costly. Then there had been legal disputes between the heirs of the last owner. One had been in Canada, one in Australia, the affair had dragged on for years. Meanwhile the damp rotted the woodwork as the mill stood empty. Purchasers don't like damp, Miss Sibley was told. But damp is, after all, to be expected if you live on an island, she replied sensibly. Then there were the trees, very large: a huge cedar, twice the height of the mill, guarded the approach bridge, some willows grew on the island, a row of Lombardy poplars screened the meadow beyond. Trees make a place dark, some people dislike it.

Miss Sibley had lived all her life in a brick street; to her, the prospect of owning twelve Lombardy poplars, five willows, and a giant cedar was intoxicating.

The word *haunted* never passed anyone's lips.

The island itself was small; not much bigger than a tennis-court. During the years that the mill had stood empty, brambles had proliferated and the place was a wilderness; Miss Sibley looked forward to turning it into a garden by and by. Meanwhile the builders used it as a dumping place for their loads of bricks and stacks of new timber. The brambles were cut and trampled down, and some of them dug up, as new drains had to be laid, and damp-proof foundations inserted; in the process of this digging a male skeleton was unearthed.

It had been buried with care, and quite deep, handsomely coffined and wrapped in some half-rotted piece of brocade material, which Dr Adams the coroner, who was also a keen local historian, inspected carefully and pronounced to be the remains of an altar-cloth or consecrated banner.

"In fact, my dear Miss Sibley, the body is probably that of a Catholic priest who died here while on an undercover mission during Queen Elizabeth's reign, and was secretly buried. The age of the remains make that the most likely hypothesis."

"But why should he be buried on my island?" crossly demanded Miss Sibley.

"Why, Jeffrey Howard, the miller at that period, had been suspected of being an undeclared Papist. This seems to confirm it. Perhaps he was giving hospitality to one of the travelling priests who rode about in disguise, saying a secret Mass here and there. I suppose there was some fatality. That would account—" began Dr Adams, and stopped short.

"So what happens now?" inquired Miss Sibley, not noticing this.

"Oh, we'll have him reburied properly in the graveyard, poor fellow," said Dr Adams cheerfully. "The vicar won't mind a bit. He'll enjoy an excuse for some research into the background of it all."

Once the coffin and its melancholy contents had been removed, Miss Sibley put the matter out of her mind. She was much too busy, buying curtain material, and discussing fitments with the builders, to trouble her head about old unhappy far-off things. Her new kitchen was taking shape, a fine spacious room with a view through dangling willow-fronds over the white, frothy, and turbulent mill-pond. The sun blazed through the wide new south window, her large modern cooker would soon keep the kitchen warm and airy.

Miss Sibley had a capacious trunk full of cake recipes which, all her life, she had been cutting out of newspapers. She could hardly wait to get started. Waffles, Aberdeen butteries, orange and walnut cake, tipsy cake, scruggin cake, apricot caramel cake, mocha layer cake, Tivoli cake, orange tea-bread, date shorties, fat rascals, cut-and-come-again cake, honey and walnut scone ring, Lancashire wakes cakes, nut crescent, currant roll-ups, rhum baba—these names sang themselves through her head like a glorious invocation.

Just wait till I can get the builders out of here, she thought. And shelves put up in the little room and my cookery books on them.

She had collected cookery books with the enthusiasm of an autograph hunter. Not a recipe had yet been tried.

To encourage them, Miss Sibley pampered her builders in every way possible. She brewed them cups of tea five or six times daily, accompanied by shop-bought biscuits. She posted letters, took messages, phoned their wives, and ran errands for them. But none of this disguised her extreme impatience to see the back of them. As soon as it was at all possible she planned to move, from her rented room over the post office, into the mill; meanwhile she visited the site daily and dug up brambles on the island. She was therefore on hand when Mr Hoskins the foreman came to say, "Beg your pardon, mum, but we found something you should see."

"And what is that?" asked Miss Sibley. The seriousness of his tone made her heart tip over most anxiously. What could the wretches have found *now*? A plague pit? A cavern under the foundation, requiring ninety tons of concrete?

Some terrible gaping crack, that would entail construction of five expensive brick buttresses?

"It's a room," said Mr Hoskins.

"A room? A *room*? Surely there are plenty of those?"

"One we didn't know of," replied Mr Hoskins, who had lived in the village all his life. "Half-way up a wall. Come and see, mum."

Her curiosity kindled, Miss Sibley came and saw.

The room was approached by a panelled door, neatly concealed at one side over the mantelshelf in a small upstairs bedroom. The panel-door was operated by a hidden spring, which one of the workmen had accidentally released. Inside, a flight of narrow dark stairs led up to a small, low, irregularly-shaped chamber with a sloped ceiling and several oak beams passing through the floor at odd angles. The place was not much larger than a coat-closet and was dimly lit by a tiny window, made of thick greenish glass tiles, which also admitted a little fresh air.

"Why has nobody ever noticed the window?" demanded Miss Sibley.

"'Tis hid by the ivy, you see, mum, and also 'tis tucked in under the overhang of the eaves, like, where you'd never notice it," Mr Hoskins pointed out.

Later, going outside, Miss Sibley verified this; and the fact that a projecting lower gable concealed the window from anyone standing on the ground.

Disappointingly, the room held no furniture.

"But we did find this," said Mr Hoskins, and handed Miss Sibley a small grimed leather-bound book. "'Twas tucked on the joist."

Opening the book, Miss Sibley found that the pages were handwritten. It seemed to be a diary.

"Thank you, Mr Hoskins," she said.

"Would you want the room decorated, miss?"

"On the whole, no, thank you, Mr Hoskins. I don't imagine I shall be using it a great deal. If you could just clear away the dust . . ."

Miss Sibley's mind was already floating back to Sicilian chocolate cheesecake.

But she did take a cursory glance at the diary, which was written in a faded brown ink, and a decidedly crabbed and difficult handwriting.

"I, Gabriel Jerome Campion, S.J. leave this journal as a memorial in case it should happen that I do not quit this place a living man. And I ask whomsoever shall find it to pray for the repose of my soul . . ."

Well of course I will do that for the poor man, thought Miss Sibley, and she methodically tied a knot in her handkerchief to remind herself.

I wonder if he was in here for very long, and what did happen to him?

"Thank you, Mr Hoskins," she repeated absently, and withdrew down the narrow approach stair to the builders' step-ladder which stood below the panel opening.

"Would you wish me to put a different fastening on the door, mum?"

"Why, no, thank you, I think the existing one will do well enough."

"Or build a flight of steps so's to reach the door?"

"No," said Miss Sibley, "as you may recall, I plan to turn this little bedroom into my cookery library, so I shall want shelves built across those two facing walls, for my cookery books. And then, you see, I'll buy one of those little library step-ladders so, if I ever should wish to enter the secret room (which is not very likely), I can use the step-ladder. Thank you, Mr Hoskins. Gracious me—it is tea-time already; I'll just run and put on the kettle."

*

Dr Adams and Mr Wakehurst the vicar were greatly excited by the discovery of the diary, news of which reached them that evening by village grape-vine; and next day Mr Wakehurst came round to ask if he might borrow the document?

"This, you know, clears up a four-hundred-year-old mystery," said he, happily. "There is a local legend about a black-coated stranger who was heard asking the way to Hasworth Mill, and was then never seen again. But that was the winter of the great flood, when the Neap overran its banks and covered all the land as far as the foot of Tripp Hill (where the deserted station now stands). Various people from the village were drowned in the floods, including Howard the miller. It was supposed that the stranger must have been drowned too, and his body washed downstream to Shoreby. Now we can guess that he had been billeted in the secret room by Howard, who no doubt proposed to see him off the premises when the coast was clear; but because of his death in the flood he never did return. So the poor priest probably starved to death. Howard's son, a sailor, who returned from the sea to claim his inheritance no doubt found and secretly interred the body. Poor fellow: what a miserable, lonely end."

"Oh, he wasn't lonely," said Miss Sibley. "Somebody called Mr Watkyn kept him company. He wrote, several times, in his diary, 'I don't know how I should have managed to remain tranquil and composed without the company of my dear and charming Watkyn.'"

"Indeed?" exclaimed the vicar, with the liveliest curiosity. "Now I *do* wonder who Watkyn can have been?"

"Another priest, I daresay," remarked Miss Sibley without a great deal of interest, and she handed Mr Wakehurst the fragile and grimy little volume. "Please do keep it, Vicar, it is of no great interest to me."

"May I really? I shall write a paper on it for the Wessex

Archaeological Society," cried the vicar joyfully, and hastened away with his treasure before she could change her mind.

At the door he turned, remembering his manners, to ask, "When do you plan to move in, Miss Sibley?"

"Why, tonight," said she. "There are still quite a few things to be done, but the kitchen stove works now, and the hot water is on, and one of the bedrooms is finished, so there is no reason why I can't sleep here. That way, I shall be even more on the spot if there are any problems—Not that I anticipate any."

Mr Wakehurst's face wore a slightly doubtful, frowning look as he crossed the three-arched bridge and looked down at the careering mill-race and swirling mill-pond. But what, after all, are ghosts? he thought. Some people never see them at all. And, as the century nears its end, they seem to be losing their power. And Miss Sibley is such a sensible, practical person, it would be a most unpardonable piece of folly to confuse her mind with ideas about things which may never happen.

Poor Father Gabriel! As good a man as ever stepped, I daresay, even if he did hold erroneous, wrong-headed religious opinions. In any case, we are all so much more ecumenical and broad-minded now.

I do wonder who Watkyn can have been? And why no other body was found? Dear me, how very, very interested Adams will be in this discovery.

Besides, nobody has actually *seen* anything in the mill. Or not that I have been told of. It is only some exaggerated stories about what people felt, or fancied they felt, or heard, or fancied they heard.

He hurried on, under a threatening and plum-coloured sky, absorbed by the diary, which he read as he walked.

"Conducted a long dialogue on transubstantiation with

Watkyn, which served to distract me from the pangs of hunger. His is a surpassingly sympathetic and comprehending nature. And his expression is so captivatingly cordial! If he chose, I know that he would confide in me all his innermost thoughts."

Can Watkyn have been a mute? wondered Mr Wakehurst. Or a foreigner, speaking no English?

"I have confessed to Watkyn not only my major transgressions, but the most minor peccadilloes, the kind of small sins which, in the presence of a confessor, one is often almost ashamed to mention. Watkyn, now, knows more of my faults than any other living being. He does not behave any less kindly. And I feel a wondrous easement of soul. Sick, enfeebled, confused as I begin to grow, I do not at all fear to meet my Maker. And it is all thanks to my good Watkyn. If only I could bestow a like grace on him!"

"Another discussion with W. on the subject of miracles," recorded Father Gabriel a day later, in a hand that was perceptibly weaker.

Now what in the world can have become of Watkyn? wondered the vicar.

"Talked to W. on the subject of Redemption . . ." The text trailed away.

Miss Sibley celebrated her first night of residence in Hasworth Mill by making a Swiss roll. Not surprisingly, it was a total disaster. What she had thought to be one of the most simple, basic, and boring of cakes is, on the contrary, the most tricky and delicate, on no account to be attempted by a beginner. The flour must be of a special kind, the eggs carefully chosen, the oven well-trained, familiar to the cook, and under perfect control. Not one of these factors obtained at the Mill. It was the first time Miss Sibley had used her new cooker, which was not yet correctly adjusted, the flour was damp and in any case not a good brand. The eggs were a mixed lot. The cake turned out sodden, leathery, and had to be scraped from the bottom of the pan, like badly-laid cement. Not surprisingly, after eating a mouthful or two, Miss Sibley went to bed very quenched and dejected, and then found it almost impossible to fall asleep in her bare and paint-scented bedroom.

A gusty and fidgety wind had blown up. As Miss Sibley sat after supper in her warm kitchen she could see, through the great pane of clear glass, long dangling fronds of the willows in wild and eldritch motion, blown and wrung and swung like witches' locks. And after she retired to bed, her high window, facing out over the water-meadow, showed the row of Lombardy poplars like a maniac keep-fit class, violently bowing and bending their slender shafts in each and every direction.

Miss Sibley could not hear the wind for, to anybody inside the mill house, the roar of water drowned any external sound. But, as the gale increased, she *could* hear that, somewhere withindoors, a door had begun to bang; and after ten minutes or so of increasing irritation, she left her bed to find the source of the annoyance and put a stop to it.

The offending door proved to be the one opening into her little library room.

Queer, thought Miss Sibley; the window in here is shut; why should there be a draught? Why should the door bang?

And then she noticed the high black square in the wall, the cavity where the panel door stood open. That's very peculiar, she reflected; I'm sure Mr Hoskins had left it closed when the men went off work; and *I* certainly haven't opened it; so how in the world could it have come open all by itself? But perhaps this wild and draughty wind somehow undid the catch. At any rate I may as well close it up again; it is letting a nasty lot of cold air into the upper storey.

Since the panel-door and its catch were too high for her
to reach, she pushed a table, which she proposed to use as
a writing desk, across the small room, perched a chair on
the table, and then climbed up on to the chair.

She was in the act of closing the door when she thought
she heard, from inside the little upper room, a faint and
piteous moan. She paused—listened harder—but there was
no repetition of the sound.

I was mistaken, decided Miss Sibley. She closed the panel,
climbed down from the table, and was about to return to
bed when, from inside the panel, came three, loud, measured
knocks.

Bang. Bang. Bang.

Then a moment's silence. Then the three knocks again.

Bang. Bang. Bang.

Can that be the wind? Miss Sibley wondered and, after
a moment's hesitation, and just a little nervous this time,
she climbed up on to the table once more, reopened the
door, and peered inside. There was nothing to be seen.

But again, after the door was shut, before she had left the
room, she heard the three knocks: Bang. Bang. Bang.

"This is perfectly ridiculous," said Miss Sibley angrily.
"However I certainly can't lie all night listening to those
thumps, so I suppose I shall have to investigate further.
But I'm not going dressed like this."

Accordingly she returned to her bedroom, pulled on a
pair of trousers and thick cardigan, and equipped herself
with a powerful torch, which she had bought in case of any
trouble with the newly-installed electric system. Once again
she climbed on to the table, and this time scrambled right
up into the panel entrance.

No sooner was she well inside the entrance than the door
swung violently to behind her and latched itself. She heard
the spring click into place.

Miss Sibley was a calm and level-headed person. But even so, well aware there was no means of opening the panel from the inside, she felt an acute lowering of the spirits. For she recalled also that tomorrow was Saturday, when the builders did not come to the house, and that was inevitably followed by Sunday, so that it might be at least fifty hours before anybody became aware of her plight and set her free.

What was she to do in the meantime?

I may as well survey my assets, she thought sensibly, and climbed the stair into the odd-shaped little room above.

The beam of her torch, exploring it, showed that the builders had cleared away the dust and left it clean, at least, and bare. There was no indication of anything that might have caused the bangs. Furnishings there were none; Miss Sibley could sit either on the floor, or, rather uncomfortably, on one of the cross-beams or joists about a foot above floor level, which meant that she would not be able to raise her head without banging it on the roof behind her.

Oh well, she thought, at least it is a seat, and she chose the beam, reflecting, with some irony, that she had felt sorry for herself earlier, lying in a comfortable bed, because indigestion prevented her from sleeping; how luxurious, in retrospect, that bed now seemed!

Something scuttled in the corner, and she flinched uncontrollably, catching her breath in what was almost, but not quite, a scream; if there was one thing in the world that filled Miss Sibley with disgust and terror, it was a rat.

"You don't like rats, and yet you're going to live in a mill which must be full of them?" a surprised acquaintance at the bank had inquired, and Miss Sibley had pointed out that the mill had not been working as a mill for at least forty years, and had been uninhabited for a further twenty; such rats as there might once have been must surely long since have migrated to more inviting premises and choicer pickings. "I suppose there might be water rats," she said doubtfully, "but they are not nearly so disagreeable, and besides I presume they will stay in the water."

But here, now, was something moving and rustling in that speedy, furtive, stealthy, and, above all, uncontrollable and unpredictable manner so horridly characteristic of rodents; Miss Sibley gave a jump of fright and, doing so, banged her head violently on the roof-tiles above.

The pain was severe; she saw stars and tears flooded her eyes, tears of pain and shock; she gasped out her very worst expletive: "*Oh blast!*"—and then, somehow, an entirely different deluge of feeling swept over her, different from anything she had ever experienced in her life before, a drenching, mountainous weight of intolerable woe. Like a rock dislodged in a landslip, Miss Sibley toppled to the floor and lay on the boards, with her head pillowed on her arms, drowned in a tidal wave of tears, weeping her heart out.

What for? If asked she could not possibly have said: for wasted life, for love lost, young years misspent in dusty unproductive work, for chances mislaid, lapsed friendships, the irretrievable past.

How long she wept she had no notion; hours may have gone by.

But at last, at very long last, like a tiny spark at the end of an immeasurably long tunnel, came into her head a faint thought: *Yet, after all, here you are, in a mill, as you have always wanted to be, and about to begin making cakes, just as you have always planned?*

That is true, she answered, surprised, and the voice, the thought, which seemed to exist outside, rather than inside her, added: *Perhaps this oddly-shaped little room where you find yourself shut up at the moment is like a comma in your life?*

A comma?

A comma, a pause, a break between two thoughts, when you take breath, reconsider, look about, wait for something new to strike you.

Something new.

What in the world am I doing here on the floor, all quenched and draggled, Miss Sibley asked herself, and she raised her head. Unconsciously, she had laid her right arm over the joist, and she now noticed, with a frown of surprise, that there was a patch of light on her right wrist, which looked like a luminous watch.

Then, blinking the tears from her eyes, she saw that it was no such thing.

Luminous it *was*, though not very; a faint phosphorescent radiance glimmered from it, similar to that on stale fish, fish that is not all it should be. And two very bright sparks were set close together at one end; and the thing, which was about the size of a bantam's egg, suddenly moved, turning on her wrist, so that the sparks went out, and then reappeared in a different place.

Miss Sibley's first violent impulse was to shake her arm, jerk her wrist, rid herself of the thing, whatever it was— bat, vampire, death's head moth? were some of the wilder notions that flashed into her head.

The second impulse, even more powerful, born of the thought that just a moment before had come to her, was to remain quite still, hold her breath, watch, wait, listen.

She kept still. She waited. She watched the faint luminosity on her wrist.

And she was rewarded.

After a long, quiet, breathing pause, it grew brighter, and became recognisable.

Not a rat; definitely not big enough for a rat. But perhaps too large for a common house mouse?

A field mouse?

The thought slipped gently into her head, as had the suggestion about the comma. Wee, sleekit, cowering, something beastie, she thought. Field mice, I've heard, move indoors when autumn winds turn cold; perhaps this one had done that once. It must have been long, long ago, for the mouse was now completely transparent; it had started climbing gently up her arm and the stripes of the cardigan sleeve, red and blue, showed clearly through it.

Of course! Miss Sibley thought. I know who you are! You must be Mr Watkyn. Dear and charming Watkyn.

A thought like a smile passed across the space between them.

That was Gabriel, yes. He named me. And I, in turn, was able to help him. So we can open doors for one another. When he left—

Yes? When he left?

He left me changed; brought forward, you might say. In this attic here, now, there is still some residue of Gabriel: the pain, the fear; as well as the hope, comfort, friendship that we two built between us. Gabriel is buried by now in the churchyard, Watkyn is a pinch of bones and fur long since swallowed by some barn owl; but the product of them lives on and will live as long as hope lives, and hearts to feel hope.

Thank you, Watkyn, said Miss Sibley then; thank you for helping me, and I hope I too can help somebody, some day, in the same degree.

Oh, never doubt it, said the voice, closer now, and Miss Sibley lay down to sleep, comfortably, on the flat boards, with Watkyn a faint glimmer of light by her right shoulder.

On Saturday morning Mr Hoskins visited the mill to pick up a sonic measuring tool he had left there; Mr Wakehurst the vicar had come too, calling, at the same time, to thank Miss Sibley again for the immeasurably valuable gift of the diary; together, with concern, not finding the lady in her kitchen, they searched the house, and she, hearing voices, ran down the little stair and banged on the inside of the panel door until, aghast, they let her out.

"*Miss Sibley! What happened?*"

"Oh, the door blew to, in the gale, and shut me in," she said gaily. "You were quite right, Mr Hoskins; we must change the catch so that can't happen again."

"But you—you are all right? You have been there all night? You were not frightened?" asked the vicar, looking at her searchingly. "Nothing—nothing of an unfortunate nature—occurred?"

"Unfortunate? *No!* Nothing so fortunate has ever happened to me in my whole life!" she told him joyfully, thinking of her future here, decided on, it seemed, so carelessly, in such random haste. And yet what could be more appropriate than to make cakes, to bake beautiful cakes in Hasworth Mill? She would learn the necessary skill, her cakes would grow better and better; and if, at first, a few turned out badly—well, after all, who are more appreciative of cakecrumbs than mice?

Cousin Alice

When Fern Robson went to stay with her mother's sister, her aunt Twyla, it was out of acute need, not for any pleasant reason.

"She's an awkward one, Twyla Deane," sighed Mr Robson. "There's no denying that. But where else to send you, I just do not know."

Mrs Robson, Fern's mother, had been very badly injured in a coach accident, on a day's outing to Paigle Bay, and it was not even certain yet whether she would recover. She was in intensive care, in a deep coma. And her husband Sam, with a broken leg, was hobbling about in a nearby ward, not allowed out of hospital, though he was well enough to make arrangements about his daughter.

"You'll just have to go to Twyla, dearie. I'm right sorry about it, but there it is."

Fern was sorry too. Apart from the dreadful non-stop pain and fear about her mother, she hated leaving home because the month was May, and the sweetpeas were coming up in her garden patch, and the lilacs in front of the cottage and the bluebells in Slype Wood down the lane. Who'd want to go and stay on the edge of a growing town, in a house by the railway?

"Who'll feed Smokey while I'm away?"

"The neighbours. He'll manage. You be a good girl now and don't argue."

So Fern miserably packed a bag, and Tom Harman, one of the neighbours, drove her thirty miles to Haleswick and left her at Aunt Twyla's house.

Crossing Cottage, the place was called, because of the level crossing nearby. It was not a cottage really, but a bungalow, built of ugly raw red brick with a slate roof. The garden was flat and bare, not a tree in it, only some empty-looking flower-beds alternating with concrete paths and poor-looking grass. There wasn't a tree to be seen *anywhere*, in fact; close by lay timber yards and goods yards and factory sheds, a bit of waste land with junk cars and nettles, the railway, of course, and, right on the other side of Aunt Twyla's garden fence, an enormous electric pylon, towering over the squat little house, its four legs planted so far apart that the square of ground between them seemed bigger than the garden itself. There were half a dozen notices fixed on the pylon: DANGER, Keep Away, HIGH VOLTAGE, Beware, Property of the Electricity Board, TRESPASSERS WILL BE PROSECUTED.

Since almost the first thing Aunt Twyla told Fern was that she would be frizzled up like a thread in a flame if he ever touched the pylon, TRESPASSERS WILL BE PROSECUTED hardly seemed necessary, Fern thought. There wouldn't be much left of them to prosecute.

The pylon hummed to itself, now and then, a feverish mosquito sound that Fern didn't care for at all. While the hum went on, she found it hard to concentrate on her school work, hard to fall asleep at night, hard to do anything but worry about how Mother was getting on.

The other children at the Haleswick school were standoffish at first.

"Your aunt, Mrs Deane, is a queer one," they told Fern. "That's why her old man goes to sea; he goes to sea because he can't stand her."

"He goes to sea because he's a merchant seaman," said Fern reasonably. "He comes back every six months."

"He don't stay home long. She quarrels with folk, your

aunt does. Where she lived before, she quarrelled with the
neighbours so bad, she had to move."

This was true, Fern discovered; or partly true. For years,
the Deanes had lived in the High Street, in a small ancient
gabled house, next to a greengrocer's shop. But there had
been trouble. What sort of trouble, Fern could not make
out, but anyway, while Uncle Frank was off at sea, Aunt
Twyla had left the house in which her husband had been
born, and moved to Crossing Cottage.

"No neighbours to fret me here," she said tersely. "It's
better."

Aunt Twyla was a terse woman, silent, thin, and angry-
faced, only uttering when she had to; twelve hours a day
she wore an apron, and had her hair scraped back as if she
didn't care what it looked like.

It was a pity about the house in the High Street,
Fern thought. It had bow-windows, and was built of stone,
looked solid and comfortable; next door to it the green
grocer's always had beautiful high-piled fragrant
masses of pinks and roses and lilies-of-the-valley, beside
lettuce and onions and cauliflowers and fruit. Flower
and vegetables next door would be much more comfort
able than the pylon and the railway; all through each
night, trains clanked and shunted and whimpered and
flung electric flashes over Fern's bedroom ceiling. Aunt
Twyla's curtains were thin cotton; the light flashed
through.

"Don't the trains ever keep you awake?" Fern asked, but
Aunt Twyla said, "I never do sleep much."

"Mother doesn't, either."

"I know," said Twyla. Then she added slowly, "Maybe
she's making up for that now."

Fern remembered her mother saying once, "Twyla and
I used to have the same dreams. At breakfast we used

check with each other about the bits we couldn't remember. I wonder if we still dream the same things?"

What was Mother dreaming now? Fern wondered; and then, looking at Aunt Twyla, thought, Is that what she is wondering, too?

The bungalow was small and bare and flimsy; even with only two people there, it was hard to get off and be alone, because every corner seemed visible from every other corner. Unless you went into the bathroom. There were no books or pictures, and the floor was bare polished lino.

No photographs. Fern had wondered if there would be one of Alice, but there was not. Nor of Uncle Frank.

"Whatever you do, don't mention Alice," Father had warned, and Fern had promised she would not.

Alice was her cousin, Aunt Twyla's daughter, who had died in an accident seven years ago. Fern had been only three when Alice died, the same age as her cousin. Of course there wouldn't be any clothes or toys left, Aunt Twyla would have got rid of them long ago. It was all over. And had happened when the Deanes were living in the other house, the one in the High Street.

Fern used to pass the house every day, as she went to and from school. She used to look up at the windows and wonder which one had been Alice's room.

Living in a house without any upstairs was queer, and not comfortable. Fern often found herself, in Crossing Cottage, absent-mindedly listening for the sound of footsteps overhead, and almost sure that she heard them. Or footsteps coming down the stairs. She never could get used to the fact that there weren't any stairs.

Nobody lived in the High Street house now, it had been turned into estate agents' offices. There were no lights in the window at night.

Coming home late sometimes, from Guides or a school

film show, Fern would look up at the dark windows and think: Suppose Alice is still there? Not very nice for her, all alone in a dark empty house full of photographs of houses. And she sent a thought through the black empty glass of the windows: Cousin Alice? Are you there? I'm sorry we never met. It wouldn't be so miserable, staying in Crossing Cottage, if *you* were there too.

June the first was Mother's birthday. Fern sent a greetings telegram to the hospital: THINKING ABOUT YOU ALL THE TIME LOVE FERN. And Aunt Twyla rang up Father, who was still in hospital too, his leg wasn't mending as fast as it should. He said there was no change in Mother's condition. Still in a coma.

Fern went to school as usual, feeling as if lead weights were tied on her feet. Coming home, at tea-time, past Coney's vegetable and flower shop, she was reminded by the colourful, fragrant display that if it was Mother's birthday it must be Aunt Twyla's birthday too, since they were twins, so she stopped and bought a bunch of pinks. They were pink and white and frilly, and smelt powerfully sweet of clove and vanilla.

"You are Mrs Deane's niece, aren't you?" said Mr Coney, plump and grey-haired, wrapping a twist of tissue paper round the pinks. "Wasn't your mother in an accident. How is she getting on?"

The concern and kindness in her voice nearly undid Fern who had managed all through the school day to wear a crust of calm. Her lip began to quiver, she muttered, "N-not to well," and almost bolted out of the shop.

She didn't stop, as usual, to send a thought up to Cousin Alice next door, but hurried homewards, out of the cheerful High Street, into Gasworks Road, along Brewer Way, through Salt Passage, and so to Railway Approach and the flimsy iron gate of Crossing Cottage.

There had been rain during the afternoon, the cracked unmade-up footway of Railway Approach was muddy and puddly. Aunt Twyla detested wet feet making marks on the clean lino floor and, even through her fog of misery about Mother, Fern managed to remember that; she took pains to avoid the puddles and reached the garden gate with dry feet. The sloping concrete path to the front door had already dried off, but as Fern walked up it, she noticed a line of wet footprints ahead of her. Some other person evidently had *not* troubled to avoid the puddles. Some other person had feet about the same size as Fern's own. Who could it be?

Nobody—and specially not children—ever came calling at Crossing Cottage. Twyla's only visitors were men coming to read the meter and ladies selling flags in aid of cancer research.

Fern opened the door and nearly fell over her aunt, who was ironing pillow slips. There wasn't room to do more than one thing at a time in the bungalow—with the ironing-board unfolded you had to squeeze along the wall.

Fern put down her school-bag and looked round the room, which was bare and tidy. No visitor, nothing unusual.

"Is anyone here?" she couldn't help asking.

"*I'm* here. Nobody else," snapped her aunt. "Why?"

Fern was embarrassed. She was afraid Aunt Twyla might think she had expected to find a birthday party in process —which she certainly had not.

"It's just—I thought I saw—" she mumbled, and turned to look through the open front door behind her. But the line of wet footprints had dried off the path, there was nothing to be seen.

"Shut that door, such a perishing draught it makes when the back door's open," said Aunt Twyla sharply. The front and back doors were directly opposite each other, with the scullery, front room, and a bit of passage between; if all the doors happened to be open, in whatever direction the wind was blowing, it seemed to veer round and sweep through the house.

"I bought these for you, Aunt Twyla," said Fern. "Happy birthday!" And she handed her aunt the bunch of pinks.

Aunt Twyla's eyes sparked, as she turned back the tissue. "Where did you get these?" she demanded.

"Coney's, in the High Street."

"I don't want you getting things there, ever. D'you hear?"

"Why, Aunt Twyla?"

"Because I say so. I don't want you having anything to do with those Coneys. Just remember that."

Aunt Twyla walked quickly away with the pinks. She certainly did not put them into a vase. After tea, wondering what had happened to them, Fern went out into the glum little back garden, with its rotary clothes dryer, ash heap, dustbin, and empty rabbit hutch left over from the previous owner. On the other side of the fence the pylon hummed menacingly. At first Fern couldn't see the pinks, on the ash heap or anywhere about the garden; but then she noticed them lying under the pylon, midway between its four massive steel feet. Aunt Twyla must have flung them there, over the fence; they were light, she must have flung them with all her strength.

That evening, unusually, Twyla went out and left Fern alone in the bungalow. Where had Aunt Twyla gone? Was she walking fast, angrily, through the draggled fields, past the gasworks and the sewage farm? Fern lay shivering in bed, listening to the hum of the pylon and the howl of passing trains.

Next day at school, Sue Coney, who was fat and curly-headed and good-natured, and had, up to now, been rather a friend of Fern's, wrote her a note that said, "After what your aunt did, I don't want to be friends any more."

Fern hated mysteries. She went up to Sue Coney at break-time—Sue was in the class below hers—and said, "What is this about? I don't understand. What did my aunt do?"

"She knocked over our posy tubs," said Sue Coney.

On each side of the greengrocer's shop there were two big ornamental tubs, standing out on the pavement, filled with growing flowers, tulips or marigolds or lobelias, whatever was in season.

Fern had noticed, on the way to school, that the tubs had been pushed over; earth and dying plants lay scattered all over the footway. Perhaps a car had skidded and upset the tubs, Fern thought at the time.

But Sue said, "Your aunt did it."

"How do you know?"

"Dad says so."

"I don't believe it. Why should she do a thing like that?"

"Dad says it must have been her."

"Why?"

"Because of what she did before." And Sue went off to the other side of the playground.

Another girl, Tessa Leigh, explained. "There used to be a lot of trouble between your aunt and the Coneys. That was why she moved to Crossing Cottage. There was always bad feeling, over one thing or another. She complained they made too much noise—their dog bit her cat, or t'other way round—Oz Coney chopped some branches off a tree in the hedge between the gardens that Mrs Deane said was her tree—there was a row about repairs to an inside wall—they couldn't ever be friendly about anything. Of course really it all went back to little Alice."

"*What* about little Alice?" asked Fern, wondering why she found it so hard to breathe.

"That was the kid that died. Mrs Deane's little girl. She was out playing one day in the back garden—they have nice big gardens behind those houses in the High Street— she scrambled through a gap in the hedge, and went into the Coneys' garden."

"Well?"

"That was it. They had a well, a deep one. It's all filled in now, they turned it into a little garden pond, with plants and goldfish. There's a spring, you see. But in those times it was eighty feet deep, with a bucket and winding handle. Folk said it was a wishing well. They still do, as a matter of fact."

"What happened?"

"The kid fell down the well. Wasn't found till it was too late."

"How awful. Oh, how awful."

"Your aunt blamed the Coneys. Said the well should have been covered over. Said other things too—" Tessa stopped short.

How could she bear it? thought Fern. No wonder she had never been on friendly terms with the Coney family since. Though they weren't really to blame . . .

But still—to upset their tubs and throw the flowers in the road—*could* Aunt Twyla really have done a spiteful thing like that?

"I don't believe Aunt Twyla did it," Fern said to Sue Coney after school, and Sue said, "Well, Dad thinks she did. He's furious. He's going to arrange the Railway Walk. He said, if it weren't for that, he wouldn't have bothered, he was going to have let it lapse this year. But now he's going to make sure they do it."

"What on earth is the Railway Walk?"

"Your aunt bought that bungalow in a hurry from old Fred Stoppard. He was the one who built it. When he buil it, he didn't know, and he didn't tell your aunt when he sold it to her, that there's a Right of Way clean through the house."

"What does that mean?" asked Fern.

"It's like a public footpath going right through. Any person has the right to walk in at your aunt's front door and out at the back, and on through that gate in the right-hand fence, along the path that goes in a tunnel under the railway and out to the river and the sewage farm. I've heard that your uncle nearly had a fit when he came back from the sea and found what she'd got, instead of his old house in the High Street."

"But," said Fern, puzzled, "nobody *does* walk through my aunt's house."

"No, they don't, because people are a bit scared of her. Some of them even think she's a witch. Anyway, there's plenty of other ways to get to the sewage farm. But if there's a Right of Way, you're supposed to make sure it's walked along, at least once a year, and that's what Dad's always done. He's on the town council in charge of footpaths, you see. Your aunt gets riled when they come and do it, but they're allowed; she can't stop them. The councillors bring their wives and people from the Haleswick Historical and any ratepayers who want to come. They're going to do it the day after tomorrow, Sunday."

"Well, *I* think it's hateful," burst out Fern. "Specially—"

Specially when Mother's so ill, perhaps dying, she thought, but she could see that was beside the point.

"Your aunt shouldn't have knocked over those tubs of flowers."

"Nobody saw her. No one can prove she did. And anyway I'm sure she didn't."

When Fern got home that evening, Aunt Twyla was very pale, even more silent than usual, and her mouth was set in a bitter line. A letter headed Haleswick Urban District Council stood on the mantelpiece; she did not say anything about it to Fern, who had her own matter for silent thought; the line of wet footprints had been there again, ahead of her on the path as she walked up to the house. She had seen them appearing, one by one, all the way to the door.

Who had stepped through the doorway just ahead of her?

Later, as she sat trying to do her homework on the kitchen table, when the hum of the pylon died down, she felt certain that she could hear somebody moving about upstairs— opening a drawer, maybe, taking a book off a shelf or a toy from a cupboard.

But there wasn't any upstairs in the bungalow.

On Sunday morning, Fern, feeling rather sick, said, "I think I'll go out for a walk." But Aunt Twyla said, "No. You stay right here." So Fern stayed. Her mouth was dry, it was like the first day at school, only much worse.

At eleven they all arrived, quite a large group of people, wearing dark respectable clothes as if they were going to a funeral or a court case. A few carried umbrellas, because it was raining a bit. They didn't knock at the door or ring the doorbell, but walked straight in, led by Mr Coney, a tall man with light grey fluffy hair and very blue eyes like his daughter. Some of the people looked embarrassed, but he didn't; he was just very serious.

"Come for the Right of Way walk, Mrs Deane," he said.

Aunt Twyla made no answer. She was ironing curtains, and had arranged her board across the room so that there was only just enough space to edge round it.

Mr Coney made as if to lift the ironing-board. Then Aunt Twyla did speak.

"You better not touch that!" she said. "Or I'll have the law on you!"

So Mr Coney, and the rest of his twenty-nine companions,

had to edge carefully round the side of the ironing-board, step gingerly over the cord of the iron, and so through the passage, the scullery, the back door, and across the garden to the side gate that led into the lane.

"Thank you, Mrs Deane," each person said politely as he or she left.

Twyla waited until the last was out, Dr Leigh; then she went into the garden. The group were still in the lane, writing on their clipboards. Aunt Twyla said—and the words seemed to come out of her like water under fierce pressure—

"You have left filthy footprints all over my clean lino. You know what I think of you? I think you are *vermin*. You deserve every bit of bad luck that will come to you. And it can't be worse than I wish it."

Then she turned on her heel and went back into the house.

Next day at school, Fern came in for a good many cold looks. She felt this was rather hard; she was not responsible for the feud between Aunt Twyla and the Coneys, or for any part of what had happened; except, true, that she had bought that unlucky bunch of pinks.

Matters were made worse because Sue Coney, that very day, had suddenly come down with what Dr Leigh called a particularly tricky kind of virus pneumonia, and her parents were worried to death about her. No one spoke out directly, or said this was a result of Aunt Twyla's ill-wishing, but some people really thought it, and things were muttered behind hands, specially among the children at school.

Fat Ozzie Coney, Sue's retarded elder brother, who was eighteen, and worked in the brick factory, lurched threateningly up to Fern after school, and growled at her, "You better tell your aunt to take that thing off."

"What thing?" said Fern, puzzled.

"That thing she laid on our Sue! Else we'll make this place too hot to hold her."

And Ozzie giggled suddenly, as he was liable to do in the middle of any conversation, whether funny or not, and rolled his eyes sideways at Fern, and shambled away.

"Don't take too much notice of him," said Tessa. "He's always been like that."

In the evening, when Fern went home, she found Aunt Twyla grimly sticking elastic plaster over several holes in the front windows where stones had been thrown. A policeman was there, inspecting the damage. He shook his head, said it was no doubt boys at their pranks, unfortunately the police force was short-staffed, and couldn't possibly keep an eye on Crossing Cottage at all hours of the day or night, but of course they'd do their best.

He did not sound as if he himself intended to do his best.

Next day, though, there was a sudden, unexpected change. People at school were friendly again, and Mrs Coney, outside her shop arranging bunches of radishes, made a point of stopping Fern, as she walked home with Tessa, to say they were all very sorry for misjudging her aunt over those flower-tubs, but mistakes did get made sometimes, and she hoped Mrs Deane wouldn't have any hard feelings, and how was Fern's mother? She asked as if she really wanted to know, but Fern could only reply that her mother was still much the same.

"Oh, dear, that's too bad." Mrs Coney sounded honestly sorry.

"Father says we need a miracle," Fern muttered. "What about Sue, Mrs Coney?"

Mrs Coney's good-natured face looked suddenly haggard.

"She's poorly. She's very poorly. If miracles are being given out, we could use one too." And she walked slowly inside, past the boxes of oranges.

"You'd think," said Tessa Leigh, "that she'd wish on her wishing well."

"Wishing well—? Oh! In the garden. But it doesn't really work, does it?"

"Of course it works!" said Tessa, rather indignantly. "I've wished for lots of things, when I went to tea with Sue, and always got them. A pair of green sandals—and a fine day on my birthday—and to come top in maths—"

"You can't prove—"

"Can't prove? Who needs to? I know!"

Perhaps you need to believe in it, Fern thought, and Mrs Coney doesn't. But I would. Oh, I think I'd believe.

She turned back and went into the shop.

"Mrs Coney—might I have a wish on your wishing well?"

Mrs Coney was serving a customer with four pounds of potatoes, a melon, and some rhubarb. She said absently, "Of course, love. Help yourself. Down the path at the side and through the green gate."

She was wrapping up the rhubarb in newspaper. Fern read the headline on it: BOYS OWN UP TO HIGH STREET VANDALISM.

"Shocking, isn't it, the things those young tearaways get up to? Lucky Sergeant Ferson caught them at it," the customer said.

Fern ran down the little snicket path beside the Coneys' house, through the green gate, and made her way to the end of the narrow, quiet garden. There was a pear tree, and a quince tree, a patch of bright green mossy lawn, and a forsythia, just shedding its yellow petals and beginning to put out new green leaves. The pool was under the pear tree, ringed by spears of iris, and with drifted white pear-blossom floating on its dark green water.

Fern knelt on the brick paving at the edge and looked in. She could see her own reflection, sliced neatly in two by a goldfish who swam across. The reflection looked much younger than she felt.

She put her hand in the cold water. I ought to drop something in, she thought. I haven't any money. What do I have in my school-bag that would do? And remembered her ivory penknife that Granny Sands had given her; it had been Granny's and Great-granny's, it had a large blade and a small, and she loved it dearly.

In it went.

"Mother," whispered Fern. "Oh, *Mother* . . . Sue . . ." and then, for some reason, she was hardly sure why, she whispered, "Alice . . . Cousin Alice," and went on crouching in silence for a while, staring down into the murky water, until a fish jumped for a fly, with a sudden plop, and startled her.

She was late home, and Aunt Twyla was cross.

"Wondering where you'd got to," she snapped. "That Oz Coney's been around, mumbling and muttering and acting peculiar. I don't like his looks. Never have—" and then she bit off something she might have been going to say and slapped a pair of plates down on the table.

"That's strange," said Fern, and gave Aunt Twyla Mr Coney's apologetic message. But Twyla sniffed.

"No more than she ought. They caught the two boys who upset Coney's tubs—cops found 'em kicking over litter bins brought them in to the station for questioning, and one of them blew the gaff on the other. Nasty little scum—I hope they get sent to preventive."

"Oh, I'm glad," said Fern. "Then—" She was beginning to say, "Then no one can go on thinking you did it—" but changed her mind and said instead, "Perhaps they were the ones that broke your windows."

"*Perhaps*—" said Aunt Twyla sourly.

After supper she remarked, "It's odd—I keep thinking

can hear somebody upstairs. I must be going daft in my old age."

"Maybe it's the pylon humming," said Fern uneasily. For no particular reason, she added, "When does Uncle Frank next come home?"

"Not for another six weeks—I think I'll go to the phone-box on the corner and ring up to ask after your mother. You'd best go to bed."

"I'll wait up till you come back," said Fern. She felt very reluctant to get undressed and lie under the covers in the dark, in her tiny box bedroom with its window looking towards the pylon and the railway.

She locked herself in the bathroom, ran the tap to drown the hum of the pylon, brushed her teeth for a very long time, washed her face over and over, then came out, hoping that Aunt Twyla would be home already, that she would have better news—

The lights were off in the front room, but the passage one, still on, threw some light in each direction. Fern felt a draught, and, over the smell of soap and toothpaste, caught another smell—sharp, strong, choking. She walked into the front room and a dark, bulky figure suddenly unbent, from something it had been doing low down, knocked against the corner of the table, and let out a hoarse, frightened cry. Fern heard a mighty whoosh! like the bark of an enormous dog, a sheet of flame swept across the room, and table-cloth, chair-covers, curtains all caught fire together.

Fern, not far from the back door, ran for it, then spun round, thinking crazily, "Alice! I must get Cousin Alice out!"

But the front room was already a dazzling cave of gold and scarlet flame; nobody was going to come out of there. Fern ran into the pitch-dark garden and cannoned into somebody—a man; she let out a yelp as he grabbed her, demanding, "Is that the girl? Are you all right? Thank god! Oh, thank god! But your aunt—where is she?"

"She went to phone—she'll be at the front—"

It was Mr Coney.

What in the world was he doing here?

Before they could get round to the front they saw something terrible—a flaming creature that raced across the garden, howling, flung itself through the rickety fence, and collapsed on the ground between the pylon's huge legs, rolling and moaning, "Help me! Help me!"

"*Ozzie!*" screamed Mr Coney.

Another figure ran after the first carrying a bundle of something dark and thick which it flung over the burning, rolling creature—then knelt and thumped, beat, thumped again, pressing out the flames. Mr Coney ran to help, ducking under the pylon, taking no notice of the DANGER signs.

"Is that you—Mrs Deane?" Fern heard him gasp. And heard Aunt Twyla's dour reply, "Who did you expect? Cinderella? Take a hand with this groundsheet, Bob Coney."

Fire engines had arrived at the front of the house—which by now was burning so hard that there seemed no possible chance of saving it; all the firemen could do was play their hoses around and stop the fire from spreading to the timber yard or the pylon.

An ambulance carried away Ozzie Coney, who was severely burned. His clothes reeked of petrol, and an empty petrol-can was found at the starting point of the fire. A police officer travelled with Ozzie in the ambulance.

"If it hadn't been for Mrs Deane and her groundsheet, your son would be dead," he had told Mr Coney, who looked terrible, Fern observed—shocked, wretched, suddenly an old man.

"I don't know what to say," he muttered to Aunt Twyla. "You saved him—how can I thank you? I—I only hope you don't think Mary and I egged him on to do this awful thing—?"

"Well I don't," said Aunt Twyla, roundly and surprisingly. "I've thought plenty hard things of you in the past, Bob Coney, but I never thought you'd take a hand in *arson*."

"He was bumbling away after tea, talking to himself, something about Crossing Cottage and then the fuel for the mower—it was only later I suddenly put two and two together, guessed what he might have in mind, and came hell for leather after him. The poor daft boy got a notion in his head you'd had a hand in our Sue's illness."

Aunt Twyla laughed shortly as she turned to watch her house burning.

"If I'd got the powers some folks credit me with, I'd be able to stop this, eh?"

They stood in silence for a moment or two, looking at the roaring flames. Behind them the pylon shone like a scarlet brooch against the black sky.

"I'd best be away to the hospital," said Mr Coney at length. "See to my poor stupid boy. But Mary said, Mrs Deane—if anything happened—would you and your niece come and put up at our house, we've beds for you both—"

"Oh," she said, "but you've a sick young one—"

"No, Sue's made the turn, Leigh says, just this evening, she's out of danger; that's why I feel so terrible, what that boy of ours did. *Please*, Mrs Deane—Mary wouldn't take no for an answer."

"Then we'll say thank you, and kindly. Come along, Fern. One thing," said Aunt Twyla with rare cheerfulness, "we've naught to carry but ourselves." And indeed she walked along Brewery Way and Gasworks Road as lightly as if she had tossed aside a whole lifetime's load of heavy luggage.

Fern had something to carry; she had picked it up off the front path as they left—something that shone in the firelight and caught her eye.

"What do you think this is, Aunt Twyla?" she asked, as they reached the brighter lights of the High Street.

"That? Let's see. Why—no! *I don't believe it!*" whispered Twyla.

She stared at the thing in Fern's hand as if her eyes were still dazzled by the fire, stung by the smoke, and could hardly see what lay in front of them. It was a small mother-of-pearl fish, with an ivory-and-silver ring attached to it, and a white satin ribbon tied to the ring.

"It belonged to Alice," whispered Twyla. "It was her teething ring."

Alice.

For the first time since the fire Fern fetched up the courage to ask, "Aunt Twyla? Did you get through to the hospital? Is there—"

"They said she'll be all right," said Twyla slowly. "Just this evening she opened her eyes, quite sensible, and asked for a cup of tea."

Mrs Coney welcomed them in, couldn't make enough of them. She gave them hot drinks laced with sherry, lent them night-wear, put hot water bottles in two beds, side by side in her spare bedroom. Sue, she said, was getting perkier all the time; and Bob had phoned from Haleswick Hospital to say that although Ozzie's burns were very bad—he'd been taken off to a special Burns Centre—he would probably pull through.

"I don't know how to tell you how bad I feel about your house, Mrs Deane. Our poor backward boy—I'm bound to say—I do blame ourselves too—he grew up among people thinking hard thoughts, hearing hard words spoken. We'll try to put that right now."

"There's been fault on both sides," said Aunt Twyla.

"One thing Bob did say—did you know the house next door is coming up for sale?"

"Let's hope the insurance money will stretch to cover it," said Aunt Twyla. And she did a thing she had not done, perhaps for years, thought Fern; she smiled.

"We'd best get to bed—thank you, Mary; it's been a long day."

Safe in bed, sandwiched with hot water bottles, Fern murmured, "Goodnight Aunt Twyla." And wondered if Twyla and her mother would be sharing dreams tonight.

"Sleep well, Fern." After a moment, Twyla said, "My daughter Alice's little room was just the other side of this wall."

Cousin Alice, thought Fern. Goodnight, Cousin Alice. Sleep well. You'll be glad to be back in your own home again. You'll rest better there.

The Legacy

When Paul Fox bought the house called The Legacy, he reckoned that he had acquired a rare bargain. True, the house, a large plain eighteenth-century mansion which had stood empty for fifteen years, was derelict, and in need of total renovation; but the stone outer wall and Horsham roof were sound, the garden, if neglected, was large, and the house was within easy walking distance of the town centre. And Spyre Market was a charming little place, half town, half village, bustling with antique shops, only just beginning to be taken notice of by the developers. Paul felt sure that in The Legacy he had an excellent investment. Refurbish the house, put the garden in order, and in a few years he could sell at a huge profit. Meanwhile he'd live there himself and use the place as a base for a bit of antique dealing; not a shop (the terms of the purchase precluded that) but some gentlemanly viewing and overseas sales to transatlantic or Japanese customers. Antique furniture always looked twice as desirable when observed in a home setting with roses outside the window and so forth.

Accordingly The Legacy was set in order; local builders were not available but Fox brought in Joliffe's, a firm that he had used before for similar jobs, from the county town twenty miles away.

As to why such an eligible house had stood empty for so long, until the attic floor fell straight through to the cellar, Fox did not particularly inquire, nor did anybody come forward to proffer information. The former owners had been eccentrics, he vaguely gathered, had laid some sort of

injunction that the place was to be left empty, and it took
a long time for this legal barrier to be done away with; they
had been a very odd pair, had no telephone for fear of
disturbing the birds, for the same reason kept a letter-box
up at the top of the drive, so postmen need not come down
to the house, ate only tinned food, for which they shopped
once a month, and were hardly ever seen about the town.
Nobody, still around, seemed to have known them inti-
mately.

The only person, Fox gathered, who might be able to tell
him anything about this couple, the Batesons, currently lay
at death's door in the local Cottage Hospital. This was a
Commander Marchbanks, now in his nineties, father of the
present Attorney General and grandfather of several rising
young politicians.

Bearing a bunch of grapes, Fox went to call on the
commander. (He never had the least objection to pushing
in where angels feared to tread if it was likely to furnish him
with information that might be commercially or socially
useful.)

The commander, propped against pillows, was certainly
an impressive figure. He had a long distinguished
face, a drooping white moustache, and an ironic expression.

"I suppose the Batesons were great gardeners?" suggested
Fox politely.

The commander grinned, showing a double row of
smoke-stained teeth, all his own. "Oh, no, I wouldn't call
them that. No, no ... I remember once when Charley
Bateson sawed off the branch he had his ladder propped
against ... No, they were certainly no great shakes as
gardeners."

"Why were they so hermitlike in their habits?"

"Oh—" said the old man vaguely. "One is, as one grows

older, don't you know? There aren't so many people one
cares to be acquainted with. All one's real friends are
dead . . ."

He studied his thick-skinned visitor with evident amuse-
ment.

"Is it true that Mrs Bateson died in the garden?"

"Yes, perfectly true. She survived Charley by a couple of
years. First she ran him over—"

"Ran him over?"

"Backing the car, in the dark, don't you know, so as to
get through the narrow gate. Lots of wives run over their
husbands," the old man remarked with his grin. "Accidental
death, it was brought in, of course. She went on living there
alone, but, after a bit, she took up residence in the Angel
Hotel. Only went to the house by daylight, to feed the birds,
and so forth. Then, one morning, she was found on a bench
in the garden. I found her, 's a matter of fact. Her expression
was quite calm; well," he corrected himself, "moderately
calm. She'd never been back to the Angel the previous
night. Natural causes, they brought in, that time. Well,
everything's natural, in a manner o' speaking, ain't it?" He
grinned again. "Moved in yet, have ye? Comfortable, is it
there? Devilish *un*comfortable in the Batesons' day, it was
—ghastly bad taste they had; all Benares trays and potted
palms. Heh, heh, heh! Still, he had a very sound taste in
port, did old Charley. Put the garden in order yet, have
ye?"

"It's a terrible job. The brambles were rooted six feet
deep—"

"Trouble with moles, you're bound to have, too. The
Batesons always had shocking trouble with moles. Well,
well, well! Thanks for the grapes!"

Fox gathered that the audience was dismissed.

And when he would have gone back next week, to ask the

old boy's view about a really interesting discovery, he was told that Commander Marchbanks had died.

"Didn't you see it in the local paper?" said the matron coldly.

But Fox only read the bits about property in the local paper.

The interesting discovery had been made by the builders.

Commander Marchbanks, Fox rapidly realised, had been absolutely right about the mole problem. In among the huge blackberry thickets, wherever space availed, there were whole colonies of monumental molehills and runways. The only thing to do if one wanted a decent lawn, which Fox certainly did, was to dig up the whole area in front of the house and cover it, half an inch deep, with strong metal mesh. No mole could fight its way upward through that; if they chose to burrow underneath it, that was their affair. But presumably, in an area several hundred yards square, the moles would, by and by, if they were unable to surface, die from lack of air.

So the site was excavated. Up came the bramble roots, deep and knobbed, and thick yellow mats of nettle roots; up came old bits of broken china, half bricks, mysterious rusty portions of old garden tools and window fastenings.

And, in the middle of the area, a stone slab was revealed.

"Here lyes the bodie of Samuel Fych, dyed in his sinnes 1612," it said unequivocally.

Paul Fox was really sorry that the old commander was not still around to offer suggestions about this interesting find. For the annals of the town were completely mute and blank as to the identity or history of Samuel Fych; nor were the county archives of any greater help. Local historians were interested but uninformed. And Fox was unable to discover anything useful in the history of the house; it had been built comparatively recently, only two hundred years ago, on the site of an earlier structure. But what that had been, nobody was able to tell him.

Meanwhile, what to do about the slab? It was a nuisance, lying just where it did; the builders would either have to prise it up, or cut an oblong gap in the mole-proof mesh to accommodate it—which would destroy the whole purpose of the mesh. If the moles could get through at that point, they would soon be burrowing about all over the place.

"Oh, take it up, take it up!" said Paul at last impatiently. "You can set it, upright, in the garden wall where it's crumbling badly; that's what they do in graveyards, when they turn them into parks."

The garden was surrounded by high stone walls, all crumbling to some degree; the stone slab looked very well, set vertically in one of them, and cleaned up a bit. Fox forgot to inquire whether the builders had dug down, at all, under where the slab had lain, but assumed they had not, as nobody made any further allusion to the matter.

The builders were an excellent firm, and had done several previous jobs for Fox; but he never remembered one where they had whipped through a piece of renovation with such remarkable speed; all the work was completed between March and the end of September. It was as if they wanted to leave the site before the shorter evenings began. One young bricklayer, in fact, was heard to say something about "not fancying it in that cellar much" but he was soon paid off and sent about his business. "Not a good workman," the boss said. "Casual. Slipshod."

On the day Fox moved into the house he recorded an interview with the local TV station. (He had friends, or at least acquaintances, in all kinds of handy quarters, well placed to receive or pass on news as to possible business deals.) The two useful minutes on the local network ad-

miringly described and displayed the sympathetic resto-
ration that had been carried out, mentioned the possibility
of a Heritage Award for the work, congratulated Mr Fox
on having rescued the derelict house for his own private
occupation, not just for vulgar profit (or not just yet at any
rate) and, to conclude, mentioned the interesting memorial
stone that had been discovered. "If any of our viewers can
throw light on this find," the announcer said, "we, or Mr
Fox, will be glad to hear from them." And then passed on
to the horrible results of an oil spill on the local beaches.

The first week or so of Fox's occupancy was spent in
arranging a carefully chosen consignment of appropriate
furniture. Nothing too antique—a bit of Hepplewhite, some
good rugs of course, minor watercolours on the walls, a
print or two, chinaware in the kitchen, and a nice French
country table. Fox did notice that the newly-installed central
heating creaked a great deal, but that was bound to be so,
at first, the builders assured him, in a building where,
of necessity, all the woodwork was brand new. (The old
woodwork had had to be burned. It was past even using for
firewood.) Also, when the wind was in the north, as it mostly
seemed to be, the double glazing on the windows and
draught-proofing round the doors let out extraordinary
banshee screeches and mumbles; the screeches Paul found
he could tolerate better than the mumbles, which sounded
exactly like a petulant halfwit continually maundering away
to himself.

A telephone had been installed (with none of the usual
delay) and a TV set and aerial delivered; Paul had stipulated
that the latter should be supplied in time for him to watch
his own recorded interview which, when it was screened,
seemed to him (as is so often the case) remarkably short,
shallow, and scrappy.

After the screening, however, several neighbours recognised and congratulated him in the street; and, about two nights later, the telephone rang.

"—Hallo?" said Fox, who had not yet memorised his new number.

"Saw you on TV!" drawled a faint, mocking voice—this was a long-distance call, evidently, interrupted by a lot of static. For all its broken and muffled quality the voice was vaguely familiar—could it be that of Commander March-banks? But no, he was dead, of course. It was the slightly derisive tone that had recalled the old man.

"Nice thing you've made of the house—very nice—" the voice said, amid crackles. "All right if I drop in one evening?"

"Of course, come in for a drink," said Fox automatically—this might be a potential customer—"but—forgive me—I didn't catch your name?"

Now, however, the voice vanished completely, and Fox was left with a dead line. Irritably he replaced the receiver —still, if he was interested, the chappie would phone again—and went back to the television set. This, as the installing engineer had prophesied, was suffering from what he had called teething troubles. That is, any picture tended to dissolve into swimming blankness. Twiddling the controls for ten minutes together, Fox could achieve nothing but a kind of cylindrical dark shape in the middle of the screen, which occasionally almost formed itself into a human image approaching, then receded again into a blurred distance.

Get back TV engineer, scribbled Paul on his list of things to be done. *Have draught-proofing re-tested*—for the banshee scream and maniac murmur were even worse, and beginning to get him down. Also the boards through which heating pipes ran, continually clicked as if giant death-watch beetles were munching them; but there was nothing to be done about that. *Get more mole bombs*, Paul wrote. For the moles, deprived of their playground in front of the house, were determinedly tunnelling along each side of the metal mesh, raising a molehill every metre or so, seemingly bent on boring their way under the house itself. Paul buried barbed wire, broken glass, holly prickles, and gorse branches in their runways (following the advice of different experts) but the only things that seemed to slow them down at all were the smoke bombs, which, when lit and tucked into the burrows, evoked spurts of black smoke from all over the ground; evidently the network of runways was as complicated as it was well established. After a vigorous treatment with these, the moles would stay quiet for a few days, regrouping perhaps.

Meanwhile, indoors, Paul had observed a queer thing.

At the head of the brand-new staircase he had caused to be inserted a large new window, giving light along both the upstairs and downstairs hallways. This window faced east; sometimes the sun shone through it, sometimes the moon. At these times, walking downstairs, Paul would see his own shadow, thrown ahead of him.

But twice, lately, approaching the head of the stairs along the right-angled upper hall, glancing over the banisters, he had seen a man's shadow cast down the staircase *before* he himself had reached the stair.

As if somebody were standing outside the window, looking in. Which was preposterous, for it was on the second floor, eighteen feet above ground.

Then, of course, Fox himself reached the top of the stairs and there was his own shadow, obscuring the other one. And running down rather quickly, he tried to put the odd phenomenon out of his mind. It was probably, must be, an optical illusion.

It would be pleasant, he thought, to get somebody, some

friend, to come and stay for a few days. After all, The Legacy was rather a large house to occupy on one's own.

But all his friends seemed to be out of town, or out of sorts, or out of touch. It was surprising how one did lose touch with people, after a year or two.

Another very odd thing was the habit the TV had of coming on all by itself. He would walk into the lounge and immediately his eye would be caught by the eerie glimmer of the bluish, pearly screen, with that vague dark indeterminate shape in the middle—like a person's body all wrapped up in bandages. He would have been certain that he'd switched the set off.

Fox took to pulling out the plug and aerial cord when he left the room; but just the same, when he returned, three times out of four, the set would be switched on again. No sound: just the vague, trembling image.

Doorbell was another note that he scribbled on his list of things to be done. The builders, curse them, after having been all over the place, hammering away, week after week, until he longed to see the back of them, had now vanished without trace, leaving a maddening legacy of small unfinished items and little faults that needed putting right. "*Legacy*" thought Fox. Ha! very appropriate. There was this bell, for example; the same bell rang, in the middle of the house, for both front and back-door buttons, a good loud bell, since Fox was somewhat hard of hearing.

But, due to an electrical fault somewhere, presumably, it would ring, two or three times a day, with that irritating loud buzz, when there was no person at either door. Paul would hurry from one entrance to the other—but no, there was not a soul to be seen.

That must definitely be dealt with.

*

He took to locking his bedroom door at night. A ridiculous, old-maidish habit—but the house did stand somewhat isolated, and there had been several burglaries recently—now the village was becoming such a known centre of the antiques trade; this precaution was, he felt, only sensible.

So it was particularly demoralising, one morning, to get up and find that the shoes he had worn the previous evening stood where he had left them the night before, neatly aligned in front of the bedroom radiator, and were, both of them, stuffed as tight as they could hold with the foil tops off milk bottles. *Crammed* with the things! What could you make of that? Some people saved foil bottle-tops and strung them on strings as bird-scarers, but Fox had never done so; he threw them out with the rubbish; never had more than a couple in the kitchen. So where the *devil* had all those come from? And who had stuffed them all into his shoes? In a locked room? In the middle of the night?

And—more unnerving still—when Fox went to open the bedroom door he found that the key was missing. Not in the lock, not to be found anywhere. Mercifully—for his predicament might otherwise have been quite serious, no one these days came near the house for days together—he had a complete spare set of house keys in his bureau drawer which the—which whoever had played this singularly pointless and silly practical joke must not have known about—so he was able to let himself out and go down to imbibe a breakfast which consisted entirely of Irish coffee. Fox was becoming rattled. And more so, when, glancing up at his charmingly-arranged kitchen dresser, with all the willow-pattern and Lowestoft, he saw that, up on the top shelf, crammed between two beautiful blue-and-white Chinese ginger jars, leaned a massive dirty old pewter meat-cover, which had *certainly* not been there the night before.

He climbed on a chair, lifted it down, and surveyed it with indignant disgust. Whoever put it there might have washed it before doing so! It was still covered in traces of earth, as if just dug up. An empty snail shell adhered to the under surface. No doubt it might fetch a fair enough price as old pewter, but it was quite *rudely* out of place among his carefully chosen chinaware—which begged the question of who, *who*, had set it up there between last night and this morning? Was it some practical joker among the builders who had retained a key to the house? The lad who had been sacked for bad workmanship, perhaps?

But Joliffe, the head of the building firm, when finally run to ground by phone on a far-distant site, disclaimed all knowledge of extra house keys. Mr Fox had been handed all five, he said; there were no more. And anyway young Andy Heather could not have played the joke; he was in jail, serving five days for drunkenness and disorder. The pranks—harmless enough, they sounded—must have been perpetrated by some of Mr Fox's friends. And Joliffe excused himself quickly, before Fox could raise the matter of the doorbell, the draught-proofing, and the cellar door, which would never stay closed. Continually came open with a loud click.

I'll go up to London for the weekend, Fox decided. Leave early tomorrow morning. And I'll put the house on the market, quietly. Take a loss on it, but never mind. No sense in staying here with all this bother. Something (he did not put it more specifically than that), something is just trying to make it inconvenient for me to stay here. Inconvenient! It makes Borley Rectory seem like the Hilton. Well—I can take a hint. I'll leave tomorrow morning. Early.

Rinsing his coffee-pot he looked through the window over the kitchen sink, and started, almost dropping the jug. For a moment, he thought he had seen the same swaddled shape that showed on the TV screen, only outside the window now, peering in.

But then of course with relief he remembered that it was the new little, well-grown cypress tree which he had planted there yesterday, dripping quietly out there in the October mist. Nothing worse than that. It was quite shaming how a few odd, unrelated incidents could make you jumpy in your nerves.

Fox would have liked to go out for the day, over to an antique-dealers' fair that was being held at Sanditon; but, unfortunately, he had to wait in for the inspector from the Gas Board, who was due to come that day to inspect all the installations.

After the manner of his kind, this individual did not turn up until half-past five in the evening, so there was the day wasted. Even more annoying, when Fox was down in the cellar with the inspector, looking at the gas boiler, the phone rang. Fox raced up the cellar stairs, but got there too late, and there was no message on the answering machine, though the button glowed red; only the word "Wait" abruptly cut off. So many people were still absurdly put off by these useful devices, could think of nothing sensible to say.

The gas inspector, having given his okay to the place, was invited by Fox to have a drink. Fox indeed made quite a point of it, but the man said no thanks, he had to get home, his wife would have dinner waiting. So Fox walked him to his van.

"Trouble with moles, I see," the man remarked as he backed on the turnaround.

The lines of hillocks had almost reached the house now.

Fox debated eating out at a pub, but the thought of returning to the empty dark house was a deterrent; he decided to make himself a frozen TV dinner and turn in early.

In his bath, after having carried out this programme, he

noticed that the wind was rising; the gauze bathroom curtain suddenly billowed inward on a wild flapping curve.

But how could it do that when the window was not only closed, but double glazed?

Fox, locking his bedroom door, putting the key in his pyjama pocket, heard, downstairs, the cellar door click open again.

A moment later, under the covers by now, he heard a slow, heavy step ascending the stairs.

Fox's body, like that of Mrs Bateson, was found on a seat outside in the garden.

But, unlike Mrs Bateson, his expression was not even moderately calm.

The house known as The Legacy is again up for sale.

IN BLACK AND WHITE

Jan Mark

Illustrated by Neil Reed

Contents

In Black and White

Jenny Fielding is Mrs Sanderson, now. She has a husband, two daughters, Julia and Margery, and three grandchildren. On the sideboard in the living room stand photographs of them all; daughters, sons-in-law, granddaughters, grandson. Every year Julia and Margery send new school photographs of Angus, Alice and Rose. Mrs Sanderson arranges them on the sideboard and puts last year's photographs in her dressing-table drawer.

On the wall, above the sideboard, hangs Mr Sanderson's school photograph. It is black and white and a metre long, the whole school in it together. One after another Angus and Alice and Rose have asked, 'Grandpa, how was it done?' and Mr Sanderson explains that once upon a time all school photographs were like that, and had to be taken with a special camera. Everybody was arranged in a huge semicircle – there were seven hundred people at his school, and the camera, which was clockwork, slowly turned, panning from one end of the curve to the other. The real miracle is that, in the photograph, everyone is standing in a straight line while the building behind them looks curved. Grandpa tries to show them why, but they can never quite understand.

'You had to stand absolutely still,' Mr Sanderson says, 'because you could never be sure when the camera was pointing exactly at you.'

Angus and Alice and Rose love it when he gets to that point because they know what is coming next. Mr Sanderson is in the middle of the fourth row, looking very young and serious, with a surprising amount of hair, but at either end of the second row are the Schofeldt Triplets.

'Really, they were twins, Marcus and Ben,' Mr Sanderson tells them, 'and they were standing one each end of the row. When the camera got half-way round Ben left his place and ran along the back of the others, faster than the camera was moving, and went to stand beside Marcus at the other end. They got into a terrible row when they were found out, but we all thought they were heroes because we'd been forbidden to do it.'

Then Angus, Alice and Rose look closely at Grandpa's school photograph to admire the three identical and heroic Schofeldt Twins, Ben at one end, Ben and Marcus at the other.

'Lots of school photographs had mysterious identical twins at each end,' Grandpa boasts, 'but I bet ours was the only one with triplets.'

'Did you have a school photograph, Granny?' Rose asks.

'I did once,' Mrs Sanderson says, vaguely, 'but I must have lost it.'

She hates lying, but if she told the truth about her school photograph no one would believe her anyway, so she pretends it is lost. But at the back of her dressing-table drawer, where Angus and Alice and Rose also lie, growing older and larger each year, is Jenny Fielding's school photograph, still rolled into a cylinder as it was on the day she first brought it home, forty years ago. She has never shown it to anyone since.

Jenny was thirteen, in the third year, when the notice was given out in assembly that the photographer was coming the following Monday. Miss Shaw, the form teacher, had a few words of her own to add when they returned to the classroom.

'You will all make sure that your uniforms are clean and pressed, that your hair is tidy – you'd better plait yours, Maureen Blake – and your shoes polished. I do not *care* if nobody can see your feet. There will be a rehearsal on Friday, so that each girl knows where she is to stand. And wherever you stand on Friday,' said Miss Shaw, fixing them with an iron gaze, 'you will stand on Monday. On these occasions there are always certain stupid people who imagine that it is amusing to run from one end of the line to the other in order to appear twice. Anyone who does that will be dealt with severely. Do I make myself clear?'

3a gazed back at her unblinkingly. Miss Shaw, as always, had made herself very clear. But in the back row Jenny's great friend Margery Fletcher turned her head slightly and muttered to Jenny, 'I bet it will be one of us. I have a feeling.'

'Did you speak, Margery?' Miss Shaw inquired, knowing perfectly well.

'I just said I thought I might get my hair cut,' Margery said, pleasantly. 'For the photograph, you know.'

'An excellent idea,' Miss Shaw said. Margery's hair, like Jenny's, was wild and dark and curly. They were very alike in other ways, too; exactly the same height, short and stocky, and were often mistaken for each other by people who saw them misbehaving from a distance. Margery misbehaved far more frequently, and far more inventively, than Jenny, but when Jenny was falsely accused Margery always raised her hand and owned up. And on the rarer occasions when the mistake was in Jenny's favour, Jenny did the same. That was why they were best friends, faithful and true. They went everywhere together, near enough.

It had come as a surprise to no one when the announcement was made in assembly; bush telegraph had seen to that. Everybody had known for weeks that the photographer was due and some people even claimed – wrongly as it turned out – to know the date. So it was already public knowledge that after the rehearsal on Friday morning the lottery would take place. They had to wait until Friday to find out who would be in it.

Friday involved a great deal of standing about in a chilly damp wind on the lawn in front of the school. In the centre of the lawn stood a long curved row of eighty chairs, with a row of benches behind them and a row of tables behind that. One after another the classes stepped forward to take their places. On the chairs sat the sixth form with the teachers in the middle and the Headmistress in the very centre. In front of them the second years knelt upright, the most uncomfortable position of all, and right at the front sat the first years, cross-legged and trying not to show their knickers. Because they were only first years people thought that they were too young to care.

The third years stood on the grass behind the sixth form and staff, the fourth year stood behind them on the benches, and at the back the fifth forms teetered on the tables. Symmetry was all. The tallest in every group stood in the middle, the shortest at the sides, and so it was that Jenny and Margery found themselves facing each other across the grass at opposite ends of the third year, and Jenny was remembering what Margery had said last week: 'I bet it will be one of us.' There was a very good chance that it would be, one chance in four, but if it were, Jenny would be the one. Jenny was on the left, the end that the camera started from.

The entrants for the lottery met at the back of the sports pavilion after lunch; Jenny from the third year, one from the second year, one from the fourth and one from the fifth; all the left-hand tail-enders, except for the first year who were considered too young to be trusted, and the sixth who were above such things. Glenda Alcott, the fifth former, was there before them, holding her blue felt school hat in which lay four tightly folded pieces of paper.

'Now then,' Glenda said, 'three of these are blank and one carries the Black Spot. Whoever draws the Black Spot is the one who changes ends. As soon as the camera is pointing to the middle you leave your place and run round to the other end of the line. You know you'll get into a row afterwards. Are you prepared to risk it?'

The other three nodded solemnly.

'All right, then. Draw your papers.'

Madeline Enderby from the second year drew first, then Jenny, then Dawn Fuggle from the fourth and that left one paper in the hat for Glenda and she took it out last of all.

Madeline, Dawn and Glenda looked at each other before they looked at their papers, smiling but grim, as if they had been drawing lots to see who should go to the guillotine, but Jenny just stared at her folded paper, remembering what Margery had said: 'I bet it will be one of us. I have a feeling.' Margery had had feelings before, and they had come true. She had had a feeling before the carol concert last year, that she would be singing the descant in *Adeste Fideles*, and when Susan Beale lost her voice just before they were due to start it had been Margery who was called out to take her place. Then she had had a feeling about the geometry exam that everyone had been so worried about before Easter. 'I have a feeling there won't be an exam,' said Margery, who had done no revision, and on the morning that it was due to take place, Miss Ogden's briefcase, containing the papers, was stolen on the train.

'I have a feeling Cranmer House won't win the acting prize this year,' Margery said, the day before the drama competition, although Cranmer House were a dead cert, and sure enough, on the day, Cranmer went to pieces and fluffed their lines and missed their cues and the cup was awarded to Becket House. Margery and Jenny were in Becket.

Margery's feelings always seemed to involve misfortune for someone, Jenny sometimes reflected, but you couldn't blame Margery for that. *She* hadn't given Susan laryngitis, or nicked Miss Ogden's briefcase. Margery hadn't nobbled the entire cast of Cranmer's play.

'Open your papers,' Glenda said, and Jenny unfolded the little wad in her hand. She hardly needed to look; she knew that it would be her paper that bore the Black Spot.

'You can't back out now,' Dawn said, half envious, half relieved, when Jenny continued to stare at the paper in her palm.

'Remember what I said,' Glenda was admonishing

her. 'Wait until the camera's half-way round in case you're still in shot, then run like hell.' Madeline gasped. She was only a second year. It seemed to her a very desperate thing that grown-up Glenda should say 'hell'.

'And another thing,' Glenda said. 'Don't tell anybody else who's won, except you, Jenny. You must appoint a liaison officer. If you're going to be feeble and come down with something at the last moment you must let us know before Monday lunchtime, so that we three can draw again.'

Jenny knew that there was no chance that she would come down with anything or Margery would have mentioned it, but she had to do what Glenda said, just in case. 'Will you be my liaison officer?' Jenny asked Margery, who showed no surprise when Jenny silently handed her the Black Spot.

'No need,' Margery said. 'If anything happens to you I'll run instead.'

'But you'd have to swap ends,' Jenny said. 'It doesn't work if you run the other way. You don't show up at all.'

'That won't be hard,' Margery said. 'People will think it's you anyway. They usually do. Actually,' she added, 'I have a feeling I may have to do it.'

'Why, am I going to drop dead before Monday?' Jenny snapped. Suddenly she felt that she had had enough of Margery and her feelings.

'Only joking,' Margery said, but Jenny had turned away with an angry flounce. During country dancing that afternoon, she chose Diana Sullivan for her partner, leaving Margery to the mercies of Galumphing Gertie the Games Mistress, who always stomped in enthusiastically to help out anyone who didn't have a partner, and at the end of the afternoon she went straight home alone instead of waiting for Margery who was in a different set for maths.

On Monday morning she made herself especially tidy, as demanded, for the photograph. Rumour had it that school photographs were always taken on Mondays so that even the scruffiest girls might look half-way presentable before they went downhill during the week.

Waiting in the form room for assembly they preened and checked each other out, even though there was the whole morning and lunch to get through before it was time for the photograph, so Jenny had only just noticed that Margery was not in the room before Miss Shaw appeared at the door and beckoned her out.

'Jenny, dear,' Miss Shaw said, as they stood in the corridor, 'I wanted a word with you before I told the others – I know Margery is a very special friend of yours.'

Jenny did not have feelings, not the way Margery did, but she knew what was coming.

'Margery had an accident yesterday,' Miss Shaw said. 'She was out for a drive with some family friends and the car door wasn't properly shut. Margery was thrown out into the road when they took a bend too sharply. She's in hospital. I'm afraid she's badly hurt.'

Jenny, excused assembly, went to sit in the cloakroom and listened to the swarming sound of rubber-shod feet as class after class converged upon the hall. The Headmistress must have made an announcement – perhaps they had all said a prayer for Margery's recovery – for at break the news was all round the school. Glenda Alcott came to find Jenny.

'You needn't run if you don't want to,' Glenda said, kindly. 'We'll understand.'

'I'll be all right,' Jenny said, 'Margery wouldn't want me to back out,' but she wasn't too bothered by what Margery would have wanted. All she knew was that if she had the photograph to worry about she might not have to think of Margery herself, lying in the hospital. 'A coma,' Miss Shaw had said. 'Severe head injuries.'

While they were all lining up after lunch, to go out on to the field, Glenda sought her out again.

'Listen,' she said, 'someone told me – someone who *knows* –' she added defiantly, 'that they do it twice, just in case anyone does run.'

'Margery had a feeling they'd do that,' Jenny said.

'The first time they don't run the film. Then if you leave your place you get caught and sent back and you don't dare try it again when they go for the take,' Glenda said. 'That's how they did it at my brother's school. They did it last time we had one here, too, but I didn't realize why. I was only a first year, then.'

If it had been Glenda alone who'd said it, Jenny would probably have doubted, and panicked, and spoiled her chance by running too soon, but as they stood there, tier upon tier, as they had on Friday, she looked across that great curve to the place where Margery ought to have been standing, and did not move. And Margery and Glenda had been right. After the camera had swept round, and while they all stood there frozen and smirking, the little photographer blew his whistle, said, 'All right, ladies, let's do it once more, to make sure,' and redirected the camera, on its tripod, towards Jenny's end of the line. He sounded his whistle again to warn them that he was ready to start and very slowly the camera began to turn a second time. Jenny thought how sinister it looked, clicking round on its

plate, but the first time she had counted the seconds until it seemed to have reached the Headmistress, slap in the middle of the curve, and now, when the moment came, she took a step backwards, turned and began to run.

She hadn't thought before about what it would be like behind the curve. The backs of the fifth years, standing on their tables, reared eight feet above her, blotting out the sun; a palisade of legs, a swathe of skirts, a battlement of heads. The curve seemed endless, for she couldn't *see* the end of it, and the camera was so far ahead of her. In her mind's eye she could see that, the little black eye, inexorably turning, and she ran faster, racing her hidden adversary on the other side of the curve.

Three yards from the end of the line she slipped. The grass was damp where it had lain all day in the shade, her foot skidded from under her and, as she was off-balance already, leaning forward for the final effort, she fell flat, heavily, and lay there winded, all the air slammed out of her lungs. She thought she was going to die, but suddenly she was able to breathe again and scrambled to her feet. But it was too late to run on. As she rose upright the wall of backs relaxed, there was a surge of muted laughter and conversation. The camera had got there first, the photographer had won and the photograph was over. Glenda Alcott, who had seen her leave and had, of course, been able to see also that she had not arrived at the far end, jumped down from the table and hurried round to find out what had happened.

'Did you fall? Bad luck. Hey, don't cry,' Glenda said, when she found Jenny weeping on the grass. Madeline and Dawn, the other tail-enders, were not so charitable.

'If you couldn't do it you might have said, and one of us could have run,' Madeline grumbled.

'I tried. I did try,' Jenny wept.

'Jenny has something on her mind,' Glenda said, severely, and the other two, remembering what it must be, became all at once very serious.

Jenny's mother came up to the school at the end of the afternoon, to meet Jenny and take her home. Jenny was far too old to be taken to and from school, but her mother had something to tell her. Margery had died at just after two o'clock, while they were having the photograph taken.

Everyone at school, girls and teachers, was kind and sympathetic to Jenny – until the photographs arrived, and then the storm broke, for there was Jenny, standing on the left-hand side of the picture, and there, in all her guilt, at the far end, was Jenny again, looking a little dishevelled and blurred, as though she had moved at the wrong moment.

'It isn't me,' Jenny kept saying.

'The truth, if you please,' said first Miss Shaw and then the Headmistress. 'Are you going to tell me that you didn't leave your place?'

'Yes, I did,' Jenny said. 'I did go, I did run round, but I never got there. I fell over.'

She was, as promised, severely dealt with; barred from this and banned from that, and everyone despised her for not admitting to what she had done, when the evidence was there in black and white, for anyone to see; except for three people. Glenda Alcott, Madeline Enderby and Dawn Fuggle had all seen her leave her place, had all been watching the far end to see her arrive, and they alone knew that she had never got there. Lesley Wilson, the girl who was standing next but one at the end of the line and who had, on the day, been at the very end, to start with, said, 'Of course you were standing next to me. I felt your arm. Only I thought at first it was Margery – I mean, it should have been Margery, shouldn't it?'

Glenda borrowed a magnifying glass and they stud ied that indistinct little figure at the right-hand end o the photograph. 'It *could* be you,' she said, finally. Wha she didn't say, and what they were all thinking, was, 'It could be Margery.'

'She said if anything happened to me she'd be there in my place,' Jenny said. 'She had a feeling.'

This is why Mrs Sanderson keeps her school photograph in a drawer instead of hanging it on the wall beside her husband's. Even now, forty years later, she can't bring herself to explain.

Old Money

*I*t couldn't happen now. If we found it now we'd
throw it away without a second thought – well,
perhaps one second thought. Money's still tight; but
. . . ten pence . . . it wouldn't be the end of the world.

The point is, though, in 1956 ten pence was two
shillings, and although two shillings wasn't a fortune it
was still a fortnight's pocket-money. Look at the next
ten pence piece you come by. If it's an old one, more
than twenty years old, it won't say ten pence on the
back, it will say two shillings, and the two shilling piece
we got from Mr Tate back in 1956 was old even in those
days. It didn't have the Queen's head on it, or her
father's, George VI. The head belonged to *his* father,
George V, an elderly man with a little beard. It was
very worn down and discoloured, but you could just
make out the beard, and in any case, we recognized him
at once. George V came to the throne in 1910 and died
in 1936, but there were still plenty of coins around with
his head on them. Victoria turned up sometimes, too.

Gary said he reckoned that Mr Tate had probably
had the coin since 1910 anyway. He was only joking
but when we thought about it afterwards we began to
wonder if it wasn't the simple truth.

Mr Tate lived farther down the street in a corner
house, and everyone said he was a miser. We knew all
about misers from comics. They were bitter and twisted
and cruel to orphans; also they wore fingerless mittens

and hoarded their money in bags with £ signs on, rather as burglars wore striped sweaters and carried bags marked S W A G. Gary's Uncle Timothy was a burglar but he wore dungarees and looked just like a mechanic, which is what he was in his spare time. When he was inside, Gary's mum said he was working up north which, in a way, was true; Durham Gaol.

Mr Tate didn't dress the part either, and wore a hard blue suit. His gloves were tan leather, with fingers, but although he went to work every day, no one seemed to know what he did for a living. His house was shabby and unpainted – although that was nothing unusual in our street – and when he went to the Corner Stores for groceries he never bought more than yesterday's bread and cheap cheese. And he looked miserable, which is where the word comes from, I suppose. A miser is miserable in spite of having money. We were miserable a lot of the time, too; from not having it.

But that Saturday we did have money; two half-crowns – five shillings – oh, all right, twenty-five pence, which Gary Sutton's mum had given him to buy a jar of mustard pickle and some potatoes from the Corner Stores. Mr Tate was ahead of us, buying his bread and cheese which he paid for – we saw him – with a two shilling piece. We saw it because Mrs Goldman looked at it very hard before she put it in the till.

'What's wrong? It's a perfectly good one,' Mr Tate said testily. He said everything testily, as if he expected to be contradicted.

Mrs Goldman held it up to the light and we noticed how black it looked, but it sounded OK when she rang it on the counter and put it in the till. Mr Tate had been scowling across the counter at her, but as the till drawer closed he suddenly smiled, raised his hat, which he hadn't taken off when he went in, and almost bowed out of the shop.

'Must have been drinking,' Mrs Goldman said, half to herself. 'Now, what can I do for you boys?'

'A-jar-of-mustard-pickle-and-ten-pounds-of-good-King-Edwards,' Gary recited.

'What d'you mean, *good* King Edwards?' Mrs Goldman demanded, heaving herself round the counter to reach the potato sack. 'When has your mother ever had a bad potato from me, young man?'

The spuds and pickles came to two and elevenpence halfpenny – just short of fifteen p if you want to know – and Gary handed her the two half-crowns. In return Mrs Goldman gave him a halfpenny and a two shilling piece, the very two shillings that Mr Tate had just given *her*. We were ready to swear to that, afterwards.

She was glaring something awful while she was holding out the money, because Gary didn't take it at first. He looked hard at the two bob, and I looked, too. It *seemed* OK, but it was very black, as if it had been dipped in something that had started to make it change colour.

'It's a perfectly good one,' Mrs Goldman snapped, exactly as Mr Tate had done. We jumped. Mrs Goldman always grumbled at us but that was only force of habit. We never did anything to offend her – unlike Bobby Daniels – and she often gave us broken biscuits. But now she looked really angry, angry and frightened, as though she couldn't wait for us to go. Her hand, with the two coins in the palm, was shaking, and the halfpenny chattered against the two bob bit.

Gary picked them up and dropped them in his

pocket, we took a handle of the shopping bag each and went out of the shop in a hurry. As we left we heard Mrs Goldman call out, as she usually did, 'Goodbye, boys. See you soon!'

'She's changed her tune,' I said. Gary shrugged, moodily. He was slouching and the shopping bag dipped annoyingly on his side, so that the lumpy King Edwards banged against my legs.

'Quit shoving!' Gary snarled, when I jerked at the bag to level it out.

'What's eating you?' I said. Gary had been in a perfectly good mood five minutes before. Now he was scowling, but not angrily, almost as if he was trying not to cry; the same expression he wore when Mr Carter whacked him at school. It was a look that got him accused of dumb insolence and whacked again. He drew his eyebrows together and glared at the ground, while the King Edwards knocked dents in my left leg.

He didn't tell me what was eating him, but he was my mate. I couldn't let him suffer in silence (this is something you only learn to do as you get older) so I kept on at him all the way up the road.

'What's the matter? It wasn't old Ma Goldman, was it? Did Old Tate put the Evil Eye on you?' I didn't know what the Evil Eye was, but catching Mr Tate's eye was usually enough to make you wish you'd been looking the other way.

'Shurrup,' Gary growled, and gave the shopping bag a violent shrug. I felt the edge of the pickle jar bite into my ankle.

'Carry it yourself, then!' I yelled, and letting go of the handle I stormed off ahead of him. I half expected him to shy a King Edward at me and my neck muscles tensed, but instead he called out, 'No, Brian! Wait!'

It wasn't so much a call as a howl. I looked round. Gary was standing in the middle of the pavement looking as miserable as an abandoned dog. I could almost see his drooping tail. There was no way I could leave him there. I went back, picked up the dangling handle, and we walked on.

'Sorry,' Gary muttered.

'What's the matter?'

'I don't know.' He finally looked me in the eye. 'I feel horrible.'

'Ill? You got a pain?'

'No . . . just horrible.' There was a tear on the side of his nose.

We were level with his front door by then. There weren't any front gardens in our street so we went straight in; as straight as we could, that is. Gary's brother was mending his bike in the hall and a clothes horse hung with airing sheets blocked the doorway of the living-room. Gary's sister had the treadle sewing machine out in the middle of the room and his mum was ironing in the kitchen. You couldn't take more than three steps in any direction and there were babies and toys underfoot.

Gary usually trod his way through this maze like a cat stepping round broken glass on top of a wall, but today I distinctly saw him tread on a teddy bear and kick his little sister, though I couldn't be sure whether he did it on purpose or from carelessness, but we left a trail of wailing babies in our wake. Instead of stopping to comfort them as he normally did he just kept going, barging between obstacles until we reached the kitchen table, where he dumped the shopping bag.

'Got the pickles?' his mum said. She could see the potatoes spilling out of the overturned bag. 'Got the change?'

Gary delved into his pocket and dropped the two coins on the table. And smiled. In that second his whole mood changed, his frown vanished, his shoulders straightened. 'Two and a ha'penny, all present and correct,' he said. His mother leaned over and eyed the two bob bit suspiciously.

'Is that a dud?'

'No, just dirty.'

'Put it in the tin, then.'

Gary's mum kept her loose change in a cocoa tin on a shelf above the coke boiler, so that the money in it was always slightly and mysteriously warm. Gary reached it down and looked inside.

'Can I have my pocket money?'

His mum slammed down the iron.

'*Already?*'

'I haven't had last week's yet.' They enjoyed this exchange regularly on Saturdays, so Gary was quite cheerful about it. That was why I was watching him. Only minutes ago he had acted as if he had been told that he had no more than weeks to live, now he was grinning as usual, hands in pockets, ready to take on all comers.

'What's in the tin?' his mum said.

'Two and six, two threepenny bits and three pennies,' Gary said. 'Give us the half dollar, eh, Mum?'

'You're joking,' his mum said, flatly, although of course he was. 'Take the ninepence.'

'Oh Mum. It's *two weeks*.' He was looking at the two shilling piece we'd got from the shop.

'Are you sure?'

'Would I lie?' He turned up his eyeballs, all holy.

'OK, take the two bob. But don't tell your dad.' Officially Gary had ninepence a week, not a shilling. The extra threepence was always a matter for negotiation, or bribery.

Gary meticulously dropped the odd halfpenny into the tin, put it back on the shelf, scooped up the two bob and we zipped out of the back door.

'What d'you say?' Mrs Sutton yelled after us.

'Ta,' said Gary. Anyone would think she'd kept the two shillings and given him the halfpenny. He was right down in the mouth again, dragging his feet as we crossed the Suttons' yard and went through the gate into the back lane. He shoved his hands deeper into his pockets and kicked at a stone. I thought he must have been putting on an act for his mum, because now he looked as miserable again as he had when we came in off the street.

'Come on,' I said, 'let's go up the rec.'

'I don't care where we go,' Gary said, but he plodded after me, head down, and I heard his heels dragging in the dirt.

I couldn't understand it. Gary had a temper, like the rest of us, but he wasn't moody, never sulked, and if anything was bothering him he talked about it – to me at any rate. After all, I was his best mate. But today he wasn't talking, he never said a word all the way to the rec, though I thought he might say something when he saw who was there ahead of us.

The rec was a couple of scrubby grass acres which in summer baked so hard that you could understand how people made bricks with mud. You could break an arm falling over on it and where a long drop was involved, necks were at risk. A pair of swings stood in one corner, with a slide which was useless for sliding *down* because most people walked *up* it, and a see-saw with deep pits under each end where generations of feet had dug into the earth. Suspended upside down from the crossbar of one of the swings was Trevor Passmore. If he'd been hanging by the neck we wouldn't have objected, but he was hanging by his knees; when he saw us he swung himself down and strutted towards us.

We stood in awe of Trevor Passmore, partly because he was a lot bigger than us, and partly because he said that underpants were sissy and refused to wear any. He was tough. We had to believe it, because of the under-pants and because he kept telling us so, but he wasn't a bully. He nagged.

'Bet you can't walk down to Woolworth's with your eyes shut,' he would taunt us. 'Bet you can't climb over the fence on to the railway. Bet you can't stand on your head for half an hour.' There was no point in telling him that we didn't much want to do any of these reckless things; he just kept on at us until we tried, and failed, and then he nagged some more, to prove his superiority.

Now he came up to us and said, 'Bet you can't hang upside down from them swings.'

Gary stared at him mournfully and started to walk on, but Trevor dodged in front of him. 'Yer scared. Yer scared. Bet you can't hang upside down from them swings. Bet you can't. Bet you can't.'

'Go and chase yourself,' I said. I said it because Gary hadn't. It was usually Gary who retaliated when Passmore got going, but Gary, sunk in gloom, just kept scuffling over the scorched grass, head down, shoulders hunched.

'Bet you can't. Bet yer scared, bet you wouldn't *dare* hang upside down from them swings,' Passmore intoned, lolloping round us like an incompetent wolf. 'Bet you can't, bet you, betcha, betch.'

At last Gary raised his heavy head, gave Passmore a long, serious look like a man who has received his death warrant and therefore has nothing more to dread, and wordlessly changed direction towards the swings. When he reached the hard asphalt pad where they stood he looked up at the crossbar – he might have been a condemned criminal staring at the gallows – and dragged his hands out of his pockets.

'Hold that for us,' he said, and dropped into my hands the contents of his trouser pockets. Then with one bound he was swarming up the support of the left hand swing. But I wasn't looking at him. I wasn't looking at anything. Just standing upright seemed to require a terrible effort. There was a leaden feeling at the back of my head, not a pain, but a dreadful heaviness, and I knew there was no hope.

If you've never felt like that, I can't explain it. I just knew, in that instant, that there was no point in doing anything, ever again, that nothing mattered; and I knew that I would always feel like this, for ever, until I died, and that wouldn't matter either, because I was nothing. I despised myself for not understanding it sooner.

Up above, Gary was dangling, head down, yelling insults at Passmore. I turned my eyes upward to watch him. Poor Gary. I felt like weeping. Didn't he *know* it was pointless, that whatever he did, and however well he did it, it was all meaningless? With a final jeer, Gary gripped the crossbar with his hands, swung upright and lowered himself to the ground. Passmore, thwarted, growled some kind of grudging congratulation, but Gary brushed him aside and pranced over to where I was standing.

'Not bad, eh? You can't half see a long way up there. Give us me bits and pieces.'

His voice seemed muffled, dull, and the words made no sense. I didn't expect them to. Nothing made sense. Why was I alive?

'Wake up!' Gary bawled, cheerfully. 'Give us me things!'

He held out his hands and with an immense effort I dropped into them all the objects he had given me to hold so that they would not fall out of his pockets; a gnawed stub of pencil, his Boy Scouts badge, a button off his jacket, half a hacksaw blade and two coins – an Irish penny and the two shilling piece.

Gary's hands closed over his possessions.

'That was brilliant!' I said. 'Shurrup, Passmore, you lost your bet.'

'It's nothing,' Gary said. The sad, sick look was back in his eyes. Passmore was taking his defeat like a man, bobbing up and down and trying to shake hands, but Gary just sighed and turned away. I knew how he felt.

I knew how he felt. Then I realized *why* I knew how he felt. Gary was walking away, dragging his feet again. I turned my back on Passmore and ran after him.

'Gary!'

He looked round drearily and didn't answer.

'Lend us two bob.'

I thought I was in for an argument and was trying frantically to think of a reason why I so suddenly needed money, but Gary simply held out his hand with the coin in it.

'Take it,' he said. 'Keep it. Go on. I don't want it any more.'

'No,' I said, 'you don't,' and I flicked it out of his palm with my fingernail, so fast I didn't have time to feel it. The coin spun away into the grass and Gary shot after it.

'What'd you do that for?' he yelled. 'You stupid nit! That's *two* weeks' money, that is.'

'Wait!' I grabbed his sleeve. 'Don't pick it up.'

'You want a knuckle sandwich?'

I was so relieved I nearly hugged him. 'Listen,' I said, 'why did you give it to me?'

He stopped and stared. 'You said "Lend us two bob".'

'I know, but why *did* you?'

'Did what?'

'Let me have it.'

'You're my mate.'

'That's not why,' I said. 'Go on, it isn't, is it? *Is it?*' I sounded like Passmore.

Gary stopped and thought. 'I didn't want it,' he said, at last. 'I didn't want anything. I wished I was dead.'

'Wished?'

'No . . . I just couldn't understand why I was alive.'

'I know,' I told him, 'and nor could I, while you were on that swing – while I was looking after your things.'

Gary gaped at me. 'While you were holding my money . . .'

The two bob was lying in front of us, on a patch of bald earth.

'Don't touch it,' I said. 'When did you start feeling like that?'

'When you gave it back to me, just now.'

'No, before that.'

'In the kitchen.'

'Before that.'

'In the shop.'

'When Mrs Goldman gave you the change.'

'Remember how miserable *she* was?'

'Hang about,' I said. 'Who gave it to her?'

'Old Tate,' Gary said. We looked at each other. 'You can't get much more miserable than that.'

'Yes,' I said, 'but he wasn't miserable once he'd got rid of it, was he?'

We sort of crept up on the two bob and stood watching it. What *was* that blackness on it?

'He must have had it for years,' Gary said. 'Imagine, if it made *him* feel like it made us feel. All the time.'

'Leave it there,' I said, as Gary stooped to retrieve it. 'Don't touch it.'

'Two shillings!' Gary squawked. 'Get out of it!'

'You know what'll happen if you pick it up,' I warned him.

'Perhaps we imagined it.' But he let it lie there.

'Spend it quick, then,' I said. 'Get rid of it.'

Gary looked shocked. 'I can't do that. Someone else will get it.'

'Yes,' I said, 'but they won't have it long. No one has money for long.'

'Old Tate does. Suppose some little kid got hold of it and put it in a piggy bank?'

'I wonder what Old Tate's doing now,' I said. 'Hey, what say we test it.'

Gary was prodding the coin with a twig.

'You feel anything?' I asked him, anxiously. He shook his head.

'What do you mean, test it?'

'We could give it to someone we don't like – just for a bit – just to see what happens. *Then* we could get rid of it . . . when we're sure.'

'Someone we don't like . . .' Gary was looking thoughtful. 'Passmore?'

'He's not *that* bad,' I said. 'Bobby Daniels?' To be honest, I couldn't think of anyone I disliked enough to make them go through what we'd been through.

'What about Old Carter?'

Of course; Mr Carter. And somehow, doing it to a teacher didn't seem quite so unfair. I mean, there wasn't much Mr Carter didn't know about unfairness.

'How shall we do it?'

'I'll ask him to look after my money on Monday.'

'Yes, but *how*? How do we get it to him – without carrying it?'

You won't believe how we did it. Gary stood guard over the two shillings while I went home for the coal tongs, a paper bag and some string. We picked up the coin with the tongs, dropped it in the bag, tied the neck with string and left a long end dangling. Then we tied the end to Gary's twig and walked back, holding the bag at arm's length. We looked very stupid and we didn't care. The bag spent the rest of the weekend in Gary's outside lav, on top of the cistern, out of harm's way.

On Monday morning we risked being late so as to arrive after everyone else, unobserved. Even so, we got a funny look from the caretaker when we came belting across the playground trailing the paper bag on the end of its string along the ground behind us. We had to pretend we were fooling about and kept yelling, 'Heel, Rover! Good dog! Sit!' but we weren't fooling, no way. On Sunday night we'd tossed up – the Irish penny – to see who would have to handle the coin long enough to take it up to Mr Carter's desk and hand it over. I called heads and it came up tails which was only fair, really. It *was* Gary's money, but he looked pretty sick, after registration, when he carried it to the front and laid it on Mr Carter's desk, even though we'd put it in an envelope.

I saw Gary swallow hard as he said, 'Please, Sir, will you look after this for me till dinner time?' and then he swallowed again, even harder, as Mr Carter took the envelope and shoved it in his pocket.

We had wondered if there would be a sudden dramatic change, but Mr Carter usually looked like a wet weekend anyway, and today was no exception. Even with the money in his pocket, he just went on looking like a wet weekend.

We lined up for assembly after that, and we were half-way through *Praise my Soul the King of Heaven* before Gary nudged me and nodded in Mr Carter's direction. In assembly the teachers sat on chairs alongside their classes, while we sat on the floor, and they always sat bolt upright, looking stuffed. Mr Carter wasn't bolt upright this morning, he was slumped forward with his head in his hands. We couldn't see his face and we didn't want to. When we all stood up at the end and filed out he stayed where he was, until Miss Lewis, from the third year, walked over and touched him on the shoulder. Gary and I were going out of the door by then, and Gary glanced back over his shoulder, to give me a meaningful look.

Miss Lewis took us for double maths, afterwards, then we had break, then history with Mr Bryce and English with Mr Carter. I don't think we'd ever before looked forward to an English lesson so eagerly.

It was due to start at 11.45, but it was ten to twelve before the classroom door opened and Miss Lewis walked in. No one complained. We all liked Miss Lewis better than Mr Carter, but Gary put up his hand and said, 'Please, Miss, what's happened to Sir?'

He had to ask.

We had to know.

'Mr Carter is feeling unwell,' Miss Lewis said. That didn't surprise us, but a sort of ripple ran through the class, teachers being regarded as durable and generally indestructible, except for the real softies who only lasted a term anyway.

A horrid thought struck me.

'He hasn't gone home, has he?' Good grief! If he'd left the premises – with the two bob –

'I don't see what business it is of yours, Brian,' Miss Lewis said, 'but, no, he has not.'

He must be in the staff room, then, and we could just imagine him sitting there, slouched, despairing, head in hands. We knew how he was feeling.

As soon as the dinner bell rang we hurried to the staff room, but before we got there I happened to glance out of the big window in the corridor that overlooked the front drive. At the end of the drive was Mr Carter, just turning right, into the street.

We were forbidden to leave school without permission, but we didn't stop to think about that. Without saying a word we were off, out of the end door – we didn't dare even then to use the front door, next to the Head's office – raced across the grass in front of the school, and out of the gate.

Mr Carter was well ahead of us but not walking very fast. One didn't walk fast, we knew, feeling as he must be feeling. We assumed he was heading for the bus stop, as he usually did at home time, but instead, when he got to the crossroads, by the garage, he turned left.

'Where's he off to?' Gary said, breathlessly. 'What's down there? Maybe he's going to the pub.'

There was a pub down that street, The Green Man, but Mr Carter kept right on past it, head down, shoulders hunched, and we realized he was heading for the station – only he wasn't. When he reached the station approach he crossed over it and went on, up on to the railway bridge.

'Where *is* he off to?' Gary said again. Now we were crossing the station approach, and we could see Mr

Carter's figure up ahead of us, outlined against the sky as he reached the highest part of the bridge; and then he stopped.

Gary stopped too. 'Oh God!' he said, and broke into a run, and I ran after him, for up there on the bridge Mr Carter had got one knee up on the parapet and was just drawing up the other beside it.

'Sir!' I was so frightened my voice had become a breathy squeak. 'No! *Sir!*'

Then a train went under the bridge, an express that wasn't stopping at the station, and Gary and Mr Carter vanished into a boiling cloud of steam, deceptively white and stinking of sulphur. When it cleared I saw, as I came up alongside, Gary holding Mr Carter by the belt of his raincoat, and Mr Carter climbing down off the parapet. He dusted his knees mechanically, and looked down at Gary.

'What do you want?' he asked, as if Gary's sudden arrival was the final straw, and he muttered under his breath, 'No peace. Even in my last hour, no peace . . .'

'Oh, Sir.' Gary was as frightened as I was, but it was a desperate moment. 'Oh, Sir, can I have that two bob you were keeping for me, Sir?'

Mr Carter reached into his pocket, drew out the envelope and handed it to Gary who took it by one corner, pinched in his fingernails.

Mr Carter looked slightly stunned, and shook his head like someone whose ears are full of water. 'Right,' he said briskly, and clapped his hands. 'Back to school. Can't think why we're hanging about here, can you?' and he strode off, whistling, without another glance at us.

Gary laid the envelope on the parapet.

'It was worse for him,' he said. 'It must be terrible for grown-ups. Think of Mr Tate.'

'What are we going to do with it?' I said, 'spend it?'

'We *can't*,' Gary said. 'We *can't* let it get loose. I mean, we could give it to Hitler or Stalin, people like that, but we can't just let it go. *Anyone* might get hold of it.'

I'd been thinking of perhaps putting it in the missionary box at Holy Trinity, with the vague idea of letting it leave the country, but that wouldn't solve the problem. I suddenly understood what people meant when they talked about someone turning up like a bad penny.

And so Gary performed the noblest deed of his life. He took the two bob bit, two weeks' pocket money, and dropped it in the canal. Two bob? What's ten p? I hear you ask. Well then, allowing for inflation, see how you'd feel about setting fire to a fiver.

Right. Now you know what it meant to Gary to chuck that two bob away. But he had to do it. Knowing what we did we couldn't have lived with our consciences if we'd let someone else get hold of it. Of course, for the next couple of weeks I shared my pocket money with Gary – but that came later. When we went home that afternoon Mr Tate was out on the pavement in his shirtsleeves, painting his front door bright red.

'Just a moment, lads,' he said, as we went by. I think it was the first time he'd ever spoken to us, but we stopped, out of curiosity as much as anything.

'Do you remember, on Saturday,' he said, 'you came into the corner shop just after me? I paid for some groceries with a two shilling piece, and Mrs Goldman is ready to swear that she gave it to you two as change.' He looked at us hopefully. 'You don't still have it, by any chance?'

I felt Gary jump. No doubt he felt me do the same. 'No, sorry,' he said, and added, unblushingly, 'we must have spent it.'

'Was it special, then?' I couldn't help asking.

Mr Tate looked sentimental, quite a feat for a face that had only ever looked sour. 'It was the first money I ever earned,' he said. 'I took it home to give to my mother, but she said, "No, Charles, keep it for good luck," and I've had it in my waistcoat pocket ever since. Not always the same waistcoat, ha ha,' he said. It may well have been his first joke. 'I can't think how it came to be mixed up with my loose change.'

'I'm sorry you've lost it,' Gary said.

'Can't be helped,' Mr Tate said, shrugging. He looked amazingly cheerful, in spite of his loss – or because of it for, as we very well knew, there was nothing amazing about it. I've often wondered since if he ever realized exactly the kind of luck his first wages had brought him. I've also wondered what his first employer could have been like, although I think I can guess.

Nule

The house was not old enough to be interesting, just old enough to be starting to fall apart. The few interesting things had been dealt with ages ago, when they first moved in. There was a bell-push in every room, somehow connected to a glass case in the kitchen which contained a list of names and an indicator which wavered from name to name when a button was pushed, before settling on one of them: *Parlour*; *Drawing Room*; *Master Bedroom*; *Second Bedroom*; *Back Bedroom*.

'What are they for?' said Libby one morning, after roving round the house and pushing all the buttons in turn. At that moment Martin pushed the button in the front room and the indicator slid up to *Parlour*, vibrating there while the bell rang. And rang and rang.

'To fetch up the maid,' said Mum.

'We haven't got a maid.'

'No, but you've got me,' said Mum, and tied an old sock over the bell, so that afterwards it would only whirr instead of ringing.

The mouse-holes in the kitchen looked interesting, too. The mice were bold and lounged about, making no effort at all to be timid and mouse-like. They sat on the draining board in the evenings and could scarcely be bothered to stir themselves when the light was switched on.

'Easy living has made them soft,' said Mum. 'They have a gaming-hell behind the boiler. They throw dice all day. They dance the can-can at night.'

'Come off it,' said Dad. 'You'll be finding crates of tiny gin bottles, next.'

'They dance the can-can,' Mum insisted. 'Right over my head they dance it. I can hear them. If you didn't sleep so soundly, you'd hear them too.'

'Oh, that. That's not mice,' said Dad, with a cheery smile. 'That's rats.'

Mum minded the mice less than the bells, until the day she found footprints in the frying-pan.

'Sorry, lads, the party's over,' she said to the mice, who were no doubt combing the dripping from their elegant whiskers at that very moment, and the mouse-holes were blocked up.

Dad did the blocking-up, and also some unblocking, so that after the bath no longer filled itself through the plug hole, the house stopped being interesting altogether; for a time.

Libby and Martin did what they could to improve matters. Beginning in the cupboard under the stairs, they worked their way through the house, up to the attic, looking for something; anything; tapping walls and floors, scouring cupboards, measuring and calculating, but there were no hidden cavities, no secret doors, no ambiguous bulges under the wallpaper, except where the damp got in. The cupboard below the stairs was full of old pickle jars, and what they found in the attic didn't please anyone, least of all Dad.

'That's dry rot,' he said. 'Thank God this isn't our house,' and went cantering off to visit the estate agents, Tench and Tench, in the High Street. Dad called them Shark and Shark. As he got to the gate he turned back and yelled, 'The Plague! The Plague! Put a red cross on the door!' which made Mrs Bowen, over the fence, lean right out of her landing window instead of hiding behind the curtains.

When Dad came back from the estate agents he was growling.

'Shark junior says that since the whole row is coming down inside two years, it isn't worth bothering about. I understand that the new by-pass is going to run right through the scullery.'

'What did Shark senior say?' said Mum.

'I didn't see him. I've never seen him. I don't believe that there is a Shark senior,' said Dad. 'I think he's dead. I think Young Shark keeps him in a box under the bed.'

'Don't be nasty,' said Mum, looking at Libby who worried about things under the bed even in broad daylight. 'I just hope we find a house of our own before this place collapses on our heads – and we shan't be buying it from the Sharks.'

She went back to her sewing, not in a good mood. The mice had broken out again. Libby went into the kitchen to look for them. Martin ran upstairs, rhyming:

> 'Mr Shark,
> In the dark,
> Under the bed.
> Dead.'

When he came down again, Mum was putting away the sewing and Libby was parading around the hall in a pointed hat with a veil and a long red dress that looked rich and splendid unless you knew, as Martin did, that it was made of old curtains.

The hall was dark in the rainy summer afternoon,

and Libby slid from shadow to shadow, rustling.

'What are you meant to be?' said Martin. 'An old witch?'

'I'm the Sleeping Beauty's mother,' said Libby, and lowering her head she charged along the hall, pointed hat foremost, like a unicorn.

Martin changed his mind about walking downstairs and slid down the banisters instead. He suspected that he would not be allowed to do this for much longer. Already the banister rail creaked, and who knew where the dreaded dry rot would strike next? As he reached the upright post at the bottom of the stairs, Mum came out of the back room, lugging the sewing machine, and just missed being impaled on Libby's hat.

'Stop rushing up and down,' said Mum. 'You'll ruin those clothes and I've only just finished them. Go and take them off. And you,' she said, turning to Martin, 'stop swinging on that newel post. Do you want to tear it up by the roots?'

The newel post was supposed to be holding up the banisters, but possibly it was the other way about. At the foot it was just a polished wooden post, but further up it had been turned on a lathe, with slender hips, a waist, a bust almost, and square shoulders. On top was a round ball, as big as a head.

There was another at the top of the stairs but it had lost its head. Dad called it Anne Boleyn; the one at the bottom was simply a newel post, but Libby thought that this too was its name; Nule Post, like Anne Boleyn or Libby Anderson.

Mrs Nule Post.

Lady Nule Post.

When she talked to it she just called it Nule.

The pointed hat and the old curtains were Libby's costume for the school play. Martin had managed to stay out of the school play, but he knew all of Libby's lines by heart as she chanted them round the house, up and down stairs, in a strained, jerky voice, one syllable per step.

'My-dear-we-must-in-vite-all-the-fair-ies-to-the-chris-ten-ing, Hullo, Nule, we-will-not-in-vite-the-wick-ed-fair-y!'

On the last day of term, he sat with Mum and Dad in the school hall and watched Libby go through the same routine on stage. She was word-perfect, in spite of speaking as though her shock absorbers had collapsed, but as most of the cast spoke the same way it didn't sound so very strange.

Once the holidays began Libby went back to talking like Libby, although she still wore the pointed hat and the curtains, until they began to drop to pieces. The curtains went for dusters, but the pointed hat was around for a long time until Mum picked it up and threatened, 'Take this thing away or it goes in the dustbin.'

Libby shunted up and down the stairs a few times with the hat on her head, and then Mum called out that Jane-next-door had come to play. If Libby had been at the top of the stairs, she might have left the hat on her bed, but she was almost at the bottom so she plonked it down on Nule's cannon-ball head, and went out to fight Jane over whose turn it was to kidnap the teddy-bear. She hoped it was Jane's turn. If Libby were the kidnapper, she would have to sit about for ages holding Teddy to ransom behind the water tank, while Jane galloped round the garden on her imaginary pony, whacking the hydrangea bushes with a broomstick.

The hat definitely did something for Nule. When Martin came in later by the front door, he thought at first that it was a person standing at the foot of the stairs. He had to look twice before he understood who it was. Mum saw it at the same time.

'I told Libby to put that object away or I'd throw it in the dustbin.'

'Oh, don't,' said Martin. 'Leave it for Dad to see.'

So she left it, but Martin began to get ideas. The hat made the rest of Nule look very undressed, so he fetched down the old housecoat that had been hanging behind the bathroom door when they moved in. It was purple, with blue paisleys swimming all over it, and very worn, as though it had been somebody's favourite housecoat. The sleeves had set in creases around arms belonging to someone they had never known.

Turning it front to back, he buttoned it like a bib round Nule's neck so that it hung down to the floor. He filled two gloves with screwed-up newspaper, poked them into the sleeves and pinned them there. The weight made the arms dangle and opened the creases. He put a pair of football boots under the hem of the housecoat with the toes just sticking out, and stood back to see how it looked.

As he expected, in the darkness of the hall it looked just like a person, waiting, although there was something not so much lifelike as deathlike in the hang of those dangling arms.

Mum and Libby first saw Nule as they came out of the kitchen together.

'Who on earth did this?' said Mum as they drew alongside.

'It wasn't me,' said Libby, and sounded very glad that it wasn't.

'It was you left the hat, wasn't it?'

'Yes, but not the other bits.'

'What do you think?' said Martin.

'Horrible thing,' said Mum, but she didn't ask him to take it down. Libby sidled round Nule and ran upstairs as close to the wall as she could get.

When Dad came home from work he stopped in the doorway and said, 'Hullo – who's that? Who. . . ?' before Martin put the light on and showed him.

'An idol, I suppose,' said Dad. 'Nule, god of dry rot,' and he bowed low at the foot of the stairs. At the same time the hat slipped forward slightly, as if Nule had lowered its head in acknowledgement. Martin also bowed low before reaching up to put the hat straight.

Mum and Dad seemed to think that Nule was rather funny, so it stayed at the foot of the stairs. They never bowed to it again, but Martin did, every time he went upstairs, and so did Libby. Libby didn't talk to Nule any more, but she watched it a lot. One day she said, 'Which way is it facing?'

'Forwards, of course,' said Martin, but it was hard to tell unless you looked at the feet. He drew two staring eyes and a toothy smile on a piece of paper and cut them out. They were attached to the front of Nule's head with little bits of chewing-gum.

'That's better,' said Libby, laughing, and next time she went upstairs she forgot to bow. Martin was not so sure. Nule looked ordinary now, just like a newel post wearing a housecoat, football boots and the Sleeping Beauty's mother's hat. He took off the eyes and the mouth and rubbed away the chewing-gum.

'*That's* better,' he said, while Nule stared once more without eyes, and smiled without a mouth.

Libby said nothing.

At night the house creaked.

'Thiefly footsteps,' said Libby.

'It's the furniture warping,' said Mum.

Libby thought she said that the furniture was walking, and she could well believe it. The dressing-table had feet with claws; why shouldn't it walk in the dark, tugging fretfully this way and that because the clawed feet pointed in opposite directions? The bath had feet too. Libby imagined it galloping out of the bathroom and tobogganing downstairs on its stomach, like a great white walrus plunging into the sea. If someone held the door open, it would whizz up the path and crash into the front gate. If someone held the gate open, it would shoot across the road and hit the district nurse's car, which she parked under the street light, opposite.

Libby thought of headlines in the local paper – NURSE RUN OVER BY BATH – and giggled, until she heard the creaks again. Then she hid under the bedclothes.

In his bedroom Martin heard the creaks too, but he had a different reason for worrying. In the attic where the dry rot lurked, there was a big oak wardrobe full of old dead ladies' clothes. It was directly over his head. Supposing it came through?

Next day he moved the bed.

The vacuum cleaner had lost its casters and had to be helped, by Libby pushing from behind. It skidded up the hall and knocked Nule's football boots askew.

'The Hoover doesn't like Nule either,' said Libby. Although she wouldn't talk to Nule any more she liked talking *about* it, as though that somehow made Nule safer.

'What's that?' said Mum.

'It knocked Nule's feet off.'

'Well, put them back,' said Mum, but Libby preferred not to. When Martin came in he set them side by side, but later they were kicked out of place again. If people began to complain that Nule was in the way, Nule would have to go. He got round this by putting the right boot where the left had been and the left boot on the bottom stair. When he left it, the veil on the hat was hanging down behind, but as he went upstairs after tea he noticed that it was now draped over Nule's right shoulder, as if Nule had turned its head to see where its feet were going.

That night the creaks were louder than ever, like a burglar on hefty tiptoe. Libby had mentioned thieves only that evening, and Mum had said, 'What have we got worth stealing?'

Martin felt fairly safe because he had worked out that if the wardrobe fell tonight, it would land on his chest of drawers and not on him, but what might it not bring down with it? Then he realized that the creaks were coming not from above but from below.

He held his breath. Downstairs didn't creak.

His alarm clock gleamed greenly in the dark and told him that it had gone two o'clock. Mum and Dad were asleep ages ago. Libby would sooner burst than leave her bed in the dark. Perhaps it *was* a burglar. Feeling noble and reckless he put on the bedside lamp, slid out of bed, trod silently across the carpet. He turned on the main light and opened the door. The glow shone out of the doorway and saw him as far as the landing light switch at the top of the stairs, but he never had time to turn it on. From the top of the stairs he could look down into the hall where the street light opposite shone coldly through the frosted panes of the front door.

It shone on the hall-stand where the coats hung, on the blanket chest and the brass jug that stood on it, through the white coins of the honesty plants in the brass jug, and on the broody telephone that never rang at night. It did not shine on Nule. Nule was not there.

Nule was half-way up the stairs, one hand on the banisters and one hand holding up the housecoat, clear of its boots. The veil on the hat drifted like smoke across the frosted glass of the front door. Nule creaked and came up another step.

Martin turned and fled back to the bedroom, and dived under the bedclothes, just like Libby who was three years younger and believed in ghosts.

'Were you reading in bed last night?' said Mum, prodding him awake next morning. Martin came out from under the pillow, very slowly.

'No, Mum.'

'You went to sleep with the light on. *Both* lights,' she said, leaning across to switch off the one by the bed.

'I'm sorry.'

'Perhaps you'd like to pay the next electricity bill?'

Mum had brought him a cup of tea, which meant that she had been down to the kitchen and back again, unscathed. Martin wanted to ask her if there was anything strange on the stairs, but he didn't quite know how to put it. He drank the tea, dressed, and went along the landing.

He looked down into the hall where the sun shone through the frosted glass of the front door, on to the hall-stand, the blanket chest, the honesty plants in the brass jug, and the telephone that began to ring as he looked at it. It shone on Nule, standing with its back to him at the foot of the stairs.

Mum came out of the kitchen to answer the phone and Martin went down and stood three steps up, watching Nule and waiting for Mum to finish talking. Nule looked just as it always did. Both feet were back on ground level, side by side.

'I wish you wouldn't hang about like that when I'm on the phone,' said Mum, putting down the receiver and turning round. 'Eavesdropper. Breakfast will be ready in five minutes.'

She went back into the kitchen and Martin sat on the

blanket chest, looking at Nule. It was time for Nule to go. He should walk up to Nule this minute, kick away the boots, rip off the housecoat, throw away the hat, but . . .

He stayed where he was, watching the motionless football boots, the dangling sleeves. The breeze from an open window stirred the hem of the housecoat and revealed the wooden post beneath, rooted firmly in the floor as it had been for seventy years.

There were no feet in the boots; no arms in the sleeves.

If he destroyed Nule, it would mean that he *believed* that he had seen Nule climbing the stairs last night, but if he left Nule alone, Nule might walk again.

He had a problem.

They Wait

'*I* don't like getting up in the dark,' Jenny said.

'The clocks go back tomorrow night,' Mum said. 'The mornings'll be lighter then.'

'But the evenings'll be darker,' said Mark.

Jenny said, 'I don't like going out in the dark with all those little things that squeak.'

'Mice?' said Mum, trying to button up Jenny's coat and not listening properly.

'No, not mice,' Jenny said. 'They fly.'

'Do hold still, Jen.'

'You've buttoned a loose bit of my neck into my coat,' Jenny complained.

'Well, what do you expect, wriggling about like that?'

'Flying mice,' said Mark.

'Bats,' said Mum. 'That's what you hear at night. You don't want to be afraid of bats.'

'Bats are flying mice,' Mark said. '*I* can't hear them squeak.'

'I know they're bats. That button's in the wrong hole,' Jenny said. 'Can *you* hear them squeak?'

'I'm much too old,' said Mum, who usually got quite cross if you thought that she was any kind of old. 'But when you're little you can hear all sorts of things that grown-ups can't. Anyway, there aren't any bats at this time of year.'

Jenny said, 'Can I *see* things that grown-ups can't?'

Mum was getting restless because the hands of the

kitchen clock were pointing to half past eight, and you could never be sure with that clock. It might be half past by now, but it could as easily be quarter past, or worse, twenty to nine. She said, 'Yes, I expect so, especially you – you're always seeing things. Do get a move on.'

'No I'm not,' said Jenny. 'Look, you've put your shopping bag on the Major's chair. It's right on his lap.'

Mum lifted the basket on to the table. 'See what I mean?' she said to Mark, over Jenny's head. Only Jenny could see the Major, and the Other Granny, and Mary Dog. The Major and the Other Granny were obviously people but no one, not even Jenny, was sure about Mary Dog. They had never been able to discover whether she were a person whose name happened to be Dog or a dog whose name happened to be Mary. Whoever she was, she lived under the table and rode a bicycle. The Major sat in a wicker chair and spat out of the window. Other Granny, fortunately, lived outside, in the alley, and never went visiting.

'You'd better hurry,' Mum said. 'It can't be earlier than quarter past.' The clock was very old, and had belonged to Real Granny's granny. Sometimes the hands hurried on the way downhill, rested for a bit at the bottom, and dawdled their way toward the top, so the clock was usually right on the hours, but rarely in between. Mark took Jenny by the mitten and hurried her out.

It was a dull morning, more like January than October, and last night's mist was still hanging about in the alley that led to the bus stop on the ring road. Mark trotted Jenny along the alley-way because she would keep stopping to feel sorry for the poor pale roses, with frostbitten petals, that were still growing hopefully through the gaps in Mrs Callaghan's fence. Jenny could be sorry for anything, even plants. Last summer she had taken pity on a poor hydrangea bud that was smaller than any of the others on the bush by the back door. For months she had tried to fatten it up with butter and sugar and juice squeezed out of old tea-bags, and when it went black and died she had picked it and buried it on the rockery. There was still a little cross of twigs where it lay next to the poor dead beetles and the poor dead flies.

The alley turned right and ran downhill slightly, between the backs of garages, until it came out into the open air again by Churchfield Garden. This was a little plot in the angle of Union Street and the ring road. It was fenced with flat round-headed stones, and there was a path along the edge with flower beds on either side, and a lawn in the middle, with another path running across that, and a long garden bench for people to sit on. Very few people did sit there, so it would have been a useful place to play. Mark was too old for that, but when Jenny got under her feet Mum often said, 'Why don't you go down and play in Churchfield Garden?' but Jenny never would.

'I don't like the people there,' she said.

'Has someone been bothering you?' Mum asked, anxiously.

'Oh no, but they aren't nice, those people. There's a little girl with a funny eye, and an old man with one leg, and an old woman with one tooth, and a lady with no head . . .'

'Oh,' said Mum. '*Those* sort of people. Well, ask the Major to go with you – he'll see them off.'

'The Major doesn't go out,' said Jenny. 'Anyway, he wouldn't like them either.'

Jenny would not even cross the garden by the centre path, as Mark did, even when they were late, so every morning it was Mark who ran catercorner to wave down the school coach, while Jenny galloped round the long way, on the pavement.

Mark saw her safely on board, waved goodbye, and then stood back to wait for his own transport. He was too old to be allowed a free journey to school. Either he had to catch the service bus, or, if he were lucky, he might get a lift from Tim's dad, if Tim's dad happened along first, in his car. Although the mist had dispersed here, on the edge of town, he could see that it must be still quite thick out in the country, so he was not too worried when he heard the church clock strike the three-quarters. If he were late for school he could blame the National Bus Company. Tim was going to be late, too, but he could only blame his dad, and Mark, knowing Tim's dad, thought that probably this was not a very safe thing to do.

The clock that he could hear was in the tower of Holy Cross, several streets away. There had once been another church, closer to hand, but Mark had never seen it. It had stood by the burial ground until it was bombed in 1942, which was why the little park was called Churchfield Garden, and the roads on the council estate were all named after it: St Michael's Close, Church Walk, Rectory Drive and The Glebe. Jenny and Mark lived in Church Walk, and Mark knew that their house was just about where the east end of the old church had been, St Michael and All Angels. Jenny did not know that, and cared less. She still had not realized that names meant something, and thought that they were just useful noises. If their road had been called

Coathanger Walk, or Sock Street, she would not have thought it strange. No one who kept friends with a major who spat in public and a dog that rode a bicycle could think that *anything* was odd. The Other Granny did things too, out in the alley, but Mum would not let Jenny talk about her any more. So although Jenny passed the garden every day, and had invented all sorts of strange people to live in it, she never realized why it was called Churchfield Garden, and was too young to remember the time when the council workmen had come and moved all the tombstones to the edge of the plot, so that there was room to lay the lawns and the paths.

The bus was very late; perhaps it had hit a sheep out on the road across the common. But Tim's dad was late too. Perhaps the bus had hit Tim's dad. Mark found his feet turning chilly. It was not really a *cold* morning, but that corner always seemed cooler than anywhere else, always in the shadow of the trees that still grew nearby, or the old warehouse on the far side of the ring road. To keep warm he began stamping like a guardsman round the paths of Churchfield Garden, until he heard the bus growling in the distance on the other side of the bridge. Then he ran to meet it at the bus stop, but not until the very last moment. No matter how warm the day, there was always a chilly wind round the bus stop, and that morning it was bitter. Mrs Callaghan and Mrs Carter from next door, who had also come down to catch the bus to work, had walked all the way up to the lamp-post to keep warm, and had to run even further than he did.

In the evening Mark usually arrived before Jenny's coach, because his bus came round by the ring road while the school coach got stuck in the city traffic, so he waited for her, to see her across the busy road, which was kind of him because if she got there first she never waited for him, but crossed the busy road by herself and raced home as fast as she could. To save him waiting for nothing she would go upstairs and flash her bedroom light on and off. As you could see her bedroom window only from the other side of the road, by the bus stop next to Churchfield Garden, he had to cross over to look, although it meant loitering in that mean chill draught, and then stepping out like a lollipop man when Jenny arrived.

But tonight, when he got down from the bus and crossed the road, to Churchfield Garden, he found that he could not see the window at all. Evidently other people beside himself had complained about the wind for now, next to the bus stop, stood a new wooden shelter with a bench inside it and a timetable in a red metal frame, screwed to the outside wall. He stood first on the left side, then on the right, but no matter where he stood he could no longer see Jenny's window. After hopping about from one cold foot to the other for ten minutes, he decided that Jenny's coach could not possibly be this late, and if it were it was just too bad, and set off home. Jenny, of course, was there before him, in the living-room, being sorry for a poor doggy on television

'Don't be,' he advised her, 'it's the hero. It's bound to be all right.'

'But it's hurt its poor *paws*, and it's lost in the *snow*, Jenny whimpered.

'Yes, but in a minute it'll rescue a poor little orphan who's buried in a snow drift and someone'll give it a medal. You know it will. It happens every week.'

'But its paws hurt *now*,' Jenny wailed.

'Idiot. It's a film. It's not even a new film. It was made about twenty years ago.'

'Do dogs live for twenty years?'

'Not often,' he said, unwisely.

'You mean, it's *dead*?'

Mark gave up and went to find Mum. She was in the kitchen, frying sausages.

'Had a good day?' she asked.

'It was all right. Jason sat on my sandwiches at break, but he didn't mean to,' Mark said. 'There's a new shelter down by the bus stop.'

'I know. I saw it when I went into the town for the shopping. They'd just finished putting it up.'

'It'll keep the wind off,' Mark said. 'Did you sit in it? Were you the first? You could have officially opened it – you know: I declare this bus shelter well and truly open and may God bless all who sail in her.'

'It doesn't keep the wind off,' Mum said. 'I did sit in it, and it was even colder inside than it was out. It seems to trap the draught.'

Jenny appeared in the doorway, wiping her eyes. 'I sat in it,' she said, 'just to try it out. But it was all damp and shivery, so I came home.'

'It can't be damp,' Mum said. 'It's new.'

'It is damp – like the outside toilets at the old school.'

The outside toilets at the old school were one of the reasons that the old school had been closed.

There was no wind at all on Monday, but it was very cold. As usual Jenny was only just in time for her coach, and Tim's dad was right behind it, hooting impatiently, although the coach was not late, he was early. Mark hopped into the back seat, next to Tim. As the car and the coach moved off together, Mark glanced out of the window and saw that someone was sitting in the bus shelter, although Mrs Carter and Mrs Callaghan were standing where they usually did, out on the pavement, smacking their gloved hands together to keep warm.

That evening Mark got off the bus and saw Jenny waiting for him on the other side of the road, under the street lamp. He went after her.

'What are you doing here?'

'I didn't want to wait in the dark.'

'It's not dark, Dumbo.'

'Why's the light on, then?'

'Street lights always come on before it gets dark, don't they?'

'Well, it's lighter under the light than it is *not* under the light,' Jenny argued.

'You should have gone straight home,' Mark said. 'I wouldn't have minded. You've never waited before.'

'I didn't want to pass the bus shelter.'

'Is there someone hiding behind it?'

'There's a person in it,' Jenny said. 'A person who doesn't get on the bus.'

'Well, there isn't a bus to get on,' said Mark. 'Not till half past. Come on home now.'

'That person was there this morning,' Jenny said. 'I saw him from the coach window.'

'I saw him too,' Mark said. 'It's not the same person, nitwit.'

'It is.' Jenny clung to the lamp-post. 'It's the same person and he doesn't get on the bus.'

'There's no one there now,' Mark said. 'I just walked past it, come and look.' He got Jenny in a kind of friendly half-nelson and propelled her towards the bus shelter. 'Look,' he said, poking his head in, and hers too. 'It's empty, isn't it?'

Jenny looked unconvinced and stayed on the pavement. Mark waved his arms about. 'See? Nobody there.'

'Let's go home,' Jenny said, tugging him out again. At either end of the shelter was a little glazed window, so that people inside could see if the bus were coming, and as they turned away Mark saw what it must have been that had frightened Jenny. Some kind of warp in the glass twisted the light in such a way that it seemed as if there were a person sitting inside, but he said nothing, because Jenny saw only the things that she believed in, and no one had told her about the refraction of light.

Thursday was market day, and there was always a long queue of people waiting for Mark's bus in the

mornings. Mark joined the end of it as Jenny's school
coach drew away from the kerb, and watched Jenny's
small face peering through one of the side windows,
toward the bus shelter. There was nothing fearsome
about the bus shelter now. The day was bright, with a
little sharp wind rattling the dry leaves of the trees in
Churchfield Garden, and tossing them in handful
round the feet of the people at the head of the queue, but
it was bright enough for the queue to stand on the
pavement, and not so cold as to drive them into the bus
shelter. The bus shelter was quite empty – even ver
very old Mrs Pickles who had rheumatism and ought t
have been keeping warm, was standing in the queue
although when the bus came and Mark had settled int
his favourite seat, at the back, he could have sworn as h
looked over his shoulder that he could see the indistin
silhouettes of two people sitting together at one end
the bench inside the shelter.

His class had football that afternoon, Reds again
Greens. Greens won by five goals to three and Mark,
the Greens, scored two of those five goals. Feeling bo
and buoyant as he got off the bus, he crossed the road
the cloudy evening light to wait for Jenny in the shelte
for already a sneaky drizzle was trickling out of the sk
He had thought, when he saw it from the opposi
pavement, that the shelter was empty, but when
crossed the road he was not so sure. Instead of going
and sitting down he sauntered back and forth along t
pavement that glistened now in the light from the str
lamp, certain that there *was* somebody in it, someo
who could be seen only out of the tail of his eye; a
whoever it was waited until he had passed and th
leaned out behind him, withdrawing into the shado

again as he turned to come back. The obvious answer was, of course, to go into the bus shelter and look, since it might be someone he knew; someone from the estate, mucking about. But it might be some big tough, like Gary Callaghan or Cynthia Carter, so he contented himself with walking past, just once more, and then going to stand under the street light to wait for Jenny. When the school coach arrived, a few minutes later, he did not remain where he was but crossed over again and collected Jenny from the very step of the coach as the door swung open.

Jenny glanced across the road.

'There's a lot of people waiting for the bus,' Jenny said.

'Are there?' Mark said, grimly. 'Where?'

'In the shelter,' Jenny said.

'Then let's stop and watch them get on,' said Mark, and together they sheltered from the rain against the wall of the warehouse, and watched the real shelter, the bus shelter, across the street. From this distance he could see quite clearly that there were people in it, but he could not see the people clearly. In spite of the nearby street lamp, and the fact that daylight still lingered in the road, the inside of the shelter was thick with shadows, long solid shadows, that seemed to cast shadows themselves.

The four-thirty bus changed gear on the other side of the bridge, and as it came over the hump its headlamps shone full into the bus shelter, and the shadows shrank into the corners, but the bus did not stop, for no one wanted to get off, and no one wanted to get on. When its tail lights had disappeared round the corner, Jenny and Mark could see that the shelter was still full of people.

'Well, they didn't get on the bus,' Mark said. 'Who *are* they, Jenny?'

'They're the people who don't get on the bus,' Jenny said.

'Can you see their faces? I can't.'

'Oh yes,' Jenny said. 'I know who they are – I've seen them before. There's the man with one leg . . . and the old woman with one tooth . . . and the little girl with the funny eye . . . and the lady with no head . . .'

Mark turned on her furiously. 'You're making it up!' he shouted. 'They're the people you used to see in Churchfield Garden!'

'Yes,' Jenny said, 'and now they're in the bus shelter.'

'Come on home,' Mark said crossly, and pulled her across the road, just missing a baker's van that came unexpectedly round the corner. He let go of Jenny's hand, feeling that it was her fault that they had been nearly run over, and strode along the path that crossed the garden on the corner. To his surprise he found that Jenny was hurrying after him.

'I thought you didn't like crossing the gardens,' he snapped.

'It's all right now,' Jenny explained. 'There's nobody here. They're all in the bus shelter.'

'Who are?'

'The people who don't get on the bus.'

And they were. The people who *did* get on the bus stayed outside on the pavement, queuing in the rain and wind and even snow, all through the winter. They said that the shelter was draughty, and that there was a funny smell about it, and wasn't it *damp*? The bus shelter gradually filled up with rubbish and vanda broke the little windows at either end, and scrawled all over the outside walls, and tore the timetable from its mounting. No one ventured to scrawl on the inside walls. When the clean spring sunshine showed it up in all its desolation, people began to complain that it was an eyesore, and one day the council workmen came with a lorry and took it away.

Mark saw that it had gone one afternoon as he waited for Jenny, and wondered what had happened to the people who *didn't* get on the bus. He thought that perhaps the council workmen had taken them away with the shelter, for these days Jenny played quite happily in Churchfield Garden, and the shelter really was not needed any more for the wind seemed to have died down considerably, but after a while strange rumours began to circulate about something funny in the bus station, down near the left luggage office, and people stopped going there at night, if they could avoid it.

Birthday Girl

My last year at school, we did community service. We didn't have to, it wasn't like being sentenced by a magistrate instead of going to gaol. We volunteered and got sent to dig old ladies' gardens, and paint old ladies' kitchens and fetch old ladies' shopping. It was mainly old ladies. There weren't enough old men to go round, though some of the old ladies had already got through a couple of husbands.

'Women last longer,' said Mrs Harborough, who was arranging it all.

Me, I was sent to an old people's home with my friend Chrissy, and it was a shock. That was mostly old ladies too, and they just sat around all day watching telly in horrible chairs that were supposed to be easy to get up out of, though none of them ever seemed to go anywhere. It was a shock because when Mrs Harborough said an old people's home, I'd been thinking of Golding House at Burgate. When I was little, being old meant ending up like Mrs Galloway at Golding House.

We met Mrs Galloway only once, but we'd known Golding House for years. It was next door but one to my Auntie Margaret and we went to stay with Margaret every summer, right from when we were tiny. Just looking at her address made us think of holidays; Miss M. Gray, Ocean View, 27c Sandy Lane, Burgate, Kent. You couldn't really see the ocean from Margaret's house, but if you'd climbed on the roof you might have spotted the English Channel, because it was right at the end of the road, which really was sandy, especially after a high wind. From the first floor you couldn't see beyond the roofs of the houses along the sea front, but you could look into the gardens either side and into the garden of Golding House, which was huge, because Golding House was huge. Ocean View was even bigger, and that was why Margaret lived at 27c; because it had been divided up into three separate houses. Golding House was still all in one piece, and the sign outside said *Retirement Home*.

Well, you hear awful things about old people's homes and, like I said, the one Chrissy and I went to wasn't too wonderful, but Golding House wasn't like that. It was a really pretty house, in spite of being so big, with balconies and lots of flowers in hanging baskets, and the gravel drive was always kept nice. And at the back it was lovely, with hundreds of roses and apple trees, even though it was so near the sea, and the grass was always cut in stripes, like they do in adverts. There were wooden park benches put out, and the old ladies – there were only ever one or two old men – used to sit out there in the sun and drink cups of tea and play cards. Some of them had drinks you could see through, and I used to think it wasn't fair that they only had water, but my sister Moya said it was probably gin and tonic and why not? I used to remember that when I was trying to cheer up my old ladies. They never got any gin, believe me.

Margaret's place was tall and thin, only being a slice of a house, if you see what I mean, and when they cut it up, her slice didn't get the bathroom, so they'd built on an extension at the back and put a bathroom in that. It wasn't very nice, dank and always chilly; even the white tiles didn't brighten it up, in fact Margaret said they reminded her of a mortuary, and she said that when she could afford it she'd turn the little spare room at the side into a bathroom, and use the extension for storing all the things she had in the spare room – mostly suitcases and old furniture. Moya and I never slept in it; we had a room at the back.

I remember exactly when that bathroom was built. It was the year I was eleven and Moya was seventeen, and as soon as we arrived at Margaret's we went straight up to see it. She'd had it done beautifully, all in blue; even the soap matched; and when the water ran into the bath Moya said it was like the Mediterranean, not that she'd ever been there, but it certainly wasn't like the Channel at the end of the road.

'Baggy me first bath!' Moya said, forgetting she was seventeen, but in the end it was me that bathed first because I went to bed earlier. Moya went out for a walk down the prom, and I heard her go as I was lying there in the nice blue water, pretending it was the Mediterranean. I heard her come back, too, very late, and have words in the hall with Margaret, about the time.

Then she came upstairs, singing under her breath, and crept into our bedroom, and when she saw I was awake she told me that she'd gone all the way along to the fun fair and met this terrific boy, and she'd been walking on the beach with him and watching the moon come up.

I could not see the fun in that, then – I can now – but I was glad she'd met a nice boy because her last one had treated her rotten, and he really was nice, this one, because she married him two years later, and they're still together. How's that, then?

Anyway, the point of all this was that she didn't get her bath till next morning, and being so happy she woke up early, about six-thirty instead of half past ten like usual, and went dancing off to run her bath in her long nightie that looked a bit like a wedding dress. I prefer big T-shirts, myself.

Well, I lay there, listening to the water running, and then it stopped and the cistern hissed and plopped a bit, and Margaret's old clock in the hall began to strike seven, and then there was this most terrible scream, just one, followed by a sort of wail that ran out of breath, half-way. I ran down the landing, slap into Margaret who was coming the other way. She hammered on the bathroom door, yelling, 'Moya! Moya! What's the matter? Open up! Let us in!' and after a moment we heard a lot of scrabbling and the key turned. Margaret threw the door open and there was Moya, leaning against the wall, clutching her nightie like it was a comfort blanket, and pointing.

And we said, 'What is it? What happened?' And she said, when she got her breath back, she said, 'There was somebody in the bath!'

Margaret went straight over and checked the window catch, but Moya said, 'No, it wasn't like that. I ran the water and turned off the taps, and I was just cleaning my teeth when . . .'

'What?'

'I don't know. Something made me look round, and I saw this . . . this . . .'

'*What?*'

'There was someone lying in the bath, just lying there, under the water, on its – her – I think it was a her – on her back, under the water.

'I didn't do anything at first. I just stood here, I mean, I couldn't believe I was seeing anything, and then the clock struck and she – it – she *sat up*, out of the water, and went – like *that*.'

Moya stuck out her arms, like ghosts do in cartoons. 'And then she just disappeared.'

'Walked through the wall?' I said.

'*Nah!*' Moya was feeling better. She made as if to hit me. 'No, she just, well, disappeared, right where she was, in the bath.'

'What did she look like?' Margaret said.

'I dunno, all in white, long fair hair. I didn't really *see*. Oh, it was . . .'

'Awful?' I said. Moya looked surprised.

'No, it wasn't. I wasn't even scared.'

'What did you scream like that for, then?' Margaret snapped. 'You scared *me*.'

'I was startled. I suppose I'd started to be scared, but I wasn't really. She wasn't frightening.'

I was glad when Moya said that because I was already wondering how I was going to bring myself even to go to the loo in there, let alone lie down in the bath. Think of it. Who would I be lying down *with*? But when I went back into the bathroom later I didn't feel a thing, not fright, not anything, and after a day or two I forgot all about it. It was funny. You might have expected to see things in the old bathroom downstairs, the one like a mortuary, but not up here where it was all new and bright and sunny. Margaret never saw anything, either. She wrote afterwards, and said.

The next year I went alone. Moya had gone off to Ibiza with Tony – the boy she met – and his family, and I took the train down to Burgate alone. It was the same day as last year, that is, it was a Friday, we always went down on a Friday, but this year it was Friday 31 July, last year it had been 1 August. I had a funny feeling when I went into the bathroom for the first time, but only because I was expecting to, and only *as* I went in. There was nothing scary about it once I was in there. Margaret had had a shower put in, over the bath, so I used it, and the next day, too, after I'd been to the beach, but it turned chilly on Saturday night and when I woke up on Sunday I thought I'd have a nice hot bath, so I did. I went into the bathroom and turned on the tap, and then went along the landing for my clothes. I was just coming back, down the landing, when the clock in the hall gave a loud click. It always did that a few seconds before it began to strike, and a few seconds was all it took for me to get back into the bathroom, and there she was.

The bath was about half full, and she was lying just as Moya had said, on her back, just under the water, like she was asleep. She was a little girl, with long hair in a plait that had come untied. She was wearing something white, but I couldn't see what because the water was all stirred up around where her feet would have been, with the tap running, and then the clock began to strike, and she sat up.

I wasn't frightened, I wasn't even very surprised, so I didn't scream or hide my eyes and so I saw her properly, which Moya hadn't done. She didn't wave her arms about like a cartoon ghost, she opened her eyes and smiled, and stretched out her hands, just like she was going to hug someone, and then she disappeared; quite suddenly she wasn't there any more, and the bath had nothing but water in it. The tap was still running and the clock had just finished striking.

I still wasn't frightened, but I didn't get into the bath.
It wouldn't have seemed right.

When I'd washed I made Margaret a cup of tea and
took it along to her room and sat on the bed while she
drank it. She looked at me over the cup and said, 'Well,
what's biting you, young lady?' and I said, 'I've seen
her again.'

'Seen who?' Margaret said. She really had forgotten.

'You know, what Moya saw, last year, in the bath.'

'Are you having me on?' Margaret said. 'You don't
look like you've seen a ghost.'

I said, 'I don't *feel* like I've seen a ghost, but I did.'

'If you say so,' Margaret said. 'I've never seen
anything.'

Afterwards I went and looked in my diary which had next year's calendar in it, and last year's too. I never know why they put that in, but this time I was glad they had, because there was something to check. Last year Moya had seen – whatever she saw – on the morning of Saturday 2 August. This year I saw it on Sunday 2 August. And Margaret hadn't seen anything in between. I wondered, was our little girl a special August ghost, just showing up on one day a year? I had another year to wait, before I found out, and I often thought about it, although I never said anything, except to Moya. What I thought was, fancy haunting a *bath*.

I was feeling a bit flat when I went down to Burgate the next year – '82 that would have been. Moya had just got married to Tony and moved away, and I had a rotten cold. On Saturday morning, 31 July (I was counting, see) I stayed at home and felt miserable, while Margaret went shopping. It was one of those wet, windy, wintry days you get at the seaside in summer, all the plants knocked flat and trees leaning over. I sat in the back bedroom and stared out across next door's vegetables at the garden behind Golding House, but all the old ladies were inside and I didn't see anyone except a nurse who came scooting out with a coat over her head to fetch in someone's knitting that had been left out on a bench. It was bright red. I'd been looking at it and wondering what it could be.

Then the doorbell rang. I didn't feel like visitors but I thought Margaret might have forgotten her key so I went down to answer it. There was an elderly lady in the porch – not one of the Golding House residents, she wasn't that elderly – very posh, with lovely shoes. I always notice people's shoes.

She said, 'I'm sorry to trouble you. Is your mother at home?'

I said, 'No, but my auntie's right behind you,' and she was, just coming up the path with her shopping. We all went inside and I made tea, while Margaret got out of her wet things and the lady sat in the lounge. She'd started all over again, apologizing for troubling us, but Margaret said, 'No trouble. Just give us five minutes and we'll have a chat.'

The lady was Mrs Pugh and she'd come about her mother. I thought I'd heard her wrong at first because, frankly, she looked too old to have a mother, but it turned out that her mum, Mrs Galloway, lived at Golding House. The point was, she'd always lived in Burgate, all her life, instead of just retiring there, and she'd actually been born at Ocean View.

'Only it was called The Pines in those days,' said Mrs Pugh. 'Look,' she said, 'it's her birthday on Monday. She's eighty-six. We always take her out somewhere, but this time all she wants is to come and have a last look at this place. I'm afraid it may *be* her last chance,' Mrs Pugh said, and looked very quivery.

'Well, of course she can,' Margaret said, 'but what about the rest of the house? I've only got one end of it.'

'I know,' said Mrs Pugh, 'but this is the part she wants to see, she doesn't care about the rest.'

'I'll be at work,' Margaret said, 'but Diana here can do the honours.' She looked at me hopefully, but I'd have said yes anyway.

So that was two things happening on Monday; Mrs Galloway at ten o'clock and before that, at seven o'clock, my little girl. Because, you see, Monday was 2 August this year, and I was sure she'd be there.

This time I was ready and waiting. I set the alarm for six-thirty and long before seven I was in the bathroom, sitting on the floor opposite the end of the bath, with the door open, so as to hear the clock properly. There wasn't any water in the bath this time. I did wonder if there ought to be but I couldn't see that water had anything to do with it. The clock clicked in the hall, and she was there. She didn't suddenly appear, she was just there, lying in her nightie, like she was asleep, and as the clock began striking she opened her eyes, and sat up, and held out her arms. I was right in front of her, this time. It was as if she was holding them out to *me*. I felt so sad when she went, I said, 'Oh, wait. Don't go,' I really did. But she did go; all at once. Not there any more.

Mrs Pugh and Mrs Galloway were punctual too, on the doorstep at ten sharp. I had tea ready, but Mrs Galloway wasn't interested. You could hardly believe she'd be interested in anything, she was so ancient. I mean, I've met people who were eighty-six, and more, but they didn't look as old as Mrs Galloway, and I saw why her daughter was afraid she might not last another year.

She had a stick and leaned on Mrs Pugh, and I went first to open doors. She peered into rooms and said, 'Mmm, *that's* an improvement,' or 'Ha! Never had one of those!' or just, 'Well I'm damned,' which sounded funny coming from an old lady. Then she said, 'Let's go upstairs.'

Mrs Pugh turned a bit pale. 'Oh, Mother,' she said, 'do you think that's wise?' I could see her point. They probably had lifts at Golding House.

'Of course it's not wise,' Mrs Galloway snapped.

'Who cares if it's wise? Might as well break my neck right now as hang on in that glorified morgue next door,' and she dug her stick into the bottom step like it was the foot of Mount Everest.

It took us about five minutes to get her up those stairs. 'It'll be much worse coming down,' she promised us, when we stopped for a rest, half-way. At the top she looked along the landing, sniffed a bit and said, 'In there.'

'The bathroom?' I felt awful. I hadn't thought of her wanting the loo. Margaret still had one downstairs.

'Is it?' she said. 'Not in my day,' and poked the door open with her stick. 'This was our bedroom,' she said.

We followed her in. 'Oh, Mother,' said Mrs Pugh, 'the two of you in here . . . and all those rooms.' Of course, it had all been one house when Mrs Galloway was a girl. It did seem a bit mean sticking two kids in a room that size. I mean, it was fine as a bathroom, but –

Mrs Galloway was prodding about, holding her stick like a metal detector. 'My bed was here,' she said, pointing to the loo. 'And Queenie was by the window . . . for the fresh air.'

A bed. I don't know why I hadn't thought of it before; a bed where the bath was. I said, 'Was Queenie your sister?'

Mrs Galloway turned and looked at me. It was the first time she'd really noticed me, I think.

'My little sister,' she said. 'They put us in here out of the way. We were poor relations. No one wanted to be bothered with us after Father died.'

'Oh, Mother,' Mrs Pugh said again. She never said much else, come to think of it.

'They weren't cruel,' Mrs Galloway snapped. 'I

never said they were cruel. No one ever laid a hand on us – not for any reason,' and I knew that she meant that if they'd never been beaten, they'd never been cuddled, either. 'Poor little Queenie,' she said. Then she looked at me again, hard, and said, over her shoulder, 'You go down again, Olive. I want a word with this gal.'

'Oh, Mother –' She never actually said it, for Mrs Galloway turned right round and gave her such a look, and Mrs Pugh almost ran for it. 'We'll call when we're ready to come down,' Mrs Galloway said. She plonked herself on the edge of the bath and said, 'Well?'

'Well what?'

'Don't be silly,' she said. 'You want to ask me something. Go ahead.'

'Queenie,' I said, 'you and Queenie. Were you twins?'

'No, I was five when she was born, the year the old Queen died. She was named after her, Victoria, but I always called her Queenie. We shared the same birthday, though,' she added. 'Queenie would have been eighty-one today.'

'When did she die, then?' I said, and I meant, what year, because I thought I could guess the day, but Mrs Galloway said, 'On our birthday. I was twelve, she'd have been seven, but she never lived to see it. She had a weak heart. It wouldn't be the same now, I dare say. Blood transfusions, transplants . . . they'd operate. But Queenie, she just sat around, mostly, all pale and quiet. No one was allowed to excite her, not that much excitement ever came our way. Anything was a treat for Queenie. Some friends of my aunt's had promised us a birthday picnic – if Queenie was well enough, because they knew I'd never go without her, and she was so

excited. Just what she shouldn't have been; I don't
wonder if that wasn't what killed her. When I woke up
in the morning she was lying there in bed with her plait
all untied, and I knew she was dead. Because every
morning I'd expected her to be . . . I didn't tell anyone
immediately. Just went over and sat with her until
seven o'clock and the maids started bringing up tea.'

I began to say, 'But wasn't it at seven when – ?' and
stopped. Mrs Galloway gave me another look. I don't
think she could see much, but she could *look*.

'Go on,' she said.

I said, 'I think I've seen Queenie. Me and my sister,
we've both seen her. I saw her this morning, and last
year, and the year before. Always on 2 August, at seven
o'clock.'

'It would have been six, though,' Mrs Galloway said,
half to herself. 'We didn't have daylight saving then. So
that's why I woke up. I just missed her.' She put out her
hand and took mine, and her voice was ever so gentle
now. 'Oh, my dear,' she said, 'how does she look?'

'She looks happy,' I said. 'She's asleep, and then she
wakes and sits up, and holds out her arms, like this. And
she smiles.'

'Is that true? You're not just saying it.'

'It's true,' I said. 'She doesn't frighten us. She's
lovely.'

'Yes, she was lovely, my Queenie,' Mrs Galloway
said. And then she said, 'I always thought she'd died in
her sleep. I'm so glad she lived long enough to know it
was her birthday.

'You know why I'm here, don't you?' she said. 'I'm
not supposed to last out the year, according to the
doctors, but I reckon I might, now I know. Do you think

your auntie would object if I paid her another visit on my birthday, next year?'

'At seven o'clock?'

'At seven o'clock.'

I wish I could say that she did, but the doctors were right and she was wrong. She never did come again, but neither did Queenie. I suppose she didn't need to, any more. When I told Moya about it she said, 'Would you wait that long for me?'

Who's a Pretty Boy, Then?

Rachel's house had a very small garden. The people on the end of the terrace had a big one, round the side as well as at the back, but Rachel's house was in the middle, so there was only a small strip of garden behind, and none at all in front. Once Rachel had travelled right to the top of Debenham's, on the escalators, to where they kept all the furniture and carpets. Some of the carpets were laid out on the floor, as if they were in a real house, and there was one carpet that was as big as Rachel's whole garden; well, almost. Two of those carpets would definitely have been bigger than Rachel's garden.

Rachel's mum could have done with a bit more room because she liked growing things, and there was not much scope for gardening on a carpet, but she made the most of what space there was. Along the back fence, by the alley, there were sprouts and cabbages, with fringes of radishes and spring onions in between, and the lusty rhubarb that was trying to get out, through the palings. In the middle was a grass plot that had to be cut with shears because there wasn't enough to buy a mower for, and down either side were flowers. Mum even had little bushes growing in old buckets, on the concrete up by the back door, and there was a stringy sort of vine that did not look at all well, and that had come over the wall from Mrs Sergeant's.

'For a bit of peace,' said Mum, pruning it tenderly.

So the whole garden was a carpet of grass and plants except for one threadbare patch, the size of a large hearthrug, right next to the house. Nothing grew there.

Mum couldn't understand it. It was a good sunny spot, sheltered from the wind, but it made no difference what she planted, nothing came up. She tried carrots and lettuce first, and when they failed she put in onions, then beetroot, then marrows and finally nasturtiums which are difficult *not* to grow, but by now it was getting late in the year, and nothing was growing anywhere. Next spring she set bedding plants instead of seeds, but after a few days the plants looked poorly and lay down limp. Then she got silly and planted dandelions. 'They'll grow if nothing else does,' she said, but they didn't. Even fireweed would not grow there.

'It must be the drains,' Gran said. 'You ought to get the council to have a look. It might be typhoid.'

'I'd have thought bad drains would be good for plants,' said Mum. 'Ever see a carrot with typhoid?'

Gran sniffed.

By the time they had lived in the house for three years, Rachel's little sister Donna had been born, Gran had moved to Maidstone, Rachel was at the Junior School and Dad suddenly started to be interested in budgerigars. Gran had kept a blue budgerigar called Pip in a cage on the sideboard, but Dad did not approve of birds like that.

'Is it cruel to keep them in cages then?' Rachel asked. She thought it probably was cruel.

'I don't know about cruel,' said Dad, 'but it doesn't look natural to me, a full-grown bird standing on one leg with a bell on its head saying, "Who's a pretty boy, then?" and kissing itself in the mirror. If we have any birds they're going to behave like birds'; and on the bald patch where nothing grew, he built an aviary.

First he put down concrete, and over this went a tall enclosure of wire netting on a frame of battens, in the angle of the house and the garden wall. At one end was a wooden sentry box with perches, where the birds could sleep safe from draughts and passing rats.

'There aren't any rats round here,' said Mum.

'Livestock attracts them,' said Dad, and made all the joints and angles rat-proof. Rachel hoped there would be rats.

At the weekend Dad and Rachel took the bus out past the M2 flyover and spent the afternoon looking in the woods for good sound branches so that the birds would have somewhere to sit, like wild birds, and afterwards they went up on to the downs to find lumps of chalk, essential for healthy feathers. They had a bit of trouble on the way home with what the bus conductor referred to as half a dead tree. 'I ought to sell you a ticket for it,' he said, and there was some unpleasantness with a woman who complained that Dad had tried to put her eye out, but they brought it home safely and it was set up in the flight, which was what Dad called the open part of the aviary.

'Why's it called an aviary, Dad?' Rachel asked.

'Look it up,' said Dad, as he always did when Rachel wanted to know what words meant. She was never sure whether this was because he thought it was good for her to look things up, or because he did not know the answer. She took care not to ask him which it was. This time she fetched the dictionary and learned that the Latin word for bird was *avis*. She was pleased to know some Latin.

For a long time the dictionary had been the only book on the shelf, but now it had been joined by magazines and illustrated books about budgerigars. The birds in the pictures were brightly coloured and when Rachel leafed through the pages her eye was captured by succulent names; Lutinos, Opalines and Satinettes, Cobalts, Cinnamons and Visual Violets; glassy, glossy words with rare flavours. She imagined the dead branch in the aviary brilliant with expensive sweets like a fabulous Christmas tree.

Then the budgerigars arrived. There were six of them and they came in little cardboard boxes with holes in the sides. Dad took them into the aviary and let them loose, then he left, without the birds following him, because he had built the aviary with double doors. There was a space between them which was, he said, the air-lock. Rachel looked up air-lock and decided that he must be joking.

'What are we going to call them?' Rachel said.

'We're not going to call them anything,' Dad said. 'They don't need names. And another thing,' he said, sternly, to Rachel and Mum and Donna who had come out to watch, 'I don't want anyone trying to teach them to talk. These budgerigars are going to be as near wild as tame birds can be. There's going to be trouble if I catch any of them creeping up to me and saying, "Who's a pretty boy, then?" And no wolf-whistles.'

Mum went indoors to give Donna her lunch, but Rachel stayed close up against the wire and watched the budgerigars ('I don't want to hear anyone calling them budgies') exploring their new home, bouncing on the branches and tidying their feathers, investigating seed trays, grit pans and water pots. There was no doubt that they looked much more impressive in their aviary than Pip had done in his cage, but she could not help wondering if they wouldn't be happier with a bell or two, and a mirror.

'They don't need mirrors,' said Dad, 'they've got each other to look at.'

When the birds had settled in they began to purr and chirrup in the sunshine.

'See,' said Dad, 'they can talk to each other. There's no point in making them learn words, those squawks are all the language they need. They mean something.'

'So do words,' Rachel said.

'Not to budgerigars,' Dad said, firmly. 'You can teach a budgerigar to say the Lord's Prayer. You can teach him to sing *God Save the Queen*. You can teach him to count to a hundred backwards, but he'll never know what he's saying. They don't really *talk*, they just copy sounds.'

Rachel remembered Pip, looking sideways into his mirror and saying coyly, 'Who's a pretty boy, then?' He had always sounded as though he knew exactly what i meant, and very pleased with himself; but then, bud gerigars usually did sound pleased with themselves and they looked smug, too. Rachel thought it might b something to do with having no neck.

It was a fine August, that year. Donna sat in he pram in the middle of the grass, and squawked whe the birds squawked. She would watch them for hours a they bowed and curtsied, turned somersaults an hung by one leg. Rachel liked spying on them when the went to sleep in the shelter, with their heads turne right round and their beaks buried in their ba feathers. It gave her a furry feeling in her front teet little kittens had the same effect, and baby rabbits.

The budgerigars had been in residence for almost six weeks when Dad came home from work one evening in a bad mood. They could tell he was in a bad mood by the way he shut the kitchen door. He always came in through the back gate and paused to have a look at the birds on his way past the aviary, before coming indoors. Tonight he didn't stop in the kitchen; he went straight through to the front room where Rachel and Mum were watching television.

'Own up, then,' he said. 'Who did it?'

'Who did what?' said Mum. 'Keep your voice down or we shall have old mother Sergeant banging on the wall.'

'Who's been at those birds?'

Mrs Sergeant thumped on the wall.

'Have they got out, then?' Mum looked alarmed. 'Rachel, have you been fiddling . . . ?'

'Oh, they're all there,' said Dad, '*and one of them's talking*. Who did it?'

'What did it say?' Rachel asked. She hoped that it had not said hello. She always said it herself as she passed the aviary on her way to school; not to teach them, just to be friendly.

'I say "Good morning, ladies and gentlebirds" when I put the seed in,' Mum said. Rachel was surprised. It was not the kind of joke that Mum went in for. 'Don't tell me that *they've* been saying "Good morning, ladies and gentlebirds" too,' said Mum.

'Stop acting innocent,' said Dad. 'Come out here and listen.'

They went out to the aviary. One of the birds was white, more noticeable than the others and more

sociable. Rachel thought of it as Snowball, although s
was careful never to say so. When the white bird saw t
family standing round, it flew up to a branch and sidl
along, until it was close to the wire.

'Pretty me,' it said.

'Hear that?' Dad demanded. 'Pretty me! I'll give
pretty me. Who's been saying "Pretty me" to th
bird?'

'No,' said Rachel. 'I haven't.' She was not quite s
if this was, in fact, what the bird had said. The wo
had come out muffled and rather subdued, not at all l
Pip's self-satisfied croak. She wished it would sp
again but it only sat there on its branch, the li
wrinkled eyelids crimping up and down.

'If any of those birds says another word, *one* other wo
there'll be trouble,' said Dad. He was looking at Rac

'I never,' said Rachel.

'I suppose it was Donna, then.'

Donna hadn't even got around to saying ma-ma yet.

'Well, it wasn't me,' Mum said. 'Why don't you sell up and get canaries instead? They don't have much to say for themselves.' She went indoors.

After tea, when Dad had gone to play darts at the Man of Kent, Rachel slipped out to the aviary again. The white bird was still sitting on its twig, next to the wire. Rachel went and stood close, sucking her teeth as Gran used to do with Pip, to indicate that she was ready for a chat. The white bird opened its eyes, and its beak.

'Pity me,' it said, in its sad, hoarse voice. 'Pity me. Pity me.'

Rachel's first thought was, 'Good; it isn't copying anything I've said.' Then she began to wonder who it was copying. Surely no one would deliberately teach a budgerigar to say 'Pity me'? Perhaps Mum had said it without thinking –; people didn't say things like that without thinking. Perhaps the bird had *tried* to say 'Pretty me' but couldn't talk very well? Perhaps Mrs Sergeant had been having a go at it, over the wall.

Rachel sucked her teeth again.

'Pity me,' said the white bird. One of the green budgerigars, there were two of them, fluttered down from the topmost twig and clung with beak and claws to the wire netting. It turned its head sideways to look at her.

'Pity me,' said the green bird.

The two yellow birds clambered up from below. 'Pity me. Pity me. Pity me.' Rachel shivered. She had not noticed that the sun was down below the roofs of the houses in the next street. The aviary was in shadow and she could only just make out the shape of the blue budgerigar, hunched on its perch in the shelter, in silence, while the white, the green and the yellow birds pressed against the netting and repeated dully, 'Pity me. Pity me.'

The next day was Saturday, mild and still, and in the morning the budgerigars swung and fluttered in the aviary with never a word to say. They nibbled at chickweed, honed their beaks on cuttlefish bones and chucked millet seeds about, very busy being budgerigars; but as the day wore on an uneasy silence settled over the aviary. Birds sang in other gardens but the budgerigars fluffed themselves up, drew their spare feet into their feathers and closed their eyes. They looked, to Rachel, not so much tired as depressed. She went over to the netting, carrying Donna, and said, 'Come on, boys, cheer up.'

A yellow budgerigar opened one eye and said, 'Oh, I'm so cold. Oh, I'm so cold.'

'Pity me,' said the white bird. The others ruffled their feathers and were motionless again.

'Cross my heart,' Rachel gabbled, that evening. 'Cross my heart and cut my throat, it wasn't me.'

'None of that nonsense,' said Dad. 'I want a straight answer, yes or no. Did you or didn't you?'

'No!' Rachel yelled. She was shocked. People didn't yell at Dad. 'I never did. Anyway, if I had, I wouldn't have taught them to say things like that. I'd have taught them "Give us a kiss" and – and –'

'Who's a pretty boy, then?'

'Yes. But I *didn't*.'

It was raining on Sunday. The budgerigars stayed in their shelter and looked at the weather with their small eyes half shut, and said nothing all day. Dad was on late turn the following week, from four till midnight, so he saw the birds only in the daytime when it was bright, and they were bright, but it seemed to Rachel that they were not so bright as they had been, and after Dad left for work, wheeling his bicycle away down the alley, she visited the aviary. The birds, that had stopped flying and gibbering, settled on their twigs and shuffled towards her; all of them, all six. They looked furtive and unwell.

'Pity me,' said the white bird.

'Oh, I'm so cold,' said the two yellow birds.

'Pity me.'

'Cold as clay,' said the blue bird that had never spoken before.

'*What?*'

Rachel jumped and turned round. Mum was standing behind her, lips pressed together tight and frightened.

'What did that bird say?'

'I don't know, Mum.' She did know, but she did not want to tell.

'Don't say anything to your dad. I'm going to watch out, this evening. Someone must be coming into the garden after dark and doing this.'

Mum watched every evening that week, and caught no one, heard nothing, even though she kept up her vigil until Dad came home at midnight. By the weekend the birds had stopped squawking and flying from twig to twig. The chickweed withered untouched; the millet sprays hung neglected from the branches. On Saturday morning Dad and Mum and Rachel stood round the aviary and listened to the listless little voices droning,

'Oh, I'm so cold.' 'Pity me.' 'Oh, I'm so cold.' 'Cold as clay.' 'Pity me. Pity me.'

'This is getting beyond a joke,' Dad said, and talked of calling the police.

'Come off it,' said Mum, 'you can't call the police because your budgies are talking daft.'

'You call that talking daft?'

'No, not really, but they aren't damaged, are they? They haven't been stolen.'

'Not damaged? Look at them.'

They all looked at the bedraggled birds, with their feathers poking out at odd angles like bristles on a bottle brush, and their dreary eyes. The white budgerigar, once the most beautiful of all, had pulled out its tail feathers and slouched on its perch with all the grace of an old shuttlecock.

'What could the police do?' Mum said. 'Question them?'

Dad scowled and went to consult his budgerigar books. Later he went shopping and came home with cod-liver oil and fortified seed and a mineral block like a lump of grey Edinburgh rock.

'To cheer them up,' he said.

'They'd probably fancy a nip of whisky, sooner,' said Mum. 'Wouldn't you?'

They had not cheered up by Sunday evening, and on Monday, the last day of October, Dad was back at work. He was on the night shift now, and did not leave home until twenty to twelve. Rachel heard him go, kept awake by the continual opening and closing all evening of the back door, as Mum and Dad took turns to leap out on the intruder; but they didn't catch anyone. When Dad's rear light had turned left at the end of the alley, Rachel crept downstairs. Mum was clearing up, before going to bed, but she sat down at the table when Rachel padded into the kitchen. She sighed.

'I don't know.'

'I'm sorry, Mum. I couldn't sleep. The back door . . .'

'I didn't mean you, it's those blooming budgies. We've been in and out a dozen times this evening, and we haven't heard anyone.'

'I don't think there's anyone to hear,' said Rachel.

'You get along to bed,' Mum said, crossly. 'You'll be having me see things, next.'

Rachel said, 'I don't think there's anything to see, either. I don't think there's anything at all, and only the birds can hear it. Are you going out to look?'

'No,' said Mum. 'Not on your life – and neither are you.'

When Dad came home from work next morning, he found Mum and Rachel standing by the aviary, watching the budgerigars that drooped on their branches.

'Oh, I'm so cold,' said one.

'I shall always be very cold,' said another, 'cold as clay.'

'I shall always be here,' said a third.

'I shall never go away,' said the white bird.

'Pity me.'

'Pity me.'

'No,' said Dad, for the twentieth time. 'No!' he shouted. 'We are not moving. I never heard such nonsense. We're staying here.'

'Right,' said Mum, 'then it's up to you. Either those birds go or I do.'

The budgerigars were sold to good homes and went to live in cages with bells and mirrors. Donna missed them very much, so instead of the budgerigars they got a Hartz Roller canary that lived up to its name by standing on its toes all day and yelling 'Rrrrrrrrrrrrrrr-rrrrr' on a very high note. Dad broke up the aviary and on the place where nothing would grow he put down crazy paving in five different cheerful colours with a little pond in the middle. He called it a patio and to decorate it he bought a plastic orange tree in a pot and a plaster stork to stand by the pond. Rachel didn't much like the look of the patio, but the orange tree did not die, and the stork never said a word.

Grow Your Own

'**T**his year,' said Dad, at the beginning of February, 'we'll have the lawn up.'

'You've been saying that for three years,' Mum said. 'I'll kind of miss it when it goes.'

'This year I mean it,' Dad said. 'This year it's curtains for the lawn.'

'Where shall we play, then?' Andy, who had been slouching with his nose almost in his cornflakes, reared up, bristling. 'You won't let us play in the street. It's not fair. We shan't have anywhere.'

Andy could be depended upon to see the worst side of any situation. Susan, who always took her lead from Andy, put down her spoon, carefully, and prepared to weep, looking round first to see if anyone would notice. Jean, who had heard it all before, went on eating.

'Anyone would think,' Dad said, 'that I was going to pull the house down and put you out on the street. All we are going to do is move the path, dig up the lawn and lay a new one, where the path is now. You'll still have plenty of room to play.'

'All?' Mum said.

'We?' said Jean.

'You'll help, won't you, Jeannie,' Dad said bracingly, but with a pleading look in his eye. 'And you little ones can have a plot each of your own to grow what you like.'

Susan slammed her tear ducts into reverse and beamed. 'Can I grow a tree?'

'A little one.'

'I want to grow a huge tree.'

'The garden's too small for that. A big tree takes too much nourishment from the soil.'

'You said we could grow what we liked,' Andy growled. 'I'm going to grow weeds.'

After breakfast Jean went out with Dad to look at the lawn. It had been a sorry sight when they first moved to the house, and it looked even sorrier now, after three years of Andy and Susan, bicycles, footballs, roller skates and Andy's misguided attempt to light a camp fire and roast potatoes.

Jean carried the trug freighted with stakes and twine. Dad had the retractable tape measure that the little ones were forbidden to touch, because it whipped back into its case like a recoiling rattlesnake. He let it out to its fullest extent, four metres, and prowled about, frowning, occasionally prodding the earth with a gardening cane. Jean drove a stake into the ground wherever he prodded, and then they strung the twine from stake to stake, which reminded Jean of those puzzles where you join up the dots, for when they had finished, the network of twine showed the outline of the new lawn and the route, across the old one, of where the path would be. Dad went into the shed to put away the tape measure on a high shelf, and Mum came down the garden to hang out the washing.

'Having fun?' Mum said, with pegs between her teeth.

'It's going to look nice,' Jean said, loyally. She had said the same thing when Dad planned the alpine garden which was where Andy and Susan had their sand pit, and when he had proposed to put up a ros arch exactly where the washing line went across. From behind a dangling double sheet Andy and Susan appeared, looking suspicious.

'I liked our lawn,' Andy said, mournfully, as if he could only just remember it but would never forget.

'Oh, come off it,' Jean said, 'it's a horrible lawn, all bald and stony. And it's full of dandelions and cats go on it. The new one will be lovely, all green and springy. You won't cut your knees if you fall over,' she added, appealing to their self-interest. She did not mention the fact that even after the new lawn was planted it would be a long while before they could play on it. There would be time enough for that in summer, when Andy got his skates out.

'Where's my bit?' Susan said. 'Daddy said I could have a bit of my own.'

'I don't know. Let's go and ask him – leave that twine alone, Andy.'

' 'snot your twine,' Andy retorted, twanging it, but only while she was watching. She turned her back and went down to the shed with Susan trotting behind.

'Dad? Sue wants to know where she can have her bit of garden.'

Dad was at the back of the shed, inspecting flower pots. He came out and stood in the doorway, considering. 'How about there?' he said, pointing to a modest corner behind the currant bushes. Susan went over to look.

'I don't like this place. There's things in it.'

'What sort of things?'

'With wings.'

'Lots of things in the garden have wings,' Dad said. 'Butterflies, ladybirds, beetles –'

'Beetles have legs.'

'And wings. Come on, Sukie, this is probably the best part of the garden. Lovely soil. And it won't matter if you grow trees down here.' This was because the plot he had earmarked for Susan was far away from everything except the shed. It was also rather shady. Very likely only a tree would grow there anyway. 'As soon as we've got the lawn up you can start digging.'

'I want *that* place.' Susan pointed towards the fence, and a cosy, sunny little nook on the far side of the shed.

'No, you can't have that. I'm going to put the compost heap there.'

'What's a compost heap?'

'We're not going to use peat and artificial fertilizers any more,' Dad said. 'We're going to make our own compost. We'll put all our grass cuttings and potato peelings and tealeaves and weeds in a big pile and they'll rot down into lovely rich soil.'

'Don't you need a bin for that?' Jean said.

'I prefer to do it the traditional way,' Dad said. 'So off you go, Sukie. Behind the currant bushes.'

'But what about the things?'

'If you're going to be a gardener,' Dad said, 'you'll have to get used to *things*.'

In spite of united opposition Dad began digging up the lawn the following Saturday. It looked like a little ploughed field, row after row of gleaming sods, neatly turned. Andy and Susan said nothing but played a pathetically shrinking game on the dwindling patch of grass, until they were huddled together in the very last corner, like castaways marooned on a rock with the tide ~ing in.

'' said Dad, when the lawn had vanished

entirely, 'we'll leave it like that until spring and the frost will break it down.'

'Frost?' said Mum. 'If we have another winter like last one –'

'There's sure to be a frost before April,' Dad said. 'No reason why you two shouldn't make a start,' he said, to the children who were sulking on the rockery. 'Do you want the spade, Andy?'

'Don't need a spade,' Andy said, kicking the rocks. 'Weeds come up on their own.'

'Don't they just,' Mum said.

Susan was staring wistfully at the place where Andy's plot would be. 'Can't I have a place where it's sunny?'

'It's mine!' Andy leaped into the centre of his territory as if prepared to defend it with his life.

'It's only sunny *now*,' Jean coaxed. 'In the morning *your* place will get the sunshine.'

Susan retreated a few paces towards the currant bushes.

'You can't see the house.'

'Yes you can.'

'Not from *my* place. It's round the corner.'

'Oh, go on, swap,' Jean said to Andy. 'You don't really care which bit you have.'

'I'm not going down by the compost heap. It'll stink,' said Andy, with some truth.

'But you're not going to grow anything anyway. Oh, come on, Andy. Don't be so mean.'

'I'm not really going to grow weeds.' Prudently keeping one foot on the plot to maintain ownership he spread out like a pair of compasses and grabbed the spade that Dad had left standing in the earth. 'I'm going to grow lovely sunflowers,' he declared, for

Susan's benefit. '*Sun*flowers need *sun*. Don't they, Jean? You've got to have *sun* to grow *sun*flowers. I can't grow *sun*flowers down by the stinky old compost heap because there won't be any *sun* there. Poor old Susan. No *sun*.'

'Oh, shut up,' Jean said, aiming a kick at him but taking care not to connect, for fear of further ructions, as Andy began to dig ferociously, like a miner whose mates are trapped by a cave-in. She went back down the path to where Susan was lurking disconsolately beside the compost heap.

So far it was scarcely more than a mole hill and so scanty that you could count the contributions; three orange peels, four days' tealeaves, two banana skins, a melon rind, potato peelings and a glossy aubergine that had secretively rotted at the back of the fridge. From a distance it all shone festively, like a bunch of unseasonable flowers.

'I don't like this place,' Susan whimpered, forlorn among the currant bushes. 'I want to change with Andy.'

'Andy won't change.' While they were talking she could hear the spade chomping energetically into the earth. 'He's already started digging.'

'I shall be sad.' There was a certain amount of threat in Susan's voice but she really did seem to be upset, not just putting it on for an act. Jean surveyed the plot behind the currant bushes. As far as she could tell the only thing wrong with it was the proximity of the compost heap, and as yet, that was much too small to ~use offence. Susan could have no idea of what it *would*
~ say in a year's time.

~v, Sukie. When you plant some flowers it

will be lovely here, too.' Jean went down on one knee beside her little sister and immediately saw why Susan was unhappy. On that eye-level the garden was entirely hidden by the currant bushes and then by the evergreen laurustinus shrubs beyond them. The house was out of sight, too. All that Susan could see when she looked round were two towering, sombre cypresses and the overhanging shed. When the compost heap rose to its full height even the view through the paling fence into Mrs Lawrence's garden next door would be obscured. Jean had never been small enough in this garden to imagine how threatened Susan felt, but she remembered the last house and the last garden where, when she was Susan's age, the sundial had reared above her like something escaped from Stonehenge. She had been so proud of climbing a tree that was, she could see now, not much taller than Dad. Couldn't *he* understand how easy it was to be frightened when you were so close to the ground? Presumably he had once been that size, too.

'I'll tell you what,' Jean said, standing up, 'I'll let you have a bit of *my* garden, up near the house. Would you like that?' Susan nodded, beginning to smile again. 'And I'll have this piece, to make up.'

'Can I grow my tree?'

Jean frowned. Her stretch of the garden was wide and shallow, laid out neatly in rows, tall plants at the back, short ones in front, and Mum said it looked like a school photograph. 'You don't really want to grow a tree. You only said that to annoy Dad.'

Susan giggled and nodded again. That was all right, then. They walked back up the garden together on the crunching cinder path that would soon go the way of the lawn. Round at the side of the house lay a stack of paving slabs bought to replace it. They paused beside Jean's plot.

'Which is my place?' Susan said.

'Here at the side, from the Michaelmas daisies down as far as Mum's roses. You mustn't touch *them*.'

She was very reluctant to give up even a centimetre of her carefully tended plot in exchange for that no man's land behind the currant bushes. The only consolation was that it was far too early in the year to think of planting anything, and that by the time April came Susan, and probably Andy too, would have lost all interest in gardening.

Long before that, though, the new garden began to take shape. Dad dug up the cinder path and laid the concrete slabs. Rain and frost broke up the clods of the old lawn and Jean's hoeing did the rest. By the end of March the site of the new lawn was raked level and the seed sown. By the end of April a fine green mist lay over it, thousands of slender grass blades. In the borders Mum's tulips flared, red and yellow; the Ville de Lyon clematis was swarming up the rose arch although it would not flower until July.

Meanwhile, at the end of the garden, the compost heap was growing too. From that first little offering of fruit and veg it had increased to half a metre in height and Dad had erected an enclosure of boards round it. Jean, sowing neat rows of land cress and lettuces, watched it rise. Its finest moment came in May when the new lawn was cut for the first time. Dad snipped daintily at the tender blades with newly sharpened shears, and collected up the fine clippings to place on the compost heap.

'I love the scent of new-cut grass,' Jean said, sprinkling the clippings over yesterday's discarded cabbage leaves and turnip tops.

'That's decomposition. Grass begins to break down organically as soon as it's cut,' Dad said. 'That's what you can smell.'

All through the summer, as the grass grew longer and stronger, there was a regular harvest of clippings for the compost heap. When Jean went down to water her salads, now she had radishes and spring onions, too, she was aware of it working away silently, turning the grass, the weeds, the kitchen refuse into the lovely rich soil that Dad had promised. Even on chilly days the compost heap felt warm and alive. She was longing for the time when they would remove the boards at the front and with a spade lift out the nourishing earth in dark slices, like Christmas pudding.

Andy's weed garden flourished for a couple of months and then he was given a skate board and forgot all about the pleasures of horticulture. Susan planted a number of interesting stones alongside Jean's tobacco plants and verbena and stuck a lopped branch from the apple tree upright in the middle of her plot.

Sometimes she ventured as far as the currant bushes to see how Jean's vegetables were coming along.

'Can I have a radish?'

'Not yet. Next week, perhaps. What's that you've got there?'

'A mouse.' Susan held it up by the tail. In fact it was two thirds of a mouse.

'Where did you find that?'

'In my garden,' Susan said. 'Do you think it was ill?'

'I should think it had a headache,' Jean said, looking at the corpse. Evidently Mrs Lawrence's cat Dennis had lost his appetite in the middle of a meal. 'Why are you carrying it around?'

'I was going to bury it,' Susan said.

'Chuck it on the compost heap,' Jean suggested. The mouse was swinging unpleasantly close to her face. 'Go on, it'll rot down with everything else.'

'Won't Daddy mind?'

'Ordinary earth's full of things that have died, isn't it?' Jean said. 'I should think that mouse would be very good for the compost.'

Susan made a dent in the latest thatch of grass clippings and laid the mouse reverently in it.

'Now wash your hands,' Jean said. The mouse had not been fresh.

When she came down later with the potato peelings from supper she noticed that the grass was looking rather scattered and the mouse had gone. Presumably Dennis had come back for second helpings.

'*Is* it all right to put meat on the compost heap?' she asked Mum, when they were washing up.

'Meat? What had you in mind, lamb chops? A few spare ribs?'

'Dead mice.'

'Why, have you got more than you can handle?'

'Susan found one that Dennis had left. I told her it could go in the compost.'

'I don't see what harm it can do,' Mum said. 'I've been chucking them on for months.'

'Mice?'

'You know what Dennis is like; mice, birds, fish . . .'

'Where's he get the fish from?'

'Dustbins, I should think. Anyway, it all goes on the heap.'

'Doesn't Dad mind?'

'Haven't told him,' Mum said.

Next time Jean encountered one of Dennis's leftovers which could, she thought, have been a rat, she scooped it up on her trowel and tipped it on to the compost heap, but this time digging a small grave first, among the cabbage leaves. She must have disturbed an air pocket, down there among the lovely rich soil, for as she turned away there came a sound from the compost heap, something between a gasp and a gulp – possibly a soft but satisfied belch.

The first frost of the year came early at the end of September, sharp and unexpected. Susan went out before breakfast to make footprints on the pale sparkling veil that was the new lawn. Jean followed her, shivering slightly, to inspect damage to plants. The low sun slid between the palings of the fence as it rose, leaving stripes of frost across the path where their shadows had lain. There was a broad white band of it where the laurustinus stood and behind the currant bushes Jean's vegetable patch was thickly iced. On the compost heap only a few crystals glittered, already melting, although the sun had not touched it yet.

Jean looked back along the path. The Michaelmas daisies had survived but the chrysanthemums' heads hung dully. The last dahlias were black and late rosebuds drooped where the cold had pinched them. Only the apples shone now in the bright air. Coming down the path Jean had seen her breath steaming, and now she noticed a faint haze above the compost heap, as if that too were breathing gently in the cold light. The end of the garden lay in deep shadow and the only thing high enough to catch the sun was the upper part of the shed. The bottom part stood in the shadow of the compost heap and from that shadow, on either side of it, lay twin pillars of shadow cast by the cypress trees, straight up and then bent at identical angles as they crossed the roof of the shed. There was no stir of wind, they did not move, but as she looked the shadow between them shifted slightly, as if something had moved on top of the compost heap.

Jean turned sharply, expecting to see Dennis the cat, or even a squirrel. Susan would like to see a squirrel. There was nothing there, but something must have *been* there for the top of the heap looked disturbed, almost churned over. All the frost had vanished suddenly, faster than it could have melted in the chilly sunlight. She edged alongside the heap and looked over the fence. How nice if it were a squirrel. But there was no trace of a squirrel over the fence in Mrs Lawrence's garden, and no cat. A trail of little cat feet ran across the white lawn between the rose bushes, but they came nowhere near the fence, nowhere near the compost heap. Jean stepped back towards the path but as she moved she knocked against the wooden boards that enclosed the heap. It wasn't a hard enough knock to dislodge anything, she thought, but the top of the heap shuddered and little clods and clumps fell away. An old green potato with sprouts like giant pincers rolled down, crabwise. From inside the mass came what sounded like a warm damp sigh. Although there was no wind a withered leaf and a shred or two of dried grass drifted to earth.

Back up the garden Susan was hovering near the blasted remains of Jean's frost-bitten plants.

'Can we dig them up now they're dead? Can we put them on the compost heap?'

'If you like.' Jean looked thoughtfully at Susan. She was five. It would be a pity to frighten her for nothing but even so . . .

'Sukie?'

'Mmmm?'

'Have you noticed anything about the compost heap?'

'It's bigger than me, now,' Susan said.

'Anything else?'

'It makes a funny noise.'

'What sort of a noise?'

'Like breathing,' Susan said. 'It's gases escaping.'

'It's what?'

'I asked Daddy. He said it must be gases escaping. Like when you eat too much and go *erp*.'

'Oh, yes. Sure.'

They went shopping that morning, but in the afternoon Susan helped Jean clear the dead plants from her flower bed. Jean cut down the chrysanthemums and separated the roots, ready to store in peat till next spring. It was growing chilly again when they went in, and darkness was falling when Jean looked out of the window and noticed that the trug containing the dead plants was still standing on the path.

She went out to fetch it and set off down the garden to the shed. Already stars were showing and a white moon rimmed the chimney stack. There would be another frost tonight, a hard one.

Jean upended the trug on the compost heap. It was

not only bigger than Susan, now, it was very nearly as tall as she was. As she opened the shed door to put away the trug, it crackled and stirred behind her.

When she looked out of the bedroom window the next morning the world was almost white. Frost lay palest green on the grass and stood thick upon twigs. Across the lawn ran a line of delicate prints from the toes of Dennis the cat, and *up* the lawn, from the direction of the shed, from the direction of the compost heap, lay a long dark track, as if something warm and heavy had passed that way, something that had moved close to the ground.

Jean threw on her dressing-gown and ran down to look, across the patio, down the steps, under the rose arch and along the path. The track on the lawn was scraped clear of frost, littered with dead leaves and bits of grass, potato peelings and dark soil, and where the lawn ended the trail went on, over the frosty rockery and under the hedge, into Mrs Lawrence's garden.

Before she reached the shed she knew that something had changed. The shed stood in full sunshine, right down to the ground, and the only shadows on it were cast by the slender palings of the fence and the two pillars of the cypress trees. There was nothing to obstruct the sunshine any more, for the rampart of boards that had enclosed the compost heap was scattered on the ground, as if something had burst them apart, and the compost heap had gone too, or rather, it had collapsed. On the earth where it had stood, a metre and a half high, lay a little pile of the rich dark soil that Dad had been looking forward to, a scattering of dead weeds and peelings, and chrysanthemum heads, the withered verbena and tobacco plants, a carrot top like an orange button. The rest of the heap was missing.

Moving very slowly, Jean went back up the garden, following the trail of earth and leaves through the frost, across the lawn, over the rockery, towards the hedge. Like the footsteps of Good King Wenceslas it seemed warm to the touch of her bare feet. On the far side of the hedge was another scattering of earth, marring the clean-swept bricks of Mrs Lawrence's patio. Round the corner of Mrs Lawrence's house came Dennis the cat, with an early morning mouse in his teeth. He laid it tenderly upon the ground and patted it with his paw. It did not respond. Dennis reared back on his haunches and took a swing at it, the mouse rose into the air and at the same moment, from behind the dustbin, something lunged out, caught the mouse with a swift clawed swipe

as it began to fall, and withdrew behind the dustbin
again. Something growled, a cat-like growl, but Dennis
was already in flight, up on the fence with eyes like
marbles, fur on end, tail like a bottle brush, all four
paws clustered together on one post.

From behind the dustbin came a throaty, satisfied
rumbling; not quite a purr. Jean leaned right over the
hedge, in time to see a bulky shape trundle from its
hideout and head through the long grass towards the
lane. It was a dark shape, low-slung, rotund and heavy
and the whispering grass stems closed behind it. It
could have been a hedgehog – a hedgehog as large as
Susan, but unlike the general run of hedgehogs, it
seemed to have acquired a taste for mice.

Welcome, Yule

Probably Emma would not have come to know Mr Jarvis, the new vicar, if someone had not tipped him off that her dad could play the organ. They never discovered who had done it, although Dad did say that whoever it was ought to be hung up by the heels and skinned with a butter knife, which would have been worth watching, but one day the vicar arrived on his motor cycle, without warning. Emma came home from school and found him in the living-room with a cup of tea at his elbow, Mum hovering and Dad cowering.

'I believe you're something of an organist,' said the vicar, to Emma's dad, who was off work with a broken finger. He was a draughtsman at Featherstone's.

'Not at the moment,' Dad said, waving his fat finger like a parsnip in its bandages.

'Well, that won't last for ever,' the vicar said.

'Nor will I,' Dad said, glumly. He hated to be ill, even on one finger. Emma loved it because she was healthy and hardly ever had a day off school.

'It would only be two weeks in three,' said Mr Jarvis. 'There's no music at Holy Communion.' He would not give in. After about an hour, Dad gave in, because his finger would keep him off the keys for at least another month and, as the vicar had said, it was only two Sundays out of three.

Ockney, Cawley and Strang shared one vicar among them. Emma lived in Strang, and the vicar did too, because it was the largest parish. It had a council estate, a factory, and the smallest Woolworth's in England, perhaps in the whole world. On Sundays he buzzed in a bee-line from church to church on his motor cycle; Holy Communion at Ockney, Matins at Strang and Evensong at Cawley. On the following Sunday they each celebrated a different service. Emma thought it was like musical chairs, and wondered what would happen if one of the churches fell down during the week, and the vicar was left stranded with a spare service and nowhere to say it. Churches had fallen down before. On the hill above Strang, between Highmead Estate and Featherstone's Marine Diesel Engines Ltd, lay the remains of St Thomas's Church. Six hundred years ago old Strang village had stood on the hill around St Thomas's, but after the Black Death, which wiped out all but seven of the parishioners, the village moved away and started again in the valley, with a new church, Holy Trinity, which showed no signs of falling down.

Up on the hill, St Thomas's slid gently back into the ground until the grass covered it, and now the local children played on the grassy lumps and bumps that had been the nave and chancel. They preferred it to the council playground where there were swings and slides and concrete pipes to crawl through. Emma herself preferred it. She did not live on the council estate, but she often went up to play at St Thomas's.

'I'm not playing on some old church,' said her cousin Naomi, when she came to stay. 'It's spooky,' Naomi said, before she had even seen it.

'It's not,' Emma said.

'I bet there's ghosts.'

'I've never seen one,' Emma retorted. 'Not up there, at any rate.'

'Where then? Bet you never.'

'Bet what you like. You wouldn't know a ghost if you saw one,' Emma said, and they went off to play in the concrete pipes.

The vicar came to see Dad in July. By September Dad couldn't pretend any longer that his finger was stiff, so all through the autumn he went down to Holy Trinity, two weeks out of three, to play the organ at Matins or Evensong. Mum and Emma, who had never been church-goers, sometimes went along too, to lend him moral support, and often Mr Jarvis visited them to discuss next week's music. Dad found himself playing the organ at choir practices as well, at weddings and funerals, and then suddenly it was November, and the vicar began to talk about Christmas carols.

Winter had come early that year. The vicar stood on the frosty doorstep, staring at the black sky and the burning blue stars, while his breath steamed in the light from the hall, and the hall grew colder and colder. Mum and Emma huddled round the boiler in the kitchen and wished that Dad were brave enough to boot the vicar out and shut the door. At last they heard the roar of his two-stroke as he shot away down the hill.

'One of these nights he'll come off at that bend by the bridge,' Mum said, hopefully, as Dad came back into the hall and shut the door.

'He thinks there'll be snow before Christmas,' Dad said, rushing to the boiler with his purple hands held out in front of him, like a rocket-powered sleepwalker. 'Says he can smell it.'

'All right for some,' Mum said. 'They've got central heating at the vicarage.'

'He wants to go carol singing,' said Dad.

'I can just see that,' said Mum. 'I can just see him belting round the county on his Yamaha, singing "Silent Night" fit to raise the dead.'

'Not by himself,' Dad said. 'He thinks we should all go out with the three church choirs and tramp round Ockney and Cawley as well. Candle lanterns and mulled ale and Jack Pewsey with his clarinet.'

'Jack plays hot jazz,' Mum pointed out.

'I should think we could cool him down enough for a few carols.'

'The weather'll do that,' Mum said.

'It had better. If it's not Jack Pewsey it'll be me with a portable harmonium and four boy scouts to pull it.'

'The Baptists at Ockney have a harmonium,' said Mum. 'It sounds like a string quartet in a drain.'

'I know – I'll go down to the Three Compasses and buy Jack a few pints,' said Dad.

Emma said, 'If you go carol singing, can I come?'

'We'll all come,' Mum said. She turned to Dad who was putting on his parka. 'The vicar wasn't here last Christmas, was he?'

'Came just before Easter. I remember the first time I saw him – lurking under the lich-gate on Good Friday.'

'Then someone ought to tell him about the Waits. He shouldn't upset the Waits.'

The vicar's idea caught on. Everybody in Ockney, Cawley and Strang wanted to go out carol singing at Christmas, although not all of them wanted to go with the vicar. Strang Women's Institute decided to dress up in Olde Tyme clothes and go round with a sled, distributing tea and sugar to the Olde Age Pensioners. Cawley Comprehensive got up a rival scheme involving Christmas puddings, while the Ockney Baptists wheeled out their portable harmonium and began rehearsing on their own account. On still evenings it could be heard even by the nightwatchman up at Featherstone's Marine Diesels. The vicar became concerned by the threat of so much competition and planned a campaign to eliminate it. He called a meeting in the parish room at Strang, to explain his strategy.

He had brought along a map of the three parishes, divided up into zones with red lines and arrows. Emma, looking at it, was reminded of a plan for battle. She could picture Mr Jarvis lying in ambush with his carol singers armed and hidden behind a hedge, waiting for the Ockney Baptists to come wheezing by. The vicar explained what the red lines were for.

'Carol singing starts a week before Christmas. The W.I. are going round Cawley and Ockney on the twentieth and twenty-third, and Strang on the twenty-second. Cawley Comp will be in Ockney on the twenty-first. Strang on the twenty-third, and at home on the twenty-second. Ockney Baptists will be in Strang on the twenty-first, and Ockney and Cawley on the twenty-second and twenty-third. How's that for dovetailing?' said the vicar.

'What about us?' Dad asked.

'Aha,' the vicar said, teeth glistening with satisfaction. 'The united church choirs will be at Ockney on the nineteenth, and Cawley on the twenty-first, but we'll be in Strang on the twentieth. That, you see – if you'll just look at this chart – gives us first crack at Ockney and Strang. No one will have been round before us.'

'And first crack at the collection,' Dad muttered.

'What about the Waits?' Emma asked. She nudged Dad. 'Mum told you to tell him about the Waits.'

Dad looked embarrassed. 'It's not that simple, Em.'

Emma could believe it. The vicar was not the kind of man to listen to things that he did not want to hear, but she was firm. She prodded her father.

'Go on, Dad.'

Dad coughed. 'Er, Mr Jarvis . . . is this absolutely final?' he asked, pointing to the map.

'And foolproof,' said the vicar. 'Why, is there a fly in the ointment? Trust you to find it.'

'Not exactly. It's just that the Waits always sing in Strang on the twentieth. It's St Thomas's Eve, you see . . .'

'Waits? Of course I know it's St Thomas's Eve. What Waits?'

'Waits. You know, the old name for carol singers,' Dad said.

'Ah, yes; Middle English, from Old Norman French *waitier* from the Old French *guaitier* . . . What about them? We've not had any complaints from them?'

'Well, you wouldn't,' Dad mumbled, 'but they might not like it.'

'Who are these Waits? A music society?'

'You could call them that,' Dad agreed.

'If they wanted to book the twentieth, they should have spoken up. I announced the provisional dates ten days ago. No one said anything. Who's their chairman, or secretary, or whatever they have?'

'I don't think they have one,' said Dad. 'They're not an official society, just local people who like to come together to sing carols on St Thomas's Eve. It's a kind of tradition,' he said, lamely.

'They're perfectly welcome to join our band,' the vicar declared, brisk and reasonable. 'I'll say as much on Sunday.'

On Sunday, at Evensong, he announced that the Waits would be very welcome to come carol singing with the united church choirs of Ockney, Cawley and Strang, on the twentieth of December, but not on any other night, and not on their own.

'We don't want clashes between rival supporters,' the vicar said, with a jolly smile. There was an uneasy, almost angry, muttering among the congregation.

'I'll be very surprised,' Mum said, under her breath, 'if anyone from Strang turns out for His Nibs on the twentieth.'

School ended on Tuesday the nineteenth, and that evening Mum and Dad and Emma wrapped up warmly, collected Jack Pewsey, who was Emma's headmaster, and Jack's clarinet, and drove over icy roads to Ockney, where they met the three choirs assembled outside the King's Head, and sang 'O Come All Ye Faithful' by way of a warm-up, before moving on to render 'The Holly and the Ivy' – with particular emphasis on the line about the playing of the merry organ – to the Baptists, practising in the chapel with their harmonium.

Next day, on the morning of the twentieth, Jack Pewsey rang up, in a hoarse voice, to say that the cold air had got to his lungs and he wouldn't be able to play his clarinet in Strang that night.

'Lungs, my foot,' said Mum. 'He doesn't want to upset the Waits, that's what.'

'Sensible fellow,' Dad said, and rang the vicar.

'I think we'll have to call it a day, tonight,' he said, but the vicar rang up the Ockney Baptists and that afternoon the pastor drove over in his minibus and unloaded the portable harmonium at Emma's front gate, just as Dad was coming home from Featherstone's.

'But won't you need it yourselves?' Dad asked, with wan hope.

'Not till Thursday, thanks to Generalissimo Jarvis,' the pastor said, leaping back into the minibus. He was an athletic man. He had unloaded the harmonium single-handed. It took the combined efforts of Mum, Dad and Emma to move it into the garage.

'No luck,' Dad said. 'I'll have to go through with it.' He looked with loathing at the minibus, skidding round the bend by the bridge. 'Why do clergymen drive so badly? I knew this mad monk in Macclesfield – had a Volvo . . .'

'We'll come too,' Emma said, firmly. If the Waits turned out for a showdown with the vicar, she wanted to be there to see it.

They gathered under a starry sky in frozen silence, by the west door of Holy Trinity. The choir from St Mary's Ockney was there, and the choir of Cawley All Saints, but from Strang there was no one but Mum, Dad, Emma and the vicar.

'I see,' said Mr Jarvis, peering into the darkness. 'I see.'

'I doubt it,' said Emma's dad, bold after a couple of whiskies with Jack Pewsey who had claimed that his tubes needed flushing and coughed hollowly to prove it. 'The Waits sing tonight.'

'And people in Strang prefer to go out with the Waits

rather than support their own church choir?'

'No one goes out with the Waits,' Dad said, 'but it's their night, and no one wants to offend them.'

'They had plenty of warning,' the vicar snapped. He turned to the four boy scouts, harnessed like reindeer to the Baptists' harmonium. 'One, two, three – *heave!*'

The choirs moved off, and did not halt until they reached the bridge where Emma's own road went round the corner.

'We'll begin with "Once in Royal David's City",' the vicar announced.

Dad unfolded his camping stool, sat down at the harmonium, and began to play. The choirs began to sing. After they had finished with Royal David's City the scouts went round knocking on doors, while Dad struck up 'Good King Wenceslas'. It was a good carol for a cold night, and the choirs sang vigorously, but at the end of every verse Emma could have sworn that somewhere, not too distant, another choir was singing 'Good King Wenceslas', four bars behind.

' "Oh Little Town of Bethlehem",' the vicar commanded, when they had finished, and they began again. This time there could be no doubt. Somewhere in the streets of Strang, another choir was singing; *not* 'O Little Town of Bethlehem'. When 'O Little Town of Bethlehem' was over, they all paused to listen. Across the frosty rooftops chimed the strains of a carol that Emma had never heard before, but rather liked:

> *'Out of your sleep arise and wake,*
> *For God mankind now hath y-take,*
> *All of a maid without any make;*
>   *Of all women she beareth the bell.*
>   *Nowell, nowell, nowell . . .'*

'It seems we have competition,' the vicar remarked, redundantly, when the carol was over. 'Time we moved on, I think.' He chivvied the scouts back into position and the group slithered over the glittering pavement in the swinging yellow light of the vicar's lantern which he bore before them, on a pole. As they went they heard, apparently from the street beyond the market, a crisp treble voice singing,

> *'Welcome be thou, heaven-king,*
> *Welcome, born in one morning,*
> *Welcome for whom we shall sing,*
> *Welcome Yule!'*

'I know the words,' the vicar said, intrigued in spite of himself, 'but I must confess that the tune is entirely unfamiliar.'

'It's the original, I'd guess,' Dad said, blandly.

They stopped at the corner by the service station. '"While Shepherds Watched",' said the vicar. In answer, and certainly in the next street, a sturdy chorus of deep male voices broke out.

> *'The boar's head in hand bear I,*
> *Bedecked with bays and rosemary,*
> *And I pray you my masters be merry . . .'*

'"While Shepherds Watched",' bellowed the vicar, so they sang it, while a single voice, sharp as splitting ice, cut through their chorus:

> *'Gabriel from heaven-king*
> *Sent to the maiden sweet,*
> *Brought he this blissful tiding,*
> *And fair he gan her greet.'*

'Move on!' the vicar shouted. 'This is getting beyond a joke. Move on!'

As they approached the deserted market square a light was seen, bobbing up Brewer's Street, above a cluster of dark figures.

'Could this be our friends, the Waits?' the vicar inquired, nastily, and raising his own lantern on its pole, he strode to meet his rivals, while the choir and the harmonium, conductorless, floundered through 'See, Amid the Winter's Snow'. Emma shuffled her cold feet in their cold boots, and stopped singing to hear what would happen. One by one the rest of the choir fell silent as the vicar and the Waits met at last, outside Woolworth's.

'Merry Christmas,' the vicar cried, not at all merry. The Waits stood and faced him, all in a lump. Their lantern shone over their heads, greenish, not glowing.

'I'm sorry it's come to a confrontation,' said the vicar, 'but we gave you plenty of warning. You were cordially invited to join us and there were notices saying as much put up in the church porch, the Post Office, and outside the police station.'

The leader of the Waits, a huge muffled man in a heavy coat, or cloak, stepped forward a pace, but still no one spoke. The vicar stepped back.

'We'd still be delighted,' he said, less certainly, 'if you'd care to join forces, but if not, I really must ask you to move on. It's not as if,' he added, 'you were even singing the same carols as us. Indeed,' he went on, 'I'm not sure that what you are singing *are* carols. I've never heard . . .'

As one man, the Waits moved; forward, sideways, and disappeared. It looked very much as if they had gone into Woolworth's, but that could not have been so, because Woolworth's closed at five-thirty, and it was now twenty minutes to nine.

'Very clever,' said the vicar. 'Most entertaining. I think this has gone far enough. Who are they?'

'Well, we don't know any of them personally,' Dad said, 'but I told you, it's an established tradition. They always come out to sing carols on St Thomas's Eve. John Aubrey mentions having seen them in – sixteen forty-seven, I think it was.'

'John Aubrey? Sixteen forty-seven? Are you trying to tell me – ?'

'That was the year Parliament abolished Christmas, but it didn't make much difference to the Waits. They kept going right through the Commonwealth, much to the annoyance of the vicar,' he added, pointedly.

'This has been going on since *sixteen forty-seven*?'

'Oh, much longer than that,' Mum chipped in. 'I imagine it really got going after the Black Death. When was that? Mid-fourteenth century?'

'*But who are they?*'

'Like I said, we don't really know any of them by name, except for the big bloke with the lantern. He's Will Plowman,' said Dad. 'Always carries the lantern, Will does.'

'Since when?'

'Since thirteen forty-eight, that's when,' Mum said. 'Good old Will. It would take more than Oliver Cromwell to make him miss his carols.'

'Carol singing as we understand it,' the vicar said, smugly, 'was unknown before the fifteenth century. How do you account for that?'

'They're a progressive crowd,' Dad said. 'They've picked up quite a lot of contemporary stuff since thirteen forty-eight. Jack Pewsey says he heard them having a go at "In the Bleak Midwinter", last year. They don't really mind what they sing, as long as it's got a good tune. The true essence of carol singing, wouldn't you say?' he asked, with a mild smile.

There were no more carols that night. There was no more singing at all, but later, in the early hours of the morning, Emma was woken by a fearful row coming from the street outside. It sounded like tin buckets being kicked downstairs, with a canteen of cutlery by way of descant. She went into her parents' room and found Mum and Dad in dressing-gowns, standing by the window, and looking down into the road.

'I could have told him this would happen,' Dad said, as Emma crept alongside.

'Yes, but I notice you didn't,' said Mum.

'No good flogging a dead horse,' Dad said. 'Still, he may pay attention next year. What on earth have they got down there?'

'Not on earth,' said Mum.

'It sounds like iron kettles and ladles.'

'I suppose it would be.'

'Rough music.'

Emma looked out into the street. In the light of the lamp by the bridge she could see a steady surge of people passing by, silent themselves but raising a deafening clangour from the pots and pans, tongs, hammers and billhooks that they carried.

'I think you'd better have another word with our Mr Jarvis in the morning,' Mum yelled, above the racket.

'Do you think it'll be necessary? After all, they've made their point. They've been carol singing for six hundred years, now. They're not going to stop because some hot-rod vicar tries to run Christmas like the Normandy landings.'

'And warn him about Midsummer's Eve.'

'Midsummer Eve's none of his business,' said Dad, 'or mine. Lord alone knows how long *that's* been going on.'

Emma slipped back to her own room and lay listening to the Waits as they came down from Strang St Thomas to play rough music round the vicarage until dawn broke on St Thomas's Day. Through the clashing of iron on iron she heard voices raised, although she could not make out the tune. Whatever they were singing, however, it was not a Christmas carol.

Efflorescence

I don't suppose the tunnel is there any more. It ran
under a stretch of disused railway line and the last
time I visited the town, about twenty years ago, there
was earth-moving equipment at work in the meadow
beyond it, and already a row of houses at the end of the
footpath. Probably the footpath is a street by now, and
no street would have fitted into that tunnel; it was only
six feet across. No, I should guess that the old line has
gone and the tunnel with it. This may be just as well.

Dennis Willis and I used to walk through the tunnel
twice a day, five days a week, on our way to school and
back. My school was Coldharbour High; Dennis went
to St Augustine's RC. For a long while this didn't
matter, but at the beginning of our second year
Dennis's twin brothers started at the infant school and
Dennis had to escort them there. Dennis thought this
was unfair. I thought it was criminally stupid, like
asking your pet baa-lamb to take the mastiffs for a walk;
not that Raymond and David were actively carni-
vorous. They did not hurl themselves at passers-by
and gnaw their ankles, they went in more for what is
known as structural damage; gate posts, bird baths,
windows. Rose bushes and milk bottles were not safe
either in their vicinity. In those days the footpath ran
alongside a row of cottages with very small unfenced
front gardens, where the milk bottles and rose bushes
were within easy reach. Dennis had his work cut out.

The upshot of all this was that Dennis had to leave home much earlier than before in order to deliver the twins to the very doorstep of their school because they could not be trusted to walk even the last hundred yards on their own. Once or twice I tried leaving early as well, to give Dennis moral support – and numerical parity, as Dennis would have it – but there were six of us at home, all leaving for various schools and jobs, and in the end I gave up because I was the youngest and always got trampled in the rush for the bathroom. All the others had not only to wash but to shave, except for my mother, of course. I saw less of Dennis on the way home, too. St Augustine's came out fifteen minutes before we did. In the good old days, B T (Before Twins), Dennis used to wait for me by the allotments, where the town end of the tunnel began, but now the extra fifteen minutes were taken up with collecting Raymond and David and somehow we usually managed to miss each other.

I'm not implying that I used to hide, mind you, and we still met in the evenings when it was fine or we didn't have too much homework. Arranging these meetings was a problem as neither of us had a phone, until Dennis discovered the loose brick. It was probably one of the twins who discovered it or more likely loosened it himself. Given time, no doubt, they would have demolished the entire tunnel, but this particular brick was on the edge, at the allotments end, and could be lifted right out. Dennis's idea was that if one of us wanted to communicate with the other he should leave a message on a piece of paper shoved in behind the brick. Each of us would check, as we went through the tunnel, to see if there were anything in the hole.

This worked for about a week until someone else discovered the loose brick. The someone else was God-frey Rains and he forged a message from Dennis for me to find on the way to school. Then he forged another one from me, which he left for Dennis the same evening. They were identical. 'See you round by the privet bush, back of the pub. 7.30.' Our writing was easy to forge as we, and Godfrey, had attended the same primary school, taught to write, as our parents had been, by ancient Miss Babbington who had herself been taught to write, so rumour had it, by the author of Genesis. When we rendezvoused innocently under the privet bush at the back of the Three Choughs, we were fallen upon by the Rains brothers, Peter Holdstock and Robert Gann. It was clear that we would have to think of something more secret than a loose brick.

This was not so easy, partly because the brick had seemed perfect and once you have enjoyed perfection anything else is bound to feel a bit of a let-down. Also, there really *was* nowhere else that would serve as a hiding place. What we needed was the kind of thing that spies use for a dead letter drop; a tele-phone box, litter bin, hollow tree, post hole, but there was nothing. Dennis and I lived on opposite sides of the estate; our routes converged only at the footpath which started out running between two chain-link fences and then lay across the meadow past the terraced row of aforementioned cottages with their gardens that had neither fences nor hedges. In case you think that this doesn't sound very cottagey, they weren't thatched country cottages with roses round the door and wall-to-wall hollyhocks; they had been built as railwaymen's dwellings in much the same style as the station only plainer, without any fancy woodwork.

The third problem was that the Rains Gang were now on to us, watching out for what Dennis called clandestine correspondence.

'What we need is a code,' Dennis said. 'Something fantastically complex to mislead the uninitiated.'

'The what?'

'The Rainses,' Dennis said.

'It needn't be *that* complex, then,' I said.

'OK, but it's got to be misleading,' said Dennis. 'It's got to be so misleading that even if they copy it down and show it to someone intelligent, they won't be able to crack it.'

'Oh, that sort of code,' I said. I was in the Scouts at the time, which Dennis was not, and I'd been thinking along the lines of knotted grass stems, bent twigs, circles of stones. I said as much. Dennis's face became pinched with scorn.

'How long do you think that kind of sign would last?' he demanded. 'The Rains Mob would kick it to *fragments*. That's what they're good at. Why do you think Newt Patrol never gets back to base when you're out tracking?'

'I'm in Beaver Patrol,' I said with dignity, for Dennis, I knew, thought little of Scouting for Boys. 'There isn't a Newt Patrol.'

'You exasperate me,' Dennis said. 'Give me a week to cogitate.' I noticed that he didn't imagine that I should be able to come up with something inside a week. Without doubt I did exasperate him. (Dennis is now Brother Dennis of that Cistercian Order commonly known as Trappists, which seems a terrible waste of a huge vocabulary.)

As it happened, it was a week to the day before Dennis and I ran into each other again, in the tunnel, on the way home from school. Dennis was there already, but I guessed that long before I saw him because as I came through the allotments I could see Raymond and David trying to impale each other on the railings that were meant to keep unauthorized persons off the embankment and away from the little black hut on the top of it, alongside the permanent way where, legend had it, a railwayman had once frozen to death during a blizzard in the middle of the last century. Such huts had little brick chimneys and looked enticingly cosy, but knowing what had happened in this one made it seem less cosy.

Raymond and David had no designs on the hut, they were occupied with the railings. There was something uncannily prehensile in the way they went up and down those railings which made me wonder if there wasn't perhaps an orang-utan a couple of generations back in the Willis family, absent-mindedly converted by missionaries. Dennis himself had long arms and rather short legs.

Dennis was under the archway with a stick of chalk, writing something on the brickwork at head height. He didn't hear me approach, owing to his ululating brothers, so I stood behind him and tried to read what he had written.

J TYF BE AE BBO AEIO R SIAOIAEAP-QVBXYZ As I watched he added, AJJOAOIU BST SO I FIAO GGT GOAT

'Goat?' I said. Dennis jumped, spun round and grinned.

'Goat,' he said, 'or toad, or deer, or seal, or –'

'Sheep?' I said.

'Not sheep.'

'Newt?'

'No.'

'Tyrannosaurus rex?'

'No,' said Dennis, 'but boot or suit or bean or soil. *Come down off of that!*' he roared suddenly, as he finally noticed what the twins were up to. 'Look, I'll come round yours this evening and show you – no I won't. I'll meet you.'

'Where?'

Dennis pointed to his row of letters, chalked on the brickwork. 'Where it says; by the phone box.'

'That says, "I'll meet you by the phone box"?'

'It says,' Dennis explained patiently, 'Tonight, 6.30, phone box.'

'All that says Tonight, 6.30, phone box? Isn't there a shorter way?'

Dennis looked hurt. 'This is Rains-proof, at least, I hope it is. Tonight will reveal all.'

'What about the goat?'

'Forget the goat,' Dennis said. 'It could just as easily be a boil.'

The phone box was the only one on the estate, nearer to my house than to Dennis's, and it was very rarely working. But it was a place where everybody met, or hung around on the off-chance of a meeting. It was said of the phone box that if you stood there long enough everyone you knew would go past eventually. This being the case it was also pretty safe. Even the Rains Gang was not foolhardy enough to attempt a frontal attack or even an outflanking manoeuvre, because at least one of my very big brothers was likely to be there, or all three of them.

I set out at 6.25, convinced that either Dennis was on to something good or else was off his trolley. He just looked smug, though, when I spotted him, sitting on the remains of the bench, by the remains of the litter bin, and ignoring the shuffling and snogging that went on all round him. When he saw me he got up and I saw he was carrying an exercise book. I was in for a period of instruction.

'Where shall we go?' I said.

'Back to yours?' he suggested.

'Well, you could have come round mine anyway,' I said, crossly. 'You needn't have hauled me out here.'

'Ah,' said Dennis, 'but I told you, didn't I, we had to see if it was Rains-proof.'

I looked round. There were no Rainses about.

'It could take *them* a week to decipher it if you just wrote it out backwards.'

'Never underestimate your adversary,' Dennis said, darkly, or as you and I might put it: the Rains Gang may not be as thick as we think.

We walked back to my house rapidly, because I was in a hurry to find out how the code worked and Dennis was dying to tell me. Also, I was only too aware that even if the Rainses hadn't cracked it, neither had I. Indoors we sat at the table and Dennis opened his book. There was the tantalizing message again.

JTYFBEAEBBOAEIORSIAOIAEAPQVBXYZA
OAOIUBSTSOIFIAOGGTGOAT

'Got it yet?' Dennis asked, after I had studied it for a few minutes.

'Almost,' I lied. Dennis smiled silently and said,

'Here's the misleading bit. This says exactly the same,' and he wrote:

LPTJROEASMIUIUIDPOIIUEOASFXPBNJO
LSAEAOIRNCCEIJOAEMPKBOIL

'Said it could just as easily be a boil,' Dennis murmured.

'That says the same? Tonight, 6.30, phone box?'

'Or,' said Dennis, 'KSVCRO –'

'All right!' I yelled. 'I give in. How's it done?'

'It's done,' said Dennis, 'on bricks.'

'Bricks?'

'Remember where I was writing it?'

'In the tunnel.'

'On the bricks,' Dennis said. 'It only works on the bricks. That's the misleading part.' I gawped at him. 'Look, when I wrote it in the tunnel it looked like this, didn't it?' He pointed to the first string of letters.

'Almost,' I said again, but this time I meant it. There *was* a difference. 'There were gaps.'

'Like this?' Dennis wrote again:

J TYF BE EA BBO AEIO R SIAOI AEAPQ
VBXYZ AJJO AOIU BST SO I FIAO GGT GOAT

'Not quite. Some of those words ran together.'

'They only looked as if they did,' Dennis said. 'I wrote one word on each brick, so of course, the four and five letter words seemed to run together. What you saw in the tunnel was:'

J TYF BE AE BBO AEIO R SIAOIAEAPQVBX
YZAJJOAOIU BST SO I FIAO GGT GOAT

'This –' he pointed to the previous line, '– is what i really says.' He added, 'You're not going to get it, ar you?'

'No,' I admitted, and then I suddenly saw what h

had done. 'Hang on!' I wrote: IOU LBW AAA

'Let's hope it never comes to that,' Dennis said. I think he was slightly sorry that I had worked out the code, but he *had* given me a lot of help. We shook hands, solemnly.

'Give it a few more days,' Dennis said. 'We'll write up another test piece and if the Rainses still don't get it, we'll put it into production.'

What Dennis wrote in the tunnel read, brick for brick; WHO GMT LEA EARO USA I BEST OMO AT EE TO UEO OU AAA IP UFO IN Z which, had Godfrey Rains been able to translate it, would have brought the gang down on us like Attila and the Huns, since it actually said, GODFREY RAINS IS A RAT. I'd been practising at home, so when I passed under the railway arch and saw Dennis's message strung out along a course of brickwork I could read it almost without hesitating, but then, I knew the brick trick. When I came home that evening Godfrey himself and Robert Gann were standing, staring at it.

'This yours?' Godfrey said, moving to block my path.

'Nah.' I joined in the staring. 'WHOGMTLE-AEAROUSAIBESTOMO . . . I best Omo? *Pufoinz?* It's a code, innit?'

Robert was copying it down on the back of his hand, but although I knew it was unlikely to get washed off I could see that there was little chance of his deciphering it before wind and rain faded it away. WHOG-MTLEAEARO . . . he printed, laboriously. Godfrey, meanwhile, tried to erase it in the hope of spoiling somebody's fun, but chalk is harder to wipe from brick than from almost anything else. Dennis's code was definitely Rains-proof.

When, after a week, we still hadn't been beaten to pulp, we put the code into operation. It wasn't merely Rains-proof, it was everybody-proof, that infuriating combination of real words, initials, acronyms and meaningless groups of letters. Sometimes a frustrated would-be cryptographer vented his spleen by interfering with our messages, but we could always spot an altered letter, and imitations were nonsense – up until just before half-term, that is. I remember the date exactly.

To foil imitators we had taken to ending messages with the date, and it was always the first thing checked. As the days shortened it was so dim in the tunnel by home-time that I now carried a torch, and had to look carefully for today's message, for by now the tunnel looked as if someone had sprayed it with alphabet soup; we had begun to write over our old white messages in red or blue chalk. I stood in the hollow darkness skimming the walls for the signal, which would be that day's date. I couldn't find it and I was just coming to the conclusion that Dennis had written nothing that day when I noticed, far up in the arch of the tunnel, a row of marks, higher than any of us could reach. I read them with ease.

LLLII LII IL LILL III

Now, according to our code, that did actually say something, and my first reaction was fury that at last someone had cracked it. Then I began to wonder; we had never done it using only two letters although that, as this proved, was perfectly possible, and the ones used here are about the simplest letters there are. Not even a baby would have had much trouble with I and L; not even a Rains. I also wondered who on earth would go all the trouble of climbing up to write on the very top of the arch – climbing up on what? Shoulders? The arch was about ten feet high. I had a vision of the Rains Gang, lightweight Godfrey perched on taller Robert or fat brother Desmond, falteringly tracing those simple letters in haste before his scaffolding collapsed. I felt betrayed – and nervous.

There was no need to write down the message; once I knew what it said I could easily re-encode it, and next morning I went round to Dennis's house and wrote it out for him.

'Someone's on to us, Den,' I said.

Dennis, refusing to panic, looked at what I had written. He said, 'On the roof of the arch, you say?'

'Right at the top of the curve.'

'Depends which way up you look at it from,' Dennis said. He turned the paper round. 'It could say, One thousand, one hundred and seventeen billion . . .' he was good at maths, too, 'seven hundred and seventeen million . . .'

'Come off it, Willis,' I snapped. 'That says eight days. You know it does.'

'Funny sort of message,' Dennis said. 'Eight days of what?'

'Eight days *to* what?'

'To the end of the month?'

'Hallowe'en,' I said.

Dennis counted. 'Thirty days hath September, April, June . . . You're right.' He looked at me uncomfortably. 'Someone's mucking about.'

'Yes, and they're mucking about with our code.'

'Let's go and look,' said Dennis.

It was dark in the tunnel even in summer. Now,

halfway through a dull autumn morning, it was gloomy, but we had the torch. I flashed it up into the tunnel's vault. The letters had faded a little, it seemed to me, since yesterday afternoon, but I hardly noticed that. Below them, on the next course but one, was a second set.

LLIII LII IL LILL III

'That doesn't say one trillion anything,' I said.

'Seven days,' Dennis muttered. He read the letters aloud, 'Lliiiliiillilliii,' a nasty gibbering whine.

'Shut up,' I said, not liking it at all. 'Someone is mucking about.'

'That's not chalk,' Dennis said. 'It's not written in chalk.'

'You can't tell from here.'

'Bend down,' said Dennis.

'What for?'

'So I can stand on your shoulders.'

'You're a stone heavier than I am,' I said. 'You bend down.'

Dennis crouched. I climbed on to his shoulders and balanced myself against the wall as Dennis slowly straightened up. Idiotic words slid past my eyes as I rose: GGA . . . OSP . . . GRAW . . . OOOI . . . MARB . . . ULP . . . Dennis turned gingerly and braced my hands against the curve of the roof.

'Can you see anything?' Dennis said.

I reached out cautiously and touched today's letters LLIII . . . 'It's not chalk.' The marks were white, but blue-white, like crystals, and when I touched them faint crust crumbled under my finger, leaving the mark on the bricks. 'It's more like salt.'

'Efflorescence,' Dennis said, predictably. He teetered and I fell off.

'Fluorescence?'

'Efflorescence. Salts coming to the surface in brick-work – well, not just in brickwork; stones, breezeblocks, even.'

'You mean it's just chance, those marks?' I'd skinned my knee.

'Damn funny chance,' Dennis growled, wiping my boot prints from his shoulders. We stood looking up at the letters.

'Could be coincidence,' I said. Dennis glared, I was pinching one of his long words. Dennis was definitely Holmes. I was only Watson.

'Coincidence, my foot,' said Dennis. 'Those marks weren't put *on* the brick – they came out of it.'

'You mean, we called them out?'

We were both staring at those lines and lines of letters.

'One thousand, one hundred and seventeen billion billion, seven hundred and seventeen billion, seven hundred and eleven million, one hundred and seventy-one thousand, one hundred and seventeen,' Dennis droned.

The next day was Sunday but I went down to the tunnel, just to check. There was a third line of letters:
LIIII LII IL LILL III

Six days.

Each line was lower than the last. By the time it had reached IILLL LII IL LILL III, two days, whatever *it* was, the words were about seven feet from the ground. You could see that in two days' time they would be at shoulder level – an adult's shoulder, that is. On the morning of the thirty-first, which was a Saturday,

Dennis and I met by prior arrangement (the usual prior
arrangement; we refused to be scared off) and went
along to the tunnel to see what was there. The inscrip-
tions of the last week seemed to glow faintly above us in
the vault, from the almost illegible LLLII LII IL LILL
III down to yesterday's, still sharp and clear: ILLLL
LII IL LILL; one day.

We looked everywhere, but there was nothing else
written that hadn't been put there by us or our envious
imitators, in chalk. We decided not to go through the
tunnel again until Monday.

That night Mum, Dad and my three brothers went to

a Hallowe'en party on the other side of town, a grown-up affair with drink; nothing in it for me. I could have gone with them but Dennis's mum said I might stay at theirs, and the two of us sat up half the night cogitating (Dennis, of course) on what might be happening in the tunnel. We were almost tempted to go out and look, and were almost glad that Dennis's mother forbade us going anywhere.

When I went home next morning the house was in an uproar. It had been a very cold night all over the region but in our house the temperature must have hit fifteen below. The garden was white with rime and every chrysanthemum, dahlia and late-flowering rose was blighted and black. The windows were thick with frost ferns and indoors the pipes had frozen. People rushed about murmuring of freak weather conditions and fires were lit, whereupon the pipes, which had burst, thawed dramatically. Plumbers were called. Gradually the house warmed up, but not before I had been into my bedroom. I have never known such cold; it took the breath away, that, and the curious marks in the ice on the window: L LLL LI II LLI IIII L

Tonight.

Neither of us ever went through the tunnel again. If it is still there I doubt if I would go through it even now. Even twenty years on it would seem like putting my luck at risk, and there were several elements of luck in the whole affair. I consider that I had a very lucky escape, although it was several weeks before I had another good night's sleep. It was luck, too, that our correspondent didn't go to Dennis's house, which he might well have done, considering it was Dennis's code that fetched him. Dennis didn't say much when I told him what had happened, but I can't help wondering if that didn't have something to do with his abandoning the idea of becoming a cryptographer and entering a monastery instead. I never spoke of it to anyone else although, much later, I asked my dad in a casual way if he knew anything about the railwayman who was alleged to have died in that little black shack beside the permanent way, just beyond the tunnel.

'He was a telegraphist,' said Dad. 'You know, dot-dot-dot-dash,' and he tapped on the table with bunched fingers, operating an imaginary buzzer. So it was sheer *bad* luck, obviously, that there should be someone using the tunnel who was not misled by Dennis's version of the Morse Code.

A BUNDLE OF NERVES
Joan Aiken

It was after him. It was gaining on him . . .
He was paralysed, unable to stir . . .

Joan Aiken shuffles the surface of the
everyday and deals out a handful of
stories that range from the weird and
fantastic to the ghostly and sharply
macabre, but all of which are firmly
rooted in the plausible.

FEET AND OTHER STORIES
Jan Mark

Nobody looks at feet.

But after being spurned by the school's tennis hero, Jane does look at feet, and makes a surprising discovery.

THE CRY OF THE WOLF
Melvin Burgess

The Hunter is a fanatic, always driven on the lookout for rare and exotic animals. Driven by an ambition to wipe out the last English wolves, the Hunter sets out on a savage quest. But he has never before had a prey like Greycub. A wolf that as a cub had been looked after by Ben and his father – his human family. A wolf that knows human needs and weaknesses. A wolf that is determined to survive.

A powerful story of courage, survival and family love in the animal kingdom, that will keep you in suspense until the very last page.

Short-listed for the Carnegie Medal.

THE GUILTY PARTY
Joan Lingard

'We're here because we're worried about having a nuclear plant on our doorstep. We're here because we think we've got a right to have a say in our future.'

Josie is a fighter – and there's nothing she won't say or do to make sure that there won't be another disaster like Chernobyl in her town. It all begins harmlessly with fly-posting and peaceful protest. But then Josie is arrested during a demonstration. Will she have the courage to go to prison for her convictions?

A Midsummer Night's Death
K. M. Peyton

Can Hugo – calm, honest, fair, intelligent, courageous Hugo – really be a perfect murderer?

When the body of the unpopular English master, Mr Robinson, is taken from the river, Jonathan doesn't feel very involved in the tragedy. But it is disturbing to discover that one of the other masters, Charles Hugo, has lied to the police about not seeing Robinson on the evening before his death. Jonathan really likes Hugo, and at first he tries to put all suspicions out of his mind. But he soon becomes convinced that the coroner's verdict of suicide is the wrong one . . .

RUNNING SCARED
Bernard Ashley

'What's it mean, Grandad? What's it all about? Cos I'm scared, really scared, I can tell you!'

When a sinister woman corners and threatens Paula – and gives her a warning to pass on to her grandad – she's pretty shaken up. What Grandad reveals to Paula, and to her alone, is that he's been an unwilling witness to an armed robbery by a ruthless local gang. And he's got a vital piece of evidence that both the police and the gang are desperate for. The crooks are prepared to go to any lengths to get what they want, and Paula finds herself in a very dangerous position: she should go to the cops and help expose the vicious gang, but she knows that doing so would endanger her family.